T0243598

THE
PROTÉGÉ

Also available by Jody Gehrman

Triple Shot Bettys
Triple Shot Bettys in Love
Confessions of a Triple Shot Betty

Audrey's Guide
Audrey's Guide to Black Magic
Audrey's Guide to Witchcraft

Other Works
The Summer We Buried
The Girls Weekend
Watch Me
The Truth About Jack
Bombshell
Babe in Boyland
Notes from the Backseat
Tart
Summer in the Land of Skin

THE
PROTÉGÉ

A NOVEL

JODY GEHRMAN

CROOKED
LANE

NEW YORK

Copyright © 2023 by Jody Gehrman

Published in the United States by Crooked Lane Books, an imprint of The Quick Brown Fox & Company LLC.

Crooked Lane Books and its logo are trademarks of The Quick Brown Fox & Company LLC.

Library of Congress Catalog-in-Publication data available upon request.

ISBN (hardcover): 978-1-63910-248-8
ISBN (ebook): 978-1-63910-249-5

Cover design by Kara Klontz

Printed in the United States.

www.crookedlanebooks.com

Crooked Lane Books
34 West 27th St., 10th Floor
New York, NY 10001

First Edition: March 2023

10 9 8 7 6 5 4 3 2 1

For my dad, Ed Gehrman,
who taught me words to live by:
*She's got everything she needs,
she's an artist, she don't look back.*

CHAPTER

1

Hannah

I'M SITTING ON the stage, contemplating Mick Lynch's skull.

It's nicely formed, as craniums go. He's bald—shaved skinhead naked, not just buzzed—so it's easy to observe its shape. The parietal bone forms one long, elegant curve from the top of his head to his occipital bun. The frontal bone, with its pronounced brow and sharp zygomatic curvature, gives his face a strong, intimidating look. We find a strong frontal bone appealing in males because of its ability to resist blunt force trauma—to survive a falling limb, a spear, a tire iron. We crave signs of strength; it means our offspring have a better chance at passing on our genes. Mick Lynch's cranium screams safety, warmth, security. Genetic success.

But what really catches my eye is his zygomatic arch—that tender, gently curved place just behind the ear. His seems to be . . . flexing. Not the bone itself, of course, but the temporalis muscles; they're hypnotically active. I watch them move as he addresses the crowd, arms outstretched like an evangelical preacher. Though I know this is scientifically inaccurate, it gives the impression his brain is too active to be caged within his skull. It's mesmerizing.

He's mesmerizing. I hate the son of a bitch, but I have to admit, he knows how to work a room.

A quick scan of the packed lecture hall confirms my suspicions. The audience can't take their eyes off him. Some of the men sit canted forward in their seats, faces eager. Others lean back, contemplating each word. The women wear faint, dreamy smiles; some flex their frontalis muscles, resulting in furrowed brows. On closer inspection, I suspect the frowners react differently to sexual stimuli than their starry-eyed sisters. The smilers enjoy the way his voice caresses them. The frowners know better.

Do I know better?

The question emerges from the dark underbelly of my mind, blindsiding me.

Of course I know better. Jesus. The guy's a first-class narcissist. He's in love with the sound of his own voice.

Granted, it does have a compelling cadence—part gospel minister, part Steve Jobs.

I force myself to focus on his lecture. I've been so fixated on Lynch's cranium, I've barely heard a word. Lynch whisks away a red velvet cloth, revealing a humanoid robot as a chorus of gasps erupts from the audience. Cheap magic tricks. Lynch is an old-time charlatan pedaling snake-oil and virility charms.

As if sensing my eyes on it, the robot whips its head around and gazes in my direction. I flinch. It has a realistic face that looks a little like my uncle Jack's—humble, unassuming, wrinkled. Designed to be disarming. It flashes me a feral grin; then it turns back to face the audience with a placid expression.

"Many people ask me, 'What if they get smarter than us and take over the planet?'" Just as Lynch poses the rhetorical question, the robot does a double take, not unlike a ventriloquist's dummy.

The audience lets out a nervous laugh.

Lynch scans the crowd, his face open, inviting. I try to pinpoint which muscles communicate that microscopic shift from stern to curious. Is it the gentle rise in the orbicularis oculi? A barely perceived tightening of the corrugator supercilii?

Lynch takes a step closer to the edge of the stage. He's a man soothing a spooked horse, reaching out a hand, meeting his audience halfway. He doesn't come on too strong. There's empathy there, a human connection; he makes each listener feel like he's speaking only to her.

He glances sideways, and our eyes meet. Is it my imagination, or is there a pulse of challenge there, a flash of hubris? When I spoke earlier, as part of the panel, I didn't inspire rapt attention. I delivered a mini-lecture on the culture of identity and bioethics in an emergent scientific discipline like AI. Eyes glazed over. I deliver information, not theatrics. Mick Lynch can work the room all he likes; it's not my strong suit, and I know it.

He turns away from me, and his gaze locks on the audience again. His volume drops to a low, confiding tone. "It's a primal fear—the lifeblood of science fiction. And yes, it's a valid question. An essential question, in fact."

The tension in the room is so palpable you can taste it. The air simmers with the electric tang of a coming storm. I can't help but wonder how the hell he does it. What is charisma, exactly? Is there a genetic predisposition for it? Can it be measured? I don't like mysteries that can't be solved. Amorphous qualities we sense but cannot quantify make me itch. Bones can be measured, weighed. Many studies indicate we can even compute beauty after adjusting for cultural norms. There's a distinct symmetry of features the majority of homo sapiens find aesthetically appealing, a specific ratio between waist and hips most men find sexually attractive. But charisma? The chemistry between speaker and audience?

Watching him, it's undeniably there—the charged, almost sexual electricity between this strange bald man and his mesmerized spectators.

"The answer is not simple, but it is definitive." Lynch beckons to his robot, who hurries to its master's side with a meek, pliable air. "We are the creators. We must remember that. We don't need to fear Roger here anymore than we fear our phones or our computers or our toasters."

Lynch gestures, and Roger instantly falls to his knees, bowing his head in a gesture of submission.

"We are the masters of this brave new world. We must find the courage to banish our irrational fears so that we may inhabit the future." He pauses, gazing out into the rapt auditorium, his blue eyes sparkling. "Thank you."

The audience explodes into applause. It's like a volatile liquid suddenly escaping, a soda shaken hard and released. They jump to their feet. I gape, unable to contain my amazement. I've delivered hundreds—maybe even thousands—of lectures. Never, in the history of my career have I inspired a standing ovation.

A queasy feeling stirs in my belly. It takes me a moment to name it.

Envy.

* * *

Winter

She's so smug. I watch her sitting there on stage, her body as motionless as a statue. She looks pretty good for forty; I'll give her that. Her shoulder-length auburn hair is shiny and well cut. The long white neck hasn't yet turned into a disgusting turkey wattle. She's skinny enough. Like most of the professors in this Nor Cal backwater think tank, she wears hardly any makeup, and her clothes are expensive but boring. I've never seen her in heels. She's big on army green and khaki, like she expects to take off on safari at any second. Tonight she's wearing knee-high boots that probably cost more than my yearly stipend, army-green fitted slacks, and a camel-colored sweater. She's totally married to her job. Everything about her screams *leading forensic anthropologist*.

I don't even know what she's doing on this panel. It's clear the robot freaks her out. When it turned and looked at her, she flinched like she expected it to spit in her face. I can't help but notice her eyes following Lynch everywhere, though. Oh, Lord, tell me she doesn't have a crush. That would be too hilarious. God, I think she does. I can't decide if that's sickening or sweet. If the two of them had a kid, it would be a total abomination, an uber genius baby with a massive brain, a Rhodes scholar by the time it hit kindergarten. Yeah, she's definitely hot for him. The way she watches him—there's something there I haven't seen before. Normally, she's cool, calculating. She's got as much warmth and humor as a crocodile. When she looks at Lynch, though, her eyes light up with pale green fire.

This is good. I can use this.

It's easy to see why Lynch has got even Dr. B lusting after him; he's sexy in a bald, sweaty, old-guy sort of way. He's got a definite Bruce Willis circa *Die Hard* appeal. He's way more fit than most of the guys on campus, young or old. You can see he's cut, even in a suit. That's another thing that sets him apart; he dresses like a man. Guess that's the UCLA influence lingering, even though he's been here since fall semester. He hasn't yet gotten the memo that Mad River University men are filthy hippies across the board, from their nasty dreads to their socks-and-Birkenstock toes. It's not just Lynch's action figure body or his suit that make him hot, though. It's his game. Every woman in this auditorium is ready to drop her panties for him. Some guys are just like that. They're tigers in a field of gazelles.

I sit back in my chair, enjoying the show. The AI is cool—whatever, boys and their toys. The real entertainment is watching Dr. B devour Lynch with her cool green eyes.

My mind wanders, dreaming up the many ways this information might prove useful in the days to come.

2

Hannah

MAD RIVER UNIVERSITY is a peculiar little campus, tucked into the wild hills above the sea, three hundred miles north of San Francisco. It was built by wunderkind architect Liam Dubois. Though the school was founded and constructed just ten years ago, Dubois has a thing for the collegiate gothic style, so it looks at least a hundred years old. An article in *Architectural Digest* described the main building, Thorn Hall, as "a cross between Hogwarts and Neuschwanstein." There are towers, finials, stone facades as intricate as lace; lancet windows, spires, and turrets give it a vaguely medieval look. Now, climbing the stone steps of Thorn Hall as the sky turns indigo, I can't help sighing with pleasure. This place is over the top, but I love it. Cantankerous gargoyles crouch on either side of the entrance, wings half extended, teeth bared.

It's a building every bit as anachronistic, guarded, and gloomy as me—and that's no small feat.

There's a catered party in Thorn Hall after Lynch's AI display. I despise these things—social gatherings in general give me heart palpitations—but my boss, Dr. Eli Balderstone, didn't give me much choice but to attend. Compulsory merrymaking. Mad River was founded by mavericks looking for an academic home that would be less mired in bureaucracy than the universities they fled. Private schools require funding, though, which means donors must be dazzled and pandered to. This shindig promises to be crawling with major donors looking to rub elbows with the brainiacs they fund. Thank God Lynch's performance ensures they'll swarm him and leave the dry academic types like myself to languish amid the canapés and bacon-wrapped figs.

Joe catches up with me just as I pass through the great stone arches of Thorn Hall. Joe's my friend, colleague, and downstairs tenant. He just moved in a few months ago, after a two-year campaign. He finally convinced me that living all alone in the woods was making me even more of a social outcast. He has a point. I do tend to isolate more than I should. Besides, the house I bought five years ago came with a self-contained apartment downstairs, complete with its own kitchen, two bedrooms, and a bathroom. It was decadent and wasteful, leaving it unoccupied.

All the same, he's living there on a trial basis. I value my solitude. Joe's presence downstairs is sometimes comforting, but it's also a little distracting. He's a musician. Two days after he moved in, I invested in an economy-sized pack of earplugs.

"Hey, Hannah." He puts a hand on my back. "Sorry, my lesson went late."

"I doubt the demo would have interested you much anyway." We continue together up the stairs toward the study, a cozy if slightly pretentious room on the second floor. Administration likes to hold parties there, especially ones involving generous benefactors.

Joe brushes a bit of lint from his blazer. "Really? Sounded kind of cool. Mr. Robot didn't impress you, huh?"

I shrug. "He's an alpha-male with delusions of grandeur. Dime a dozen."

"What about his robots, though?"

"Robot—singular." I pull a face. "It's anthropomorphic, which just seems wrong. Gives me the creeps."

He shoots me a mock-appalled look. "Dr. Bryers! I'm shocked."

"That's sarcasm. I can tell because of the movement in your orbicularis oculi."

He grins. It's a long-standing joke between us, my inability to detect subtle social nuances like sarcasm. "You seem like the last person to fall prey to base superstitions."

"I'm an anthropologist for a reason. 'Anthro' is all about man—the kind made of blood, sinew, and bones. That's my world. I'm just as susceptible to instinctive revulsion about pseudo humans as the next guy."

By now, we've reached the entrance to the study, a long, elegant room with a massive fireplace at one end. It's a gas fire—Mad River is fanatical about the environment—but it gives off a warm, golden glow just the same. Richly hued oriental rugs cover the oak floors. Oxblood leather chairs and moss-green velvet sofas abound, many of them already occupied by guests. Iron chandeliers and wall sconces add to the flattering light provided by the fireplace. In spite of my pronounced social anxiety, I can't help but feel lucky. There's a subtle glow that ignites inside me, knowing I'm welcome within this privileged space, the inner circle of an institution I consider home.

A waiter darts past with a tray. I start to reach for a glass, but he's moving too quickly and doesn't even see my outstretched hand. A huff of irritation escapes me as I spot the object of his attention. Isabella Lynch, Mick Lynch's ex-swimsuit-model wife, stands in a circle of male admirers. I recognize a couple colleagues among them: Gil Matheson from Engineering and my boss, Eli Balderstone. Isabella's wearing a dress the color of blood. Her velvety brown skin, lush black hair, and plunging neckline have drawn a crowd of men, all of whom vie for her attention like hummingbirds swooping around a trumpet vine. As the waiter arrives, several of her fans practically lunge for the chance to hand her a drink first.

Mrs. Lynch appears to enjoy the attention. Human social nuances are not my specialty, but I base my hypothesis on the way she flicks her hair over one shoulder and laughs, throwing her head back to expose her long, vulnerable neck. She's displaying typical mating ritual signifiers. I have learned these do not necessarily indicate imminent plans to copulate, unlike in the animal kingdom. They do, however, comprise the ritual we refer to as "flirtation." We humans go to great lengths to prove our ability to attract potential sexual partners, without having any serious mating intentions; that's just one of the many reasons I find human behavior fascinating and mystifying.

Joe's managed to secure two flutes of champagne. He hands one to me and follows my gaze. "Isn't that Mrs. Robot?"

"Mm. Your moniker is amusing."

"Remember that thing we talked about?"

I pull my eyes away from the spectacle of Isabella and focus on Joe. "What thing?"

"If you find something funny, it's best to . . . you know, chuckle, chortle, snort, giggle—"

"Ah, right. Don't just remark on its amusing qualities, indicate amusement with a sound or facial expression."

"Even a hearty smile will work." He grins. I grin back.

Joe sometimes refers to himself as my "trainer." He says being friends with me is a full-time job, but somebody's got to do it. Once, I heard him telling a lab tech to think of me as a brilliant but clueless alien, one who must be introduced to the customs of earthlings in a patient, methodical fashion. It doesn't escape me that my greatest strength as an anthropologist—my ability to view humans with clear-eyed objectivity—is also my greatest weakness as a friend and teacher. It's not something I worry about, though. It's just the way I'm made.

I approach the art of socializing the way others approach unpleasant but obligatory tasks such as cleaning the toilet or suffering through a root canal; I avoid it whenever possible but strive to be brave and endure it with dignity when no alternative makes itself available.

"Lester's over there. I better schmooze." Joe nods in the direction of Lester Wang, the chair of the Music Department. Joe teaches guitar and music theory at Mad River part-time. I deduce he wants to get chummy with Lester in the hopes of adding more sections, a social ritual that at least results in monetary gain.

"Go ahead."

He glances at me. "You sure you're okay on your own?"

I give him a wry look. "I'm not afraid to be left alone. You know that. I'll just blend with the natives, indulge in some participant observation."

"Become one with the wallpaper?" His eyes smile down at me, the crow's feet crinkling in that old familiar way.

"There's no wallpaper." I'm being deliberately literal this time to amuse him.

It works. He guffaws. "Be right back."

I know from experience this is a lie. Joe thrives at a party; he feeds on the energy of a buzzing room. He excels at flitting from one conversation to another, with the effort-less grace of a pollinating insect. Me, I tend to stake out one corner and observe. I could blame my observation tactics on my profession, but it would be more accurate to say I chose my profession because this has always been my way. My dad says I did it even as a baby—retreated from crowds. I was so silent and watchful, others in the room invariably forgot I was there. Once, when I was two, my Aunt Ellen actually sat on me.

"Dr. Bryers." I recognize the voice immediately—that tone, warm and rich as hot chocolate. He's standing right behind me.

I force myself to take a deep breath as I turn to face him. "Dr. Lynch."

"Thanks again for agreeing to sit on the panel."

"Accurate verb choice."

One of his eyebrows arches—the corrugated supercilii muscle, I note automatically. "Sorry, not sure I—"

"Lots of sitting. Not much talking. You obviously had that covered. But you're welcome."

He takes a step back, assessing me. Though he joined the faculty back in September—six months ago now—we've never had a proper conversation, just the two of us. I'm acutely aware of his smell. I detect something citrusy, probably an expensive aftershave. That's not what catches my attention, though. Underneath that layer of artifice, there's a scent that's pure animal—sweat and musk and salt.

I can see him considering his next words carefully. I'm a respected faculty member, one who's been here seven years. He cannot afford to alienate me. But he's also not a man accustomed to backing away from a challenge.

"It's unfortunate we didn't get to hear from you more." He's testing the waters, trying to figure out my game. "I'm sure you have valuable insights to share."

"I doubt my insights would concur with yours." Even I recognize the bitchiness in my tone.

"How interesting."

I squint at him, hunting for signs of condescension. To my surprise, he looks curious. It's that same look he gave the audience earlier—the open, childlike expression that says, *"Tell me more."* I know the difference between someone putting on an interested expression and someone who's sincere. It's in the eyes. People can do all kinds of deceptive things with their mouths, their foreheads, even their brows, but the eyes never lie.

He takes a minute step closer, peering at me. "What specifically do you disagree with? My theories, or the way I present them?"

"I find your presentation theatrical but effective. The audience responds well—that's obvious."

"And you find that suspect?"

"Of course."

"Why 'of course'?" One corner of his mouth curls upward, amused.

"It's natural to feel instinctive revulsion when one is being manipulated."

"And yet, as you say, the audience responds."

"Most people run on pure pathos. They're slaves to their emotions, as much as they'd like to think otherwise. They're too busy being seduced by your charisma to question your ethics or the soundness of your hypotheses."

"But not you." He says it softly. I can't tell if he's mocking me.

"No. I'm driven by logos." I meet his gaze head-on. "Logic tells me you're dangerous."

Instead of looking defensive, he lets out a laugh so loud and genuine, I flinch. Several people nearby turn to look, including—I can't help but notice—his wife.

"Dangerous," he repeats. "It's not the first time I've been called that, but it's never sounded so much like a compliment."

"It's not a compliment or an epithet. It's a fact."

Isabella glides toward us, a glass of wine in her hand. It's a deep, plummy red; it matches her dress, her lipstick, and her ruby earrings. My limbic cortex recognizes danger; the fight-or-flight instinct flares inside me, poised to move. Her dark eyes scan me before fixing on my face with a pleasant smile. Her mouth says "friend," but her eyes say "foe."

"Have you met my wife?" Mick reaches out a hand as she approaches, and pulls her close. "Isabella, this is Dr. Bryers."

"Yes. From the panel." She has a husky, lightly accented voice.

"Are you from Peru?" I enjoy trying to place accents. I have an excellent ear for languages.

Her eyes flash with irritation, and she glances at Mick. "Venezuela. I have been here for many years, but I never seem to lose my accent."

"It's beautiful." I'm being sincere. I hope she can tell. People say I don't express emotion well—that I have a flat, unreadable affect. Maybe that's why I like accents, especially South American ones; they always sound so expressive, the polar opposite of my colorless monotone.

Mick smiles down at her in a way most people would read as reassuring. To me it looks condescending, but I'm hypersensitive, so I could be wrong. Nothing spikes my pulse faster than a patronizing man in power, and not in a good way.

Isabella turns back to me. Her shiny dark hair swings forward as she moves, nearly covering one eye. The effect is alluring, I'm sure, but all I can think about is how a couple strands have adhered to her thickly glossed lips. I can never stand to have my hair in my face; I usually pull mine back.

"You are a professor here, yes?"

I nod. "Yes. I've been here since right after the college was founded seven years ago."

"You must have been very young." She's trying to flatter me. Personally, I've never understood why looking young is so important. It's indicative of a culture that values physical beauty and prowess over wisdom and experience. While I'm trained not to judge the prevailing values of a culture, I can't help but prefer the value systems of the Hopi or the Koreans, where the elders are treated with the reverence we Americans reserve for rock stars and super models.

"I was thirty-three," I say simply.

Isabella blinks her thickly mascaraed lashes and forms a pleasant little smile, but I can tell she's only being polite. The eyes again, telling the truth in spite of all the other facial muscles conspiring to feign interest. She is interested, but not in my academic career. She wants to know one thing: if I'm a threat to her marriage. I wish I could just tell her how base-less her fears are. Of all the women in this room, I'm the least likely to fall prey to her husband's charms.

This is why parties exhaust me. All the social niceties contrast sharply with the body language tells. My brain races, trying to make sense of the contradictions.

A waiter carrying a tray of miniature meatballs offers them to us. Isabella and Mick both take one, but I stick to my champagne. I find conversation challenging enough without adding the effort required to masticate and swallow, all while guarding against the social faux pas of talking with your mouth full.

Isabella takes a delicate bite and somehow manages not to mar her lip gloss. When she swallows, her throat moves. I find myself fixating on her sternocleidomastoid; I have to drag myself back to hear her question.

"You are teaching the robotics, like Mick?"

Lynch breathes out a little laugh. "No, Dr. Bryers is a forensic anthropologist. She studies cultural artifacts—"

"Not artifacts," I interrupt, correcting him. "Human remains."

"Dead bodies?" Isabella looks uneasy.

I focus my attention on her. "Whatever's left of the corpse, I examine to reconstruct the cause and approximate time of death. I specialize in forensic taphonomy—or, in sim-pler terms, decomposition. After just a day or two, the inter-nal organs start to break down; soon after, the body bloats, emitting blood-containing foam from the mouth and nose."

She puts down her meatball with a moue of distaste.

"Of course, anthropoid colonization affects the decom-position process—"

"Anthropoid?" she echoes, her brow furrowed.

"Bugs," Lynch clarifies. He looks like he's trying not to laugh, which I find perplexing. There's nothing especially humorous about anthropoids.

I continue my explanation, holding her gaze, though she looks increasingly queasy. "Various carrion insects are attracted to the biological and chemical changes a carcass undergoes as it decays. I examine this as well, though that's more the purview of my entomologist colleagues."

Joe finally returns from his strategic wooing of Lester Wang. He looks bright-eyed and flushed, the way he always does at a party. A quartet of stringed instruments has started playing. Joe's always in his element when there's music, booze, and beautiful people filling a room.

"Uh-oh," he says by way of greeting. He nods at Isabella. "I know that look. Is Hannah regaling you with tales of rotting flesh?"

"She asked about my work." I know I sound defensive, but I don't care. Joe has a habit of turning me into a joke to make me appear more sympathetic. I find it either charming or infuriating, depending on my mood.

Isabella laughs, and her relief is evident. Heat creeps up my neck and spreads across my face. Joe's saved these two helpless captives from my awkward social efforts. He can now translate the behavior of the alien for the puzzled earthlings.

Lynch catches my eye. I'm not sure I understand his expression, but something about his steady gaze calms me.

Joe extends a hand to Lynch, then to Isabella. "Joe Shepley."

"You are Dr. Bryers's husband?"

"No! We're friends," I say, my tone sharp.

Joe looks wounded. He recovers quickly, though, flashing a self-deprecating grin. "I'm just the dude who lives in her basement."

"It's not a basement," I correct. "He has an apartment on the first floor of my home. He just calls it a basement because he thinks it sounds amusing."

"Sorry I missed the presentation." Joe changes the subject smoothly, addressing Lynch. "I hear it was riveting."

Lynch flicks a quick look at me, then turns to Joe. "Not according to Dr. Bryers, but I don't mind. It's refreshing, talking to someone so honest."

Joe pats my arm. "Hannah's nothing if not honest."

* * *

Winter

One of the things I like best about grad school is how temporary it is. Sure, there are losers who work on their doctoral dissertations so long they become part of the landscape—scared Peter Pans cowering in the libraries, unwilling to move on—but for most of us, it's a stepping-stone. We uprooted our lives and drove U-Haul trucks to this God forsaken forest several hundred miles from civilization. We flocked here from all over the world to be mentored by these elusive geniuses, professors who are giants in their fields—never mind that outside their field nobody gives a shit. In their specialized sphere, these professors are celebrities. We came here to apprentice with the best and the brightest.

It's a lot like joining the circus. You pitch your tent for a few years, study hard, and party harder. Then, when it's all over, you tear down your tent and move on.

I like that. Temporary works for me.

Where I come from, everyone's been there forever. Nobody in Apalachicola ever leaves or returns. They're born in that sad little outpost on the edge of a humid, primeval swamp. They eat there, work there, mate there; they have ugly, wrinkled little babies, and their babies have babies; and then they die. Those people exist like trees, rooted to one spot, doomed to see the same humdrum shit day after day. It makes them boring and bored.

If there's one thing I've learned in my twenty-three years, it's that boredom breeds evil.

The other great thing about the temporary nature of grad school is that even boyfriends come with an expiration date. I wasn't planning to hook up with anyone, but Cameron makes an excellent camouflage boyfriend. He's so trustworthy and respected, he makes me disappear beside him. For my purposes, this is ideal. The day I met him, I decided to make him mine because being his girlfriend makes my mission here that much easier.

I list here—in no particular order—the main reasons he provides amazing camo:

1. He's freakishly attractive. Though I'm pretty enough, when I walk into a room with him, he's the one everyone notices first. He's four inches taller than me; since I'm five eleven, this is a definite perk. He's got dark hair, dark eyes, five o'clock shadow, and an impish, crooked grin that's just dirty enough to offset his crisp button-down shirts and trendy jeans. Most dudes in this part of the world are fugly hippies who smell like bong, so even if he's a little preppy for my taste, it's way better than the alternative.

2. Cameron went to Yale for undergrad. People remember that way more than my forgettable alma mater.

3. He can play the violin. Serious violin.

4. He's rich (see numbers two and three).

5. He's smart. Not just ace-your-GREs smart, but actually smart.

6. Luckily, he's not smart enough to know when I'm lying.

Cameron annoys me at least as often as he entertains me, but that's because of how I'm wired. I've got a very low tolerance for people's flaws. Nobody else finds him the slightest bit irritating, but I'm funny that way. Even saints could try my patience.

Most of the time, I'm able to hide this. See number six.

The truth is, Cameron has no idea who I am. I'm very careful not to reveal much. He knows I grew up in Florida, but he thinks I was an only child in a happy family. He knows my parents died in a car crash, but he thinks this happened right after I left for college. Whenever possible, I avoid talking about anything that transpired before the day I met him. I never discuss ex-boyfriends. Like most guys, he's happier believing I sprang into existence the moment he laid eyes on me. It makes things easier for both of us. *Suppressio veri*—concealment of truth. It's win–win.

After Lynch's AI lecture, Cameron and I walk through the gathering gloom toward downtown. The campus sits on a dramatic bluff above the ocean. Salt Gulch was barely more than a gas station and a post office before MRU, from what I've heard. Now it's hardly a bustling metropolis, but it's grown. Since its whole raison d'être is the university, all of the businesses are just a short walk from campus. There's a pub, a bakery, a café, a Thai restaurant, a taco joint, a few boutiques that specialize in high-end pot princess chic. There's a market called the Salt Gulch Bazaar that sells everything from bamboo T-shirts to artisanal bacon. Between these meager offerings and Amazon, we get by.

"What did you think of Lynch's demo?" Cameron's all amped. He's got that earnest, fired-up look. Whenever we go to these things, he likes to sort through the ideas afterward like a kid poring over his prize collection of baseball cards.

Sometimes, I find it a bit much. Tonight, I'm in an indulgent mood, though. Getting a glimpse of Dr. B's crush has made me generous. "He's a great speaker."

"Amazing, right? I'm dying to take one of his classes."

I snort. "Good luck with that. They fill up months in advance. Anyway, Dr. Bryers would shit a brick."

"You think?" He looks at me, eyebrows rising. "Because it's outside our program?"

"And she thinks AI is the devil."

"Really?" Cameron looks intrigued. Behind him, in the distance, the ocean churns in the twilight, glowing a luminous blue. "It's not like her to be biased about a field with so much potential."

I want to tell him he has no idea what she's capable of.

Cameron idolizes Bryers. It's one of his most irritating traits. We're both her star students, but there's a huge difference between us. He worships her; I study her. We're in our second year of the PhD program, with two more to go. I've played my cards perfectly with Bryers. She even made me her TA this year. I can never show Cameron how I really feel about her. Mostly I excel at this; sometimes it's a challenge.

We've reached the pub. Its windows are steamy, and live music pulses through the open door. A small line snakes along the sidewalk as the bouncer checks IDs. MRU is small, with only about three thousand students. Even so, the makeshift town of Salt Gulch struggles to serve us all. The nearest "big" town is Arcata, another smallish college town. It's only about twenty minutes south of us, but most of us prefer to walk home after a few beers, so we all cram into the pub every weekend.

We show the bouncer our IDs and push inside the warm, steamy room. I'm glad for the loud music. It will keep conversation to a minimum. If Cameron says anything else annoying, I can just pretend I didn't hear him.

CHAPTER

3

Hannah

"So then I slept with him."

"Wait, what? I thought he called you a cow."

"He did." Amy shrugs, pushing a strand of hair back from her face and leaning forward to take a massive bite of pastry. "What can I say? I have no standards."

"Isn't he the one who smells like mildew?"

She laughs, spraying a few crumbs of pastry before slamming a hand over her mouth. "He leaves his clothes in the wash for ages—I finally figured it out."

"He sounds disgusting."

She nods. "Pretty much."

Amy Lambert is my best friend. She's the primary medical examiner for Humboldt County, so we both poke around in human remains for a living. At thirty-four, six years younger than me, she's never been married. She dates a massive variety of losers she meets on the internet, sometimes driving all the way to San Francisco—five hours—just to hook up with guys who all sound about as appealing as her most recent conquest, who smelled like mildew.

She's self-destructive in at least five different ways, but she's also the greatest company I've ever known. Amy can make me laugh on days when nobody else can even make me smile.

"Enough about me," Amy says. "How's Joe these days?"

I shrug. "Joe's Joe."

"That's not an answer." Amy leans back in her chair. The sunlight streaming through the plate glass windows of the café caresses her long blonde hair, making it gleam. It's Saturday, and she's wearing an old gray sweatshirt with the neck cut out, *Flashdance* style. The scabby remnants of words remain on the fabric, maybe "Humboldt State," though they've worn so thin it's impossible to be sure.

"What? He's my friend, and now he's my tenant. I don't know why you insist on turning it into something it's not."

"Oh my God, you make me crazy." She lets out a groan, startling a woman at the next table. "He's clearly into you. Hey, if you guys get married, think we could be sister wives? That would be awesome."

I shake my head and stir more honey into my tea. "You're the one who likes him. You should stop pretending it's about me and just ask him out."

She tilts her head, studying me. "You really think he'd say yes?"

"You'll never find out if you don't ask."

"Well . . ." She gazes at her lap, suddenly shy. "You could ask him."

"What is this? Third grade?"

She pulls a face. "Not directly, of course, but—you know—subtly. You could put out feelers."

"Amy." I level a gaze at her. "Come on. 'Subtle' is not a word anyone would ever apply to me."

"True dat," she says, pointing a finger at me.

Amy's eyes catch on something across the room. Interest lights her face. "Don't look now, but there's that guy."

"What guy? Not Mildew Man?"

She giggles. "No. The new professor up at Mad Scientist Central. You know—the one they did a profile on in *Wired*. He's cuter than he looked in the picture."

"What's *Wired*?"

"God, Hannah, you need to read something that isn't peer reviewed." She sips her coffee, eyes still fixed across the room. "I like him. He's got heat."

"Heat?" I repeat. "What is he, a microwaved snack?"

She ignores this. "Even *you* have to know who he is. He's a total media whore. They love him. He's like the enfant terrible of the AI world. Nick something?"

I've just taken a bite of her pastry, but that stops me mid-chew. "Mick Lynch?" It comes out way too loud.

"You called?"

I turn and see Lynch standing behind me. I force myself to chew and swallow.

"Hi." It's all I can think of to say. Warmth ignites my face, burning my cheeks. Logically, I know this is just adrenaline triggering vasodilation, my veins responding to the chemical transmitter adenylyl cyclase; it doesn't keep me from feeling like a complete imbecile, though.

He smirks, obviously pleased by my discomfort. "Morning. How is the esteemed Dr. Bryers on this beautiful Saturday?"

"Fine. You?" I sound wooden and stilted, like a bad actor reading a teleprompter.

"Never been better." He acknowledges Amy with a smile and thrusts out a hand.

I stare at it, focusing on his unusually large phalanges and pronounced triquetrum. I'm hoping concrete details will help me get my vasodilation under control.

"Mick Lynch." His voice is all confidence, rich with bonhomie.

"Great to meet you. Amy Lambert." She holds out her hand and allows it to be swallowed by his. Amy's not a small woman. She's a curvy, buxom endomorph, but her hand looks like a child's in his. I wonder how he manages to accomplish the delicate work of putting together an anatomically convincing mechanical specimen with those enormous paws.

I remember social custom just in time to add something to the introduction ritual. "Dr. Lambert's chief medical examiner for the county."

He smiles. "Impressive. I guess you two have corpses in common."

"Exactly." Amy looks up at him from under her lashes. "Between the two of us, we've got hundreds of skeletons in our closets."

This idiom has always irked me. I understand the metaphor, but the idea that anyone would be careless enough to store a specimen in their closet defies logic. Lynch laughs obligingly, though, cradling his paper cup. It looks like an extra-large coffee, but even that's dwarfed by his baseball mitt hands.

"You have extremely large hands," I blurt.

Amy and Lynch both turn to me, startled.

"You'll have to excuse my friend." Amy gives me a pointed look. "She has no filter."

"Thank you. I think," Lynch says.

I shake my head. "It's an observation, not a compliment."

He looks at his hands like he's never seen them before. "I guess they are kind of big."

"Well, you know what they say about big hands." Amy laughs her dirty laugh.

I look at her blankly. "No. What do they say?"

Lynch and Amy both snigger. I look from one to the other, mystified.

Then it hits me. "Oh! You're talking about the common belief that big hands indicate a large penis. That's unsubstantiated. Some studies have found a correlation, but others have not."

Amy kicks me under the table.

"Ow!" I glare at her. "There was a study a few years back in the *Asian Journal of Andrology*. Researchers found having an index and ring finger of different lengths was the strongest indicator of a longer penis."

"Good to know." Amy gives me a "shut-the-hell-up" look.

I turn to see Lynch appraising me with those blue eyes. His whole face radiates amusement. My gaze falls on the hand wrapped around the cardboard cup; I can't help noting the difference in length between his index and ring finger is unusually pronounced.

There goes my vasodilation again.

"At least you have the grace to blush," he comments dryly.

"Like I said, no filter." Amy gives him an apologetic smile.

I don't know why it's aimed at him. If anyone deserves an apology here, it's me. She did kick me, after all.

Lynch's gaze returns to Amy. "It was nice meeting you. I should run."

"Yes! Enjoy the beautiful day."

I try to think of an appropriately trite conversation closer to add, but my mind's gone blank. Instead, my eyes fall on his hands again. I blush harder.

"Dr. Bryers," he says, "a peculiar pleasure, as always."

"Goodbye." I know my timing's off, hitting the wrong note, as usual. *God, small-talk is exhausting.*

As he strides toward the door, I see him shaking his head, that well-formed cranium rotating side to side.

"What the ever-loving fuck, Hannah?"

I spin back around to face Amy. "What?"

"Penis size? Seriously?" Her eyes are wide with incredulity. "I know you're socially challenged, but Christ, that was off the charts, even for you."

"Your joke implied the same exact thing."

"The key words there are 'joke' and 'implied.' Big difference. Ever heard of innuendo?"

"Social nuance is not my specialty," I huff.

She laughs. "No kidding."

I take another bite of her pastry. "I don't care what that man thinks of me, anyway."

"Hmm . . ." She studies me in a way I can't decipher. "Somehow, I suspect that's not quite true."

"It *is* true. He's a pompous blowhard with a God complex."

She squints, scanning my face. "I've never seen you blush like that. In fact, I'm not sure I've *ever* seen you blush *at all*."

"A reaction of the sympathetic nervous system. Not under my control."

"You know what else isn't under your control?"

I look down into my lap to avoid her gaze. "What?"

"A crush on a coworker." Her expression's gone sly and knowing.

"If you're implying what I think you're—"

"Oh my God!" she interrupts. "There you go again!"

I press my palms against my cheeks. She's right. They're feverishly hot.

*   *   *

Winter

I wake to find Cameron gazing at me. Another one of his annoying habits.

"Hey, sleepyhead." He smiles, his perfect teeth gleaming in the morning sunlight. "I made coffee. You want some?"

"French press?"

He nods. "The kind you like from Salt Gulch Bazaar. Ground the beans myself."

Before we met, Cameron drank Pepsi for breakfast. I've been slowly training him over the year and a half we've been together. When I leave him, he'll be perfect for the next girl—marriage material, in fact. It's a public service, my gift to womankind.

I sit up, rubbing my eyes. "Don't forget the cream."

"Yes, Your Highness." He trots off to his kitchen.

I watch him go, appreciating the view of his brown, muscular back. He likes to spend most of the weekend wearing nothing but boxers. At first, I found it uncouth, but I've learned to appreciate it. He really is easy on the eyes. I grab the tiny compact I keep by his bed and snap it open. I'm not as vain as some girls, but I still like to make sure I'm not hideous. It's one of the hazards of a beautiful boyfriend—wondering if you're up to snuff. My long black hair's a little tangled, but I decide it's more of a sexy bedhead look than a full-on Medusa fro. My dark eyes still bear faint traces of last night's makeup. I lick a finger, rub it along my lower lashes. *Good enough.*

As I stash the compact again, Cameron returns with two steaming mugs. I take one from him and sip. He's added a little more cream than I like, but it will do.

He climbs in beside me, clutching his coffee. "You working today?"

"Yeah. I have those exams to score, and Dr. B wants me to prep the lab."

"Bummer." He sighs.

"Why?" I look at him. "What did you have planned?"

He puts his coffee down and fondles the length of my thigh. Scooting lower, he plants a kiss on my hipbone, peeling away the elastic of my underwear just enough to ensure his lips meet bare skin. Gazing up from under his ridiculously long lashes, he murmurs, "I was hoping we could spend all weekend in bed."

This is a Cameron quirk I sometimes find exasperating, and sometimes it's sublime. It all depends on my mood. He's insatiable. For him, sex is an ever-present need urging him forward like a wolf snapping at his heels. Don't get me wrong; I have a pretty healthy libido myself. And Cameron's got moves, so it's hardly a chore, satisfying his incurable lust. But I also have shit to do. I don't plan to spend graduate school in bed, as appealing as that sometimes sounds.

"Sorry, got to work." I honey my voice just enough to take the sting out of it.

Fluffing the pillows, he settles back into position beside me, picking up his coffee again and taking a sip. We sit together in companionable silence, watching the shadows play around the room as the morning breeze riffles through the branches outside.

"Winter?"

I drink more coffee, not liking the tone of his voice. It's serious. Maybe even a little nervous. "Yeah?"

"I want to ask you something." He gazes out the window.

I risk a sideways glance at him, wary. "Okay . . ."

"I've been trying to find the right moment."

This makes me even warier. Has he found something out about my past? My vague life story has satisfied him so far, but maybe he dug around online. Maybe—by some terrible stroke of bad luck—somebody who knew me back in Florida knows him. But that's crazy. Not possible. Cameron grew up in Vermont. He did his undergrad at Yale. We didn't even exist in the same solar system until now. My heart's pounding, pumping blood through my veins so fast I feel like I might faint.

Dear God, what if he found out about Ella? I grip my mug so tightly my knuckles turn white.

I feel his hand brushing my hair over my shoulder. I can see him in my peripheral vision, peering at me, but I can't meet his eye.

"What is it?" I choke out.

"I think you should move in. With me."

It takes a long moment for his words to land. My brain spins like a hamster on a wheel. I let out my breath, and relief floods through me like a drug. He's talking again, but I can't hear what he's saying over the roar in my ears. I've missed the last couple of sentences. I force myself to tune back in.

"It doesn't have to be right away. You've already paid the full semester for your dorm room, right? But this summer, for sure. I've got plenty of room. Say yes." He leans forward, forcing me to meet his eye.

I lick my lips, my body still coming down from the spike of fear. "That's really sweet."

His brows pull together, a furrow of concern forming between them. "But . . .?"

"It's a big step, is all." I put my coffee down and hug my knees.

Now that the storm of panic has blown through, I try to focus on his question. Cameron has a great place. He occupies the entire upstairs of an old brick building in the heart of Salt Gulch. The Blackberry Bakery is downstairs, so the aroma of rising bread and chocolate chip cookies sifts up through the floorboards at all hours. It's an open-floor plan loft, its massive windows facing the sea.

His parents pay for everything. They live in a mansion on Lake Champlain, so I'm sure they consider Cameron's ocean-view apartment slumming it. He's never strapped for cash. He always pays when we go out. Living here would mean all my expenses covered—groceries, utilities, everything.

Right now I live in the dorms. I have a single, thank God, but it's still basically a shoebox. I share a bathroom with twenty other students, which is a nightmare. For most girls, Cameron's offer to shack up would be a dream come true.

The problem? I'm not most girls. Like I said, I've got shit to do. Some of it requires privacy. I may live in a shoebox, but it's my shoebox, dammit.

I'm also not sure it's a good idea to make Cameron think we're on the fast track to domestic bliss. He's in love with me. Though he'd loathe the label "traditional," deep down he still retains the old-fashioned values of his blue-blood tribe.

If I move in with him, it's only a matter of time before he produces a stunning diamond ring nestled in a velvet box, probably a family heirloom dating back to the *Mayflower*.

I may be calculating, but I do have a heart. Sure, it's battle scarred and tough as Teflon, but it's still there. I don't want to crush Cameron any more than I have to.

He squints at me. Now he's the one who's wary. "I have no idea what you're thinking right now."

"Like I said, it's a big step." I reach out and brush his cheek with my fingers. "I need some time to mull it over."

"Fair enough." His smile tries to be brave, but I can see the injured pride it covers.

Life with Cameron is a constant balancing act; I'm determined to keep him for as long as I'm here—another two and a half years. At the same time, I know it's temporary. The life he wants isn't one I can slot myself into. He'll want babies, for starters. That right there is a deal breaker. Luckily, we're still in our early twenties, so it's not a point of discussion, but I know him well enough to see the Christmas-card family portrait he holds in his imagination.

Never going to happen.

Right now, though, I need to reassure him. Luckily, I know just how to do it.

I take his coffee cup from him and set it down on the nightstand.

He looks puzzled. "What are you—"

With my palm against his chest, I push him back against the pillows. My long legs straddle him, my fingers reaching down to explore his boxers. I flash him my filthiest grin. "What was that you said about your plans for this weekend?"

He reaches up to cup my breasts. "I thought you said you had to work."

"I'm not working now, am I?" I press my hips against him, my hands raking through my hair. My body writhes as he hardens against me.

"Winter," he murmurs, gripping my ass.

"We have some time. Unless you're too busy . . ." I give him a pouty little frown.

"Never too busy for you," he breathes.

As I lean down to kiss him, my hair falls around us like a dark shroud.

4

Hannah

MONDAY MORNING, WINTER Jones, my TA, is in the classroom before me, as usual. She spent the weekend grading exams and prepping the lab. Her efficiency never ceases to impress. She's a little edgy at first glance—nose ring, tattoos, black eyeliner as bold as a Sharpie—but she's the best TA I've had in the seven years I've worked here. She's quiet when she needs to be, which is essential. My last TA was so garrulous I thought my head would explode. Meaningless chatter doesn't work for me. Winter never says a word that isn't relevant. When she does speak, it's in a calm, husky voice that's articulate and self-assured—none of this insecure upspeak so many young women employ these days. In another two and a half years, she'll have her doctorate. If she continues on the path she's laid out for herself, I may even lobby for her to teach here. She's become so indispensable, I can't imagine life without her.

I enjoy mentoring Winter. She's respectful, but never fawning. Her intelligence is self-evident, but she's not arrogant, even when she's helping the undergraduates who struggle to master the basics. I'm not maternal—the biological drive to procreate seems to have passed me by entirely, thank God—but Winter does stir a protectiveness in me that's almost motherly.

I suppose we all want to believe our work on this planet will outlive us. We want to leave a legacy. My textbooks and research might continue to inspire new generations of anthropologists after I'm gone, but that's cold comfort compared to the time-honored tradition of passing knowledge down to eager young students. Winter Jones is the protégé I've longed for my whole career.

The vast majority of my students aren't nearly as inspiring. Case in point: my Monday-morning 201 undergraduates roll into the room looking rumpled and hung over. They scroll through their phones with catatonic, vacant stares. As I take my place at the front of the room, reminding them to put their phones away, they glance up, annoyed. Apparently, the education their parents took out second mortgages to afford is interfering with their all-consuming Snapchat and Instagram addictions. The number of yawns I see in the first couple minutes of class makes me cranky. It doesn't help that I'm fighting a yawn myself. Last night, I had dark, tangled dreams; after waking with my heart pounding, I lay awake for at least two hours, listening to the wind. Now my students' lack of enthusiasm grates on me all the more because it mirrors my own.

I take a deep breath and launch into my planned lecture. Their eyes glaze over. I might as well be a TV blaring random sound bites and meaningless jingles. That's something I can't abide—boring people. I might not have Mick Lynch's charisma, but every one of my lesson plans are packed with essential information gleaned from years of intensive study and fieldwork. A couple of them glance covertly at their phones. Anger bubbles up in me. I welcome it. Most emotions are useless. Jealousy, shame, sadness, even joy—none of them qualify as productive. Give me a pure, hot dose of pissed off any day of the week. It goads me into action.

I tear up today's lesson plan and decide to improvise. Luckily, I have just the antidote to boredom.

"Okay, people. Since you're clearly not present, there's no point in going through the motions. Let's shake things up, shall we? Follow me."

A faint tremor of confusion runs through the room. My students aren't used to spontaneity. They shoot each other covert glances, eyebrows raised. They're wondering what's gotten into me.

What has *gotten into me?* I thrive on order. Somehow, today, the urge to break out of my usual staid box is too powerful to ignore.

Mick Lynch's face whips through my mind. I see him standing before his rapt audience, his expression open and vulnerable as a child's.

Go away, I tell him. *I'm working.*

I march my students down the hall, leading them from the classroom to the lab. They trail after me like sleepy ducklings. They're waking up a little more with each step, though. By the time we gather around the stainless-steel table at the center of the room, the tension is palpable.

A lumpy, human-sized shape lies beneath a thin white sheet. A few of them already look a little sick. If they are hungover, this probably won't help their delicate digestive systems, but they should have considered that before they did Jell-O shots or keg stands or whatever it is they do on Sunday nights to make them this limp and comatose Monday morning. It's one thing to study images of decomposing bodies on a screen or in a textbook. It's something else entirely to smell one.

The lab is filled with the usual potpourri of contradictory scents; there's the sharp, antiseptic perfume of bleach and disinfectant. Under that, though, is the ripe, warm smell of decay.

"John Doe arrived yesterday." I scan their faces, trying to detect if any of them are likely to be sick. Nobody looks fish-belly pale, so I continue. "Police responded on Sunday to a call from a jogger who discovered the body. During her morning run in the southeast corner of the Salt Gulch Community Forest, she noticed what looked like a human hand protruding from beneath a large blackberry bush."

I yank the sheet off. The remains of John Doe are desiccated, black. There are still a few patches of skin clinging to the skeleton, though it looks more like black plastic draped over bones than actual human flesh.

Most of the students take an instinctive step back, covering their mouths or gasping in surprise. One girl, Tess Wilcox, lets out a quick, sharp yelp of disgust. Since the body has reached the active decay stage, on the cusp of advanced decay, the smell is not nearly as pronounced as it must have been a few weeks ago, but it's far from odorless.

I search their faces, considering which of them to call on. I prefer someone composed enough to reply without any hysterics. Only one of them remains totally expressionless. Winter. Her dark eyes take in the body with calm, clinical interest. A vein in her temple throbs, but aside from that, she could be selecting avocados at a grocery store, not staring at a decomposing human corpse.

"Winter?"

"Yes, Professor?" She pivots to face me, her dark eyes alert.

"What can you tell me about John Doe?"

Her voice is cool and composed. "The skin has obviously blackened, and the flesh seems to have mostly . . . disappeared."

"Disappeared?" I echo. "Can you elaborate?"

"You said he was found in the forest, under foliage. Chances are, maggots have already consumed most of the flesh."

Garrett Abrams emits a barely audible moan.

"Good." I address the others, still scanning for anyone likely to vomit. I can't have them contaminating the evidence.

"Let's unpack that a little more, though. Can anyone tell me what Winter means when she says 'maggots'?"

They look at me blankly.

I sigh. "A more scientific name for the carrion insects responsible for the flesh that has, as she put it, 'disappeared'?"

Cal Rosenbaum raises his hand, pushing his glasses up on his nose.

"Yes, Cal?"

"Necrophagous blowflies usually get there first. It's likely they colonized John Doe's decomposing remains."

"Excellent. Yes. Anything to add to that?"

Winter speaks up again. "Their eggs are generally laid directly on or in the corpse. They complete their life-cycle there. Calliphoridae, sarcophagidae, and muscidae are typically the first to lay eggs inside the body."

"Okay, now we're getting somewhere." I look down at the corpse again, studying the sagging black skin. Grabbing a scalpel laid out on a nearby tray, I carefully peel back the epidermis to reveal the thoracic cage beneath. "So, we've established that the body was in the forest long enough to be colonized by necrophagous insects. What other clues can tell us how long it was there?"

"The body has blackened," Winter says. "It turns green and then purple before it gets this dark. Bacteria digest what's left when the insects have done their work; that's when the remains darken."

"So, we're talking about how much time?" I prompt.

She squints, thinking. "At least . . . two or three weeks? Possibly more, depending on temperature. The hair and teeth have fallen out, correct?"

I nod, prying open the mouth so they can get a better look.

"So that makes me think he's been decomposing for at least a month," Winter says.

I close the mouth, nodding again. "This varies, but—usually after three to four weeks—the hair, nails, and teeth begin to fall out. The swollen internal organs start to rupture and liquefy. The organs decompose at different rates."

Winter speaks again. "Is it true the uterus and prostate last longer than the other organs, and that helps pathologists identify a corpse's sex?"

"There are a number of other indicators; we can hypothesize with a high degree of accuracy, even if we have nothing but partial skeletal remains. To answer your question, though, the uterus and prostate tend to be more resilient than other organs, yes. They can be identified up to a year after death."

"Sexy." This from Garrett, the class clown. Though it's not funny, the class laughs, releasing some tension.

I speak over their titters, my voice stern. "I would remind you, respect is of the upmost importance here. Though it's natural for humans to seek release through gallows humor when confronting mortality, we keep that to a minimum in my lab."

Garrett looks cowed.

Softening my tone, I meet his eye. "This was a human being. It's essential to keep his humanity in mind, even though we also require clinical distance to do our job. We have the honor of examining John Doe, trying to determine who he was and how he died. That is our sacred charge. I implore you to treat it as just that: sacred."

*   *   *

Winter

As the students file out, I stay behind in the lab, staring at the body beneath the sheet. My mouth is dry, and goose bumps linger on my arms. Bryers reminds me to pull the door closed when I leave. In a tone as normal as I can manage around my thick, gritty tongue, I assure her I will.

When at last I'm alone with the body—*his* body—I pull off the sheet and force myself to look again.

It reminds me of the time I killed a bird with my sling-shot. I must have been nine or ten. Ella and I were messing around, shooting at cans, when a flurry of motion caught my eye in the trees, and I shot at it on impulse. The bird dropped to the ground, and Ella turned to me with an expression somewhere between horror and delight.

When we found its limp, feathered body bleeding into the earth, though, she started to cry. It was a little chickadee, with a black and white head and a gray body, now oozing blood. Its wings twitched a couple of times, stirring the smattering of leaves it landed on, and I realized with sick dread it was still alive. I ordered Ella to stand back, ignoring her panicky expression as she obeyed. I picked up a heavy rock and hesitated just a second before I brought it down on the tiny black-and-white head. It's one thing to kill, but it's something else to make your victim suffer. That's sadistic. Thanks to our nana, torture was something Ella and I already knew too much about, even at that age.

"You killed it," Ella whispered between pale fingers.

I shrugged, trying for tough, even though my hands still trembled. "It was dying. I had to."

"It was alive." Her gaze drifted to the canopy of oaks overhead. "And now it's dead."

Sweet Ella. How delicate she was, pure and innocent, in spite of everything we'd been through. Though we looked exactly alike—right down to our matching outfits—the darkness we lived in affected us differently. Even at nine, I could already feel it getting into my bones, my blood, infecting my dreams. Ella, on the other hand, grew more ethereal, dreamier, like a ghost drifting through the battlefield of our dilapidated family estate, immune to its rot and decay.

I force myself to breathe in the smell of the corpse before me, bringing me back to the present. Though the face is little more than bones in a blackened shell, I know it's him. It has to be. How many dead bodies can there be in the Salt Gulch Community Forest? A hysterical giggle rises inside me at the thought, but I smother it with one hand. Even though I'm alone in the lab, Bryers's warnings about gallows humor are fresh in my mind. Respect. She's always going on about respect. She has no idea. I'll teach her something about respect.

With a shudder, I recall the way "John Doe" looked at me when he died, the expression of mute betrayal on his face as I watched him gasping for breath.

What's done is done. I can't allow myself the luxury of regret. He's washed up here, in our lab, as I knew he probably would. Now I have to focus on the best way to move forward. There's a way to use him to my advantage, I'm sure of it. He'll help with my master plan, ensuring that he didn't die in vain.

* * *

After leaving the lab, I find Bryers in her office. I tap lightly on her open door until she looks up. "Professor Bryers? Do you have a minute?"

"Of course." She turns away from her computer and gestures for me to come in.

Though I've been here many times, I stare around the room, taking it in. Bryers likes it when people take the time to notice. She's got a freaky, old-fashioned, cabinet-of-curiosities vibe going in here. The walls are painted deep green, lined with thick wooden shelves displaying human bones and teeth under bell jars. Anatomical illustrations hang side by side with Día de los Muertos shadow boxes. Preserved remains marinate in glass specimen jars. I can never decide if her attention to detail is impressive or creepy. She's created her own little movie set in here, a shrine to the last hundred years of anatomical science—more evidence that she sees herself as the star of her own adventure flick.

I hand her the stack of exams I graded over the weekend.

"Thanks for doing that." She smiles. "How did they do?"

"Not bad. The usual bell curve."

"Glad to hear it. What's up?" She leans back in her leather chair, giving me her focus.

I clear my throat. "I was wondering . . . did you get a text from the summer internship I applied for?"

She looks puzzled. "A text?" As I'd hoped, she pulls her phone from her pocket and studies it.

I pluck my own phone from my bag. "Yeah, they sent me an email saying they'd text our professors about letters of rec."

"That's an odd way to do it." She sounds distracted as she scrolls through her phone.

Heart pounding, I reach out a hand. "Do you mind if I look? It might be stuck in a weird subfolder."

She hesitates for half a second. Handing someone your phone is like giving them all your secrets. Also, there's no such thing as "weird subfolders" when it comes to texts. It's a risky move, but I'm banking on the fact that Bryers—for all her brilliance—is still almost twenty years older than me, and therefore believes, consciously or unconsciously, that I have mad skills when it comes to any tech invented in the last two decades. I see the exact moment when she tells herself it's ridiculous to doubt me. This is me, her best TA, the girl who's proven herself more reliable than any student she's ever had. She hands me her phone.

Taking it with one hand, I quickly send a text on my own phone under the desk. Though the idea that we're all tech geniuses is a myth, one skill we millennials *have* mastered is sending texts on the down low. My message to the undergrad I paid fifty bucks to this morning is just one word: *Now.*

The fire alarm blares throughout the building, impossibly loud. Bryers jumps to her feet, frowning. She narrowly escaped a massive forest fire a couple years ago in Tanzania— she mentioned it once in lecture—so I knew she wouldn't hesitate. I move as if to follow her out the door, but as soon as she's halfway down the hall, I retreat to her office again and close the door behind me.

Working quickly, I install the spyware app on her phone. This puppy is virtually undetectable, and it will tell me everything: her location, her texts, social media posts (as if! Bryers would never sully herself posting on Facebook or Instagram). As soon as the app's installed, I check my own phone to make sure it's working. Voilà! The keys to the kingdom.

I allow myself a quick victory dance before putting her phone back on her desk and slipping out.

God, that alarm really is ridiculously loud. Whoever set the volume on that thing must be a sadist. Jogging down the stairs, I'm sure my eardrums will rupture.

Outside, I join the people pouring out of the building. Bryers is talking to Frankie, one of the security guards. She'll be distracted for a while. I seize the opportunity and hurry to the parking lot. Bryers always parks in the same place. Her car would be indistinguishable from others like it—the dusty green Subaru is standard hippie gear around here—except for the bumper sticker that says: "Dead men tell no tales—unless you're in forensics." I look around, making sure the coast is clear. There's a guy and a girl about fifty yards away, but their backs are to me. I pull out the small tracking device I purchased online (on Cam's laptop, just in case) and stick it to the wheel well.

If Bryers goes somewhere without her phone, I'll still know where to find her.

I walk away quickly, smiling to myself.

You can run, Bryers, but you can't hide.

5

Hannah

THAT AFTERNOON, MY attention keeps drifting back to John Doe from the Community Forest. I've waded into the never-ending tide of my emails, answering queries, selecting textbooks for next semester. All the while, though, I can feel John Doe calling to me, demanding I discover his identity and cause of death.

The sheriff's department made no secret about the significance of this body. They had a deputy sheriff go missing a couple weeks ago, and they have reason to believe this is the same guy. The corpse has deteriorated too thoroughly to identify it quickly and definitively. While every suspicious death deserves equal consideration, the tribal nature of law enforcement means they have a much more pronounced interest in this body than your average John Doe. I feel the pressure weighing down on me, ever present. A dull headache blossoms near my occipital bone.

Rubbing the tension from my neck, I decide to make a quick stop in the faculty lounge for a cup of tea. My lack of sleep last night has crept past the wall of caffeine I erected

I blink.

He grins. "Great! I knew you'd be intrigued."

"I have a body to identify."

"Won't take long."

"What could I possibly—"

"Right this way." Lynch indicates the door to the lab.

With a sigh, I walk through.

*   *   *

Lynch's workspace looks more like a demented toyshop than a lab. The walls are lined with robots in various stages of construction. I can feel their eyes on me, leering. In the center of the room are three of the stainless-steel autopsy tables we use in our lab. Instead of human remains, though, robots lie prone on two of his tables, their artificial skin peeled back in places to reveal the mechanical workings beneath.

Students in lab coats work in the far corner, talking in low tones; occasionally, they erupt in raucous laughter, something I find off-putting in this setting. A handful of Lynch's assistants sit gathered around a conference table near the large, mullioned windows; some of them have their feet propped on the table—a hideous, unsanitary habit I would never allow.

As Lynch beckons me into the room, I'm not sure where to look. Everywhere my eyes land, some fresh horror assails me: a disembodied hand with garishly painted nails; a half-completed torso with a belly button that's just *wrong*, though from this distance I can't say why; a petite female android with a smile that looks disconcertingly feral. This must be how first-timers feel in my lab, seeing corpses in various stages of decay. A queasy dread sloshes through me, slow and syrupy.

Lynch leads me to a table against the far wall. On it sits a long, lean male android with short, dark, synthetic hair and a face that's apparently still under construction.

"This is Francois." Lynch's hand reaches out to adjust a gear as effortlessly and unselfconsciously as a parent wiping food from a child's mouth.

When I don't respond, Lynch turns to me. His shrewd blue eyes study my expression. "Does Francois make you uncomfortable?"

I widen my eyes at him. "Everything about this place makes me uncomfortable."

"Really? Everything?" He looks around, as if seeing our surroundings for the first time. "Surely the lab itself puts you at ease. It's not so different from yours, after all."

A sound of disbelief escapes me. "It couldn't be more different."

"This room was modeled on your lab—the layout, the tables, even some of the equipment."

Lynch tweaks something again in the robot's mechanisms and Francois's eyes swivel toward me. I shudder.

Lynch barely manages to repress a chuckle. When my gaze snaps to his face in warning, he forces the corners of his mouth down, trying for serious.

"What, precisely, do you find so discomforting about my workspace? Can you put it into words?"

I expect to see condescension in his expression, but there's only watchful stillness. As if he sincerely wants to know.

I search for the right words. "It has to do with how they're both human and . . . not human."

"Uncanny valley."

"Sorry?"

"It's a phenomenon known as uncanny valley. The more lifelike and convincing something is, the more we fixate on the tiny things that make it different from us—the flaws, if you will. That gap between 'us' and 'them' incites instinctive revulsion. The uncanny valley."

I find I'm interested in spite of myself. "On an animal level, we're driven to uncover the distinctions, to know what is and is not authentically human."

"Yes. Exactly." He turns back to Francois, cupping the robot's shoulder. "That's why I need you to help me make his anatomy as accurate as possible."

I raise an eyebrow. I didn't see this coming.

Lynch frames the android's face with his hands. "The facial structure must be perfect. Mouth. Cheekbones. And, of course, most of all, the eyes."

"There's only so much you can do with synthetics."

Lynch whips around sharply, as if I've said something startling. "Tell me more."

"The complexity of human anatomy is beyond our wildest imagination. Right here." I gesture at the area beneath Francois's eye. "The zygomaticus minor and major work together with a subtle sophistication even the greatest clockmakers couldn't hope to achieve."

"Yes. The complexity."

"If you want realism, we have to see the muscles working beneath the skin." I reach out to trace the line of the android's jaw. "If it all looks too smooth, without the ripples of complex facial muscles subtly flexing and relaxing, he'll never be anything but a mannequin."

He studies me in silence. I can feel the air thickening between us. When I turn to meet his gaze, he surprises me yet again. His eyes fill with wistful melancholy. There's something else there too. Wonder?

"What?" I tuck a strand of hair behind my ear, suddenly self-conscious.

"Nothing." Like flipping a switch, Lynch's expression turns bland. "Sorry."

"You just—you looked—"

"I know. Bad habit."

"What is?" I feel a little lightheaded; I don't know why.

He sighs. "I'm told I have a face that says too much."

"Is that right?"

"Needless to say, I don't play poker." He holds his hands out, palms up. "I'm an open book."

I consider him. Lynch does have a dizzying array of expressions, each one more complex and nuanced than the next. Somehow, though, I can't buy the idea that this is a man without secrets.

"The human face." He shakes his head. "It's the most complicated machinery to replicate."

"I still don't see why you'd want to."

His hand reaches out and rests on Francois's shoulder with a paternal air. "Until we make them more human, they'll never reach their full potential."

"But have you truly considered that potential? How dangerous it could be?"

His smile is tinged with sadness. "Believe me, Dr. Bryers, the thought consumes me."

"Then why do you do it?"

"AI is inevitable." Lynch brushes a strand of hair back from the robot's face with unexpected tenderness. "I want to ensure we do it right."

6

Hannah

THE PUB MAY have the least imaginative name ever, but what it lacks in colorful monikers it makes up for in whimsical decor. Mr. Yamada, the owner, is obsessed with mermaids. Every inch of the dark wood walls are adorned with mermaid images from around the world. From the tacky Vegas-style life-sized mermaid statue near the door to dark depictions of skeletal sirens of the Edo period, the place is a shrine to Yamada's passion.

It's Monday night, and Joe's got his usual gig at The Pub. I don't always go, but tonight the silence at home was stifling rather than soothing. I'm in the mood to be around people— unusual for me. Even though I know I'll probably hole up in a booth by myself and barely utter a word, the muggy warmth of the bar sounds more appealing than bed and a book. I don't have class until noon tomorrow, so I can afford to stay out as late as I like.

Stepping around the glitzy mermaid standing guard near the door, I make a beeline for the bar. My eyes adjust to the dim interior. I spot Joe up on the stage and recognize the song he's playing, though I can't remember the name. He's engrossed in the music, as he always is during a performance—even a small, casual one like this. I give up on catching his eye. Leaning against the bar, I search the shadows for familiar faces. When the bartender acknowledges me with a curt nod, I order a pint of Scrimshaw and a basket of fries. The salty, fried smell of Yamada's famous katsudon perfumes the air. Within seconds, Yamada's large, cheerful face appears in the window that provides glimpses of the kitchen.

"Irrashaimasse!" he calls.

I beam at him and bow. Yamada-san knows I was in Japan over winter break, doing research. We often make small talk in Japanese when I come in. I don't know his first name, so I doubt he qualifies as a friend, but the sight of him never fails to cheer me up.

"*Konbanwa, Yamada-san,*" I call, greeting him. "*Genki desu ka?*"

"*Hai, genki desu,*" he replies.

I decide to take a seat at the bar. Usually, I need my own space. That's one of the things I like about this place; the booths, with their cracked vinyl seats and thick wooden tables, provide the buffer I need from other people. I'm trying to get better at random interactions, though, so I push myself to sit in the communal space. Amy keeps urging me to "get out of my comfort zone" and "open up more." Though I'm still not completely convinced this advice is sound, tonight I'm in the mood to live dangerously. Fries and a beer at our local pub—the same place Joe plays every Monday—hardly qualifies as risky to most people. I'm not most people, though. Baby steps, as Amy likes to say.

"Hey, Professor Bryers."

I turn to see Winter standing there, her eyes bright.

"Oh, hi."

She flags down the bartender over my shoulder, orders a beer, and perches lightly on the stool beside me. "I didn't know you hang out here."

"I'm not here often, I just . . ." I trail off. Sometimes, in the middle of trying to make small talk, my brain goes all staticky, like a radio losing its signal. It happens a lot when I'm trying to talk to students off campus. I have trouble relating to somebody in one context, then switching abruptly to another—part of the reason I'd normally sequester myself in a booth.

"Right—no, I get it." Winter nods with earnest verve, like she actually does get it, though what I said imparted almost no meaning. "Sometimes I come on Mondays, for the music."

"That's my friend," I say, nodding at Joe. Even I can hear the sliver of pride in my voice.

Her eyebrows arch. "Joe Shepley? Really? And when you say 'friend,' do you mean . . . special friend?"

I look at her blankly. "I'm not sure what you . . .?"

"As in boyfriend?" Her expression goes from playful to contrite. "Sorry—none of my business."

"Oh! I see. No. We're not sexually involved, if that's what you're asking."

She looks a little taken aback.

"He lives in my house, but downstairs."

Winter's expression grows more confused.

"Not in the basement. He likes to call it the basement, but it's not. It's the ground floor."

"Okay. Got it." She still looks a bit mystified.

In unison, we turn to survey Joe, a pretty good-looking guy, I suppose. He's in shape, with a grizzled charm most women find attractive. He's a competent musician—better than competent: talented. His knack for writing soulful lyrics goes a long way with the ladies. When he sings, you're convinced he's singing every word just for you.

"He's really good," Winter says, trying to get us back on track. "I love hearing him play. He teaches at Mad River too, right?"

"Part-time." I wonder, too late, if this sounds like I'm putting Joe down. I overcompensate. "His classes are always full. He's very popular. I have a lot of respect for him."

The polite bewilderment on her face makes me want to cringe. I get that look a lot. I can hear when I've hit the wrong note in a conversation, but it's always too late. That bell can't be un-rung.

I stare at an empty booth with longing.

Winter's just opened her mouth to say something else, probably a platitude designed to smooth over my awkwardness. I can't bear it. I scoop up my pint and fries.

"Just going to"—I nod at the booth—"while it's empty. Have a nice—uh—night."

"You too, Professor." She offers a smile that's part bemusement, part . . . what? Pity? God, I hope not.

Settling into the booth, I take a swig of beer, enjoying the cool fizz. I tell myself I'm being overly sensitive. Amy said baby steps. I spent at least seven minutes on a barstool, sitting out in the open. Okay, so the experiment couldn't exactly be called an unqualified success, but neither was it an epic fail. I tried. I was weird and flustered, but I didn't shame my ancestors. It was one pebble in the sea of awkwardness that is my life.

Okay, that's a little depressing. I probably shouldn't have come.

I take another long pull from my beer. Joe's playing "Train to Madison," one of my favorites. It's about Matty, one of his many ex-girlfriends. Most of his best songs are about his exes. Like I said, though, he sings with such conviction, every woman in the room is sure it's all about her.

My beer goes down even smoother on the third sip. The fries are hot, greasy explosions on my tongue. Delicious. I close my eyes, drinking in the pleasure of the moment.

When I open them again, Mick Lynch is sitting across from me in the booth. I blink several times. My eyelids feel like mechanical shutters, opening, closing. His presence does not compute.

"The thing about faces," he says, as if we're mid-conversation, "is that, while no two are exactly alike, they can be categorized into types. Twelve face shapes, four profiles, which some say correspond with temperament. What's your opinion on morphology?"

I clutch my beer, trying to regain my composure. "What are you doing here?"

"Here?" He looks around, as if noticing the bar for the first time. "I was walking by, and it looked cozy."

"Okay." I can feel my brow crinkling.

"Actually, it didn't look cozy." His volume drops a fraction; I have to read his lips to be sure of what he's saying under the music. "I saw you sitting here, and I like talking to you. Morphology?"

"It's interesting, from a cultural point of view." I feel much drunker than three sips of beer can account for. I keep talking, though, thinking aloud. "It dates back to the Egyptian pharaonic tradition. Ancient Greek physicians were crazy for it. During the Renaissance it went underground, discredited by the natural sciences. Scientifically speaking, most lump it together with palm reading and bloodletting these days."

"As a diagnostic tool, it's probably useless." He reaches out and seizes one of my fries, popping it in his mouth absently. His eyes scan the bar, though I can tell he doesn't see any of it. His gaze is fixed inward, working out equations. "As a starting place for facial design and personality programming, I'm thinking it might provide a handy model."

I scoff.

His eyes dart to my face, narrowing. "You disagree?"

"I just can't imagine playing God with such blithe hubris."

"Blithe hubris," he repeats, beaming. "I like that. I think I'll have that printed on a T-shirt."

"You act like these are imaginary characters you're conjuring from nothing."

"Not imaginary. They're quite real to me." He snags another fry, holding it up for inspection. "These are delicious."

"Yamada-san. You should taste his katsudon."

"Japanese guy?" Lynch pops the fry in his mouth and chews.

I nod. This conversation is very peculiar. I glance at Joe. His eyes are closed, and he's singing into the microphone like he's in love with it. I don't think he's spotted me.

"Man, I love a good katsudon. I lived on that stuff in Tokyo."

"You were in Japan?"

He nods. "Taught there for a couple semesters."

"I was there over winter break."

"Really?" His eyebrows arch. "Doing what?"

"Fulbright." I can't deny it: I love saying this word. Something about Lynch makes me want to impress him. Talking to him, all my modesty dissipates. My sheen of social decorum—thin at the best of times—evaporates, leaving a reckless, childish desire to do whatever it takes to hold his attention, as though I'm a little girl spinning crazily to make the adults notice me.

"Dr. Bryers." He gives me an inscrutable look.

"What?" Heat crawls up my neck and pools in my cheeks.

He shakes his head. "You never cease to fascinate."

"That's agentless passive."

"Sorry?"

My overheated face burns even hotter. I'm grateful for the dim pub, the shadowy booth. "No agent by-phrase. In your sentence."

"You a linguist too?" Lynch asks.

I shrug. "I've always liked languages."

"Nihongo wa?" ["Do you speak Japanese?"]

"Ma-ma," I reply. ["So-so."]

"*You* fascinate *me*." His blue eyes hold my gaze with a steady intensity. "Does that eliminate the agentless passive issue?"

I don't reply. The silence seems to stretch between us, elastic.

"Didn't know you were here." I look up to see Joe's affable face. He scoots in beside me, takes a sip of my beer. "How's it going? Is it Nick?"

"Mick. Joe, right?"

Joe nods. An awkward silence blooms between the three of us. Somebody feeds the jukebox. A Patsy Cline song bursts through the speakers, but even that can't break the spell.

Joe looks at me. "Did I know you were coming?"

"No." I trace the perspiration on my pint of beer. "I'm being spontaneous."

"Not exactly your specialty." Joe shoots a conspiratorial glance at Lynch, who stares at him blankly.

Lynch stands, brushing grains of salt from his fingers. "*Ja, mata,*" he says. ["See you later."]

I don't even have time to respond before he's out the door.

Joe watches him go. "That guy's weird."

"You think?" My voice sounds funny.

"Almost as weird as you." He musses my hair. "You need anything from the bar? I'm going to get a beer."

"No. I'm good."

He stands, scanning the room. I can tell his attention has already moved on. I can't help but wonder: if Lynch hadn't come in, would Joe have taken a break and acknowledged me?

As Joe saunters over to the bar, I catch Winter watching us from across the room. She's at a table in the corner with a group of other students. The guy next to her is laughing so hard he has to wipe away tears. When she sees I've noticed her, she looks away.

* * *

Winter

Sun Tze wrote *The Art of War* at least twenty-five hundred years ago. You'd think that would nullify its relevance in the twenty-first century. You'd be wrong. I live by it.

As I watch Bryers from across the pub, I review the work's most essential lessons:

1. Choose your battles; timing is essential.
2. Know yourself; know the enemy.
3. All warfare is based on deception.

It's no accident that Bryers doesn't give me much thought. I'm her Girl Friday, her trusty servant. I show up before I'm supposed to. I do everything she asks, and then I do just a little more. Not too much. I can't look too eager. Overstepping our carefully prescribed teacher–student rituals would draw attention. It's a must that I become as invisible yet as essential as her own right hand. Well, in her case, her left hand. She's a leftie.

"Know the enemy."

I must study her without appearing to study her. *"All warfare is based on deception."*

Tonight, as I sat in Cameron's living room, watching people without much interest through his wall of windows, a gift fell into my lap. I spotted Dr. B striding down the street. She always walks with purpose, like there's a crime scene she needs to investigate, a precious artifact she must unearth before marauders get to it. She sees herself as the star of her own *Indiana Jones*–style adventure. I can't decide if this is sweet or pathetic.

Cameron was immersed in a paper for biostats, buried under a mountain of research. I told him I had to go out for a minute. Mild surprise registered on his face, like a sleepwalker turning lucid, but then he grunted in the affirmative and dove back into his work.

I slipped out and hurried down the street. Concealing myself behind a group of tipsy undergrads, I followed Bryers into the pub. We chatted at the bar for a minute or two. She's so damn awkward. It's one of my favorite things about her—her total lack of social filters. Any number of priceless gems might slip through that wide-open net. Though she's guarded as a rule, especially at school, she's so off-balance in any other context, she's liable to say anything.

I found a rowdy booth filled with bio-chem acquaintances and used them as camouflage. Then I began watching her in earnest.

Now, keeping my gaze trained on her from across the crowded bar, three vital scraps of information emerge:

1. Bryers is definitely hot for Lynch. I suspected as much, but tonight confirmed it. Her body language, seated across from him, was unmistakable. Nervous babbling? Check. Dilated pupils? Check. Playing with her hair? Never would have thought it possible with cool, distant Dr. B, but checkety-check-check.
2. Joe Shepley, the part-time music prof half the female undergrads have crushes on, is hot for Bryers. His strategic break just in time to kill the vibe between Bryers and Lynch made that crystal clear.
3. Bryers is immune to Shepley's charms. She may not even realize he's angling to get in her pants. She thinks he's just the dude who lives in her basement. Correction: ground-floor apartment. God, she's priceless.

I sip my IPA, considering. The last year and a half has been all about reconnaissance. My whole reason for choosing MRU was Dr. Bryers. Our history runs deep. Of course, she doesn't know this. She thinks we met for the first time sixteen months ago, when I showed up in her evolutionary biology course, all bright-eyed and eager to learn.

She doesn't remember the first time we met, when I was just a thirteen-year-old traumatized orphan in Apalachicola. I legally changed my name two years ago—went with my middle name, Winter. I kept Jones, since it's the ultimate surname for hiding in plain sight. She might have recognized me if I still went by Bekkah Jones. I couldn't risk that.

Who knows, though? Maybe the cases all blur together for Bryers. Maybe she doesn't understand the trail of heartbreak and devastation she leaves in her wake.

"Timing is everything. Know your enemy; know yourself. All warfare is based on deception."

7

Hannah

AMY'S TEXTED ME three times to apologize for being late. She knows lack of punctuality is my least favorite of her many annoying qualities. She's learned to grovel, and I've learned to meet her in my office, where at least if she keeps me waiting I'll have plenty to keep me busy. Today we're supposed to meet here before heading downtown for lunch. Last night she went out with a guy named Gavin—an ear, nose, and throat specialist. Normally, she goes for fringy types: out-of-work mimes, political activists, documentary film-makers who've never actually made any films. Given how late she is and how thoroughly she's groveled, I'm guessing she slept with him. Her new year's resolution was to stop sleeping with guys on the first date. It's now March, and so far she has failed to live up to this resolution even once.

When I hear a knock on my door, I call out, "Come in, you lazy slut!"

The door opens behind me. I'm engrossed in adding the last few lines to an email and don't turn around. "So . . . what? You slept with him, right? Or at least gave him a blow job."

A husky, accented voice says, "Excuse me?"

I spin around in my chair, surprise sending a jolt of adrenaline straight through me. It's not Amy standing in the doorway, eyes wide. Of course it isn't. It's Lynch's wife—what was her name? Isadora? Esme? Dammit, I'm such an idiot.

"I'm so sorry! I thought you were my friend."

"Is not a problem." Her smirk is unmistakable. "Sounds like quite a friend."

"She is. And she's late. Again." I stand, removing a stack of textbooks from the chair opposite my desk and gesturing. "Have a seat."

She sits, smoothing her flawless floral sundress over her knees. She's just as beautiful as I remember—maybe more so. Her satiny shoulders gleam beneath spaghetti straps. Lush black hair frames her face. My mind races to remember her name, but the harder I try, the further it drifts away from me.

"Excuse my intrusion, Dr. Bryers. Is it Hannah? May I call you Hannah?"

I nod, taking a seat behind my desk. "Of course! I'm sorry, I know we met the other night, but I can't remember your name."

"Isabella Lynch." Is it my imagination, or does she place special emphasis on her last name?

"Right! Of course. What can I do for you, Isabella?"

She reaches into her expensive-looking leather purse and plucks an envelope from its depths. "I want to invite you to our home."

I take the envelope from her. It's hot pink, made of stiff, expensive stationery. With one finger I break the seal and slide the invitation out. It's adorned with champagne flutes, and the words "You're Invited" are printed in embossed metallic gold.

"I'm ashamed that we are just now getting around to inviting our neighbors and friends for the—how do you say? House heating party?"

For a second I'm baffled. Then I get it. "Oh! House-warming, yes."

She laughs. It's a musical laugh, delicate as wind chimes and feminine as lace. One manicured hand reaches up to cover her mouth. "I am always butchering the English."

"Not at all! I find malapropisms deeply charming."

She blinks at me. I think she's trying to decide if I've insulted her.

"Sorry. It's an unusual word. It means . . . um . . . when you get something wrong. In English." She looks unconvinced, so I keep talking. "It comes from Mrs. Malaprop, a character in Richard Sheridan's play *The Rivals*, an eighteenth-century comedy. She always got things wrong. Mrs. Malaprop."

"Perhaps that should be my name." She smiles, but her eyes are cold.

"No! I'm sure Isabelle suits you much better."

"Isabella," she corrects. Her accent caresses each syllable.

"See? I'm the one getting things wrong. Your name, no less, which is much more important than some random term for a social gathering. I'm more Mrs. Malaprop than you—socially anyway." Inside my head, a voice is crying, *Shut the hell up!* I tidy some papers on my desk. "So, what do you think of Salt Gulch? Do you like it?"

Her gaze moves around my office. She takes everything in with a shrewd, calculating eye, like an art dealer assessing a collection, mentally tallying its value. I get the feeling her appraisal will be low. "It is good, I suppose. Mick likes it. But Mick loves every place."

"You moved here from LA, right?"

She nods. "Westwood. You know it?"

"Not really." I shrug. "I've been there for a conference, but that's about it. Do you miss it?"

"I would like to say no." Isabella's face is wistful. "But, yes. I do miss it. We had many friends there—very interna-tional, UCLA."

"Of course."

"Here, I just . . ." She hesitates. "It is not easy to make friends in a town so small. I suppose that is odd, since you can know everybody much more quickly, but I feel a bit like fish out of water."

"I understand." I try to school my features into compassionate warmth, but I'm not sure I succeed. There's something about this woman that rubs me the wrong way. I don't think it's just garden-variety female envy. She is certainly beautiful enough to inspire petty rivalry. Her perfect complexion makes me feel sallow and wrinkled by comparison; her bombshell body makes my own figure seem scrawny, boyish. My instinctive wariness of her comes from something else, though. I sense she's here with an agenda. Not knowing what this agenda might be puts me on edge.

"Knock, knock!" Amy pokes her head around the half-open door. "There you are. Shit, I'm so sorry! Don't be pissed, okay?"

I tilt my head toward Isabella, and Amy cringes. "Sorry! You're with a student. I'll wait out here."

"That is very flattering." Isabella flicks her hair over her shoulder. "I am not a student, but thank you; this makes my day."

"Amy, this is Isabella Lynch. Her husband is the new AI professor?"

"Right!" Amy reaches out one hand. "Nice to meet you."

Isabella shoots me a sly grin. "The 'lazy slut'?"

"Exactly." I laugh.

Amy looks a little taken aback. I give her a look that says, *"I'll explain later."*

Isabella stands, smoothing her dress again, though it's still remarkably wrinkle-free. I've never understood women who can maintain such perfection. "Well, I have stayed too long. Forgive me. Thank you for making time in your busy schedule."

After she leaves, I can still smell Isabella's expensive perfume—something sharp and floral, probably laced with ambergris, from the intestines of some hapless sperm whale.

Amy raises her eyebrows. "'Lazy slut'?"

"Well, you are, aren't you?"

Her chin lifts in defiance. Then her head wilts. "Yes. Dammit. The ear, nose, and throat specialist was actually kind of hot. For an ear, nose, and throat specialist, anyway."

"I'm not sure what that means."

She shuts the door and whispers, "So, that was Dr. Robot's hot wife?"

"His name is Lynch, not—"

"Man, what a power couple," Amy says, ignoring me. "You know she's sniffing out her competition, right?"

"That's ridiculous." I grab my bag and keys.

Amy looks unconvinced. "Please! Don't even try for naive. It's not a good look on you."

"She invited me to a party at their house." I hand her the invitation.

"Uh-huh. Exactly. Wants to keep an eye on you. Remind you her sexy husband's unavailable."

"I'm sure that's not true." Even as I say it, though, I wonder. Amy has a habit of cutting through all the shit and hitting the truth square-on. Can she see something I'm ignoring? I'm not exactly known for my intuition, but even I sensed Isabella had an ulterior motive.

With one hand, I open the door and let Amy step out into the hallway. "Well, her husband is safe with me."

Amy throws me a look over her shoulder, clearly unconvinced.

*   *   *

The Lynches' home is so over-the-top feminine it makes me itch. I'm not exclusively masculine in my decorating choices, but next to this place, my home looks positively macho. I favor jewel tones, anatomic prints, antique globes, leather-bound first editions. Isabella Lynch, on the other hand, never met a floral print she didn't like. I have to believe this house is all her; the thought of Mick Lynch choosing any of this makes me want to laugh. The overstuffed couches are a soft peach linen with white blossoms; the throw pillows feature birds of paradise; the curtains drip with lilacs; even the rugs depict pastel hydrangeas and peonies. Should your eye happen to find a flower-free zone on which to rest, you can bet that space will be filled with lace. Elaborate lace tablecloths, lace runners for the coffee tables, lace liners for the curtains, lace doilies.

Joe offered to come along as my date. Not a date-date, mind you. He knows I feel obligated to attend, and also how social events give me hives. We have a standing agreement that he'll serve as my liaison at faculty social gatherings, where he can steer me away from potential faux pas and translate my alien tendencies with his usual garrulous ease.

Lynch has invited a number of grad students as well; Winter mentioned she and Cameron plan to attend. This makes me even more nervous, since faculty gatherings don't include students as a general rule. The more nebulous the etiquette, the more likely I am to experience deer-in-the-headlights panic.

The second we walk in the door, I want to turn around and march back to the car. All my life, ritualized femininity has made me uncomfortable. Maybe I have an estrogen deficiency. Being raised by my father and older brothers rendered me allergic to female customs. My mother died when I was just a baby. As I got older, rather than try to fill her shoes as the only female left in the house, I blended in with the boys, so stepping into the land of women always feels treacherous. Men, at least, tend to communicate in a direct way. Women's conversational patterns and body language leave me mystified. As we enter the Lynches' home, the scent of cloying air freshener mixes with the brittle sound of women's high-pitched laughter; a cold sweat immediately breaks out all over my body.

Joe puts a steadying hand on my arm. "You okay?"

"Maybe we should just go." My eyes dart from one floral surface to another. I know I probably look like a spooked horse, but I can't help it. The urge to flee is primal.

"You're fine," Joe soothes, nudging me gently toward the backyard, where everyone seems to be gathered. A bright pink sign on the front door declared "Come on in—we're out back!" Even that brand of casual, hospitable welcome makes me uneasy.

We pass through the living room, then the kitchen, which is open, light, and airy. Once again, the floral and lace theme continues, this time with a vaguely French vibe. Huge copper pots hang from a rack suspended over the kitchen island. Framed prints of Monet adorn the yellow walls. A gaggle of women in sundresses huddle together near the French doors. Joe greets them with his usual bonhomie as we pass through the doors onto the patio. Sunlight illuminates the garden, a riot of flowers in every possible hue, from ballet slipper pink to lapis lazuli.

"Ah, here they are! Welcome! Bienvenido!" Isabella detaches herself from Gil Matheson, one of my coworkers, and glides over to us. Her smile is so huge, and her lipstick so red, she looks like she's ready to host a cooking show. Not surprisingly, she wears a floral dress with a dramatic plunging neckline. In my usual Sunday outfit of jeans and T-shirt, I feel dowdy and mannish.

Joe kisses Isabella on the cheek with just the right touch of European courtliness. "Thanks so much for inviting us. Your home is beautiful."

"Hello." I try for a hug, but somehow my hair tangles in Isabella's enormous hoop earrings. I have to disentangle myself carefully. "God, sorry! Jesus, that's—oops, careful."

Off to a stellar start, as usual.

Isabella pretends not to be annoyed by the fact that I almost ripped her earlobe off within minutes of my arrival. "You are here just in time! We are about to serve dessert. It is my very special double-chocolate, better-than-sex cheesecake."

"An enticing offer," Joe purrs.

I look at him. He's devouring Isabella with his eyes. His gaze rakes up and down her body, catching on her cleavage. Joe can be such a dick. Outrage at his obvious sexism shoots through me. I hope it doesn't show on my face. The only thing worse than watching your plus one ogle another woman is letting everyone see how much it bothers you.

"That does sound delicious." My tone is flat as I glare at Joe, and then I wrench my gaze away to look at Isabella. She really is beautiful, all coppery skin and sharp cheekbones. "I need to urinate. Can I use your toilet?"

Joe and Isabella both laugh like I've said something hilarious.

I look from one to the other, puzzled. "What?"

"TMI, Hannah." Joe gives me a patronizing smile.

"I have no idea what that means."

"Too much information," Isabella says, one hand on my arm. "I may be a Miss Malaprop, but I do know that one."

Heat rises in my face. The man who is supposed to be my friend is laughing at me with this flower-obsessed ex-model—it's too much. I walk away, intent only on escape.

"Down the hall, last door on the left," she calls after me.

There are more women in dresses between me and the French doors now. One of them throws back her head and laughs like a hyena. Why does everyone seem to know the garden-party dress code except me? That old familiar feeling washes over me—the humiliation of not knowing the rules, not knowing the etiquette, making a fool of myself. A dark ember of shame smolders inside me.

When I finally reach the bathroom, I yank the door closed behind me, locking it. The large, luxurious room has been decorated in—you guessed it—more flowers. Sprawling wild rose wallpaper. Deep red tile floor. A line of floral bath products on a glass shelf. One of those massive basins that's big enough to bathe a child in. When I've finished peeing, I wash my hands with the rose-shaped soap.

The woman is obsessed.

I take a deep breath and stare at myself in the mirror. Why did I even come here? I never should have shown Joe the invitation. As soon as he saw it, he started campaigning for us to go. After all, they're new in town, he'd insisted. We should make them feel welcome. Didn't I remember how hard it was to make friends when I first moved to the area? He claimed it took him over a year to feel connected when he moved here from Chicago. This is absurd. He can land in any town and know everyone within a week. Although, now that I think of it, I've got Amy—one real friend. Joe's got truckloads of acquaintances, but I can't think of anyone he'd tell his secrets to. I'd take Amy over an army of generic half friends any day.

The thought of Amy calms me a little. She would be in hysterics over Isabella's floral mania. I realize it's childish to comfort myself by mentally sniggering at the woman who just sniggered at me, but let's face it: we're all children inside.

I can handle this. I've trekked through war-torn Darfur, examined skeletons by moonlight in Romania, braved the horrors of mass graves in Chechnya. I can endure laughing women in sundresses.

Another idea occurs to me. Maybe Amy's right, and Isabella really does feel threatened by me. If that's the case, my job is to put her mind at ease. Being ogled by my "date" should remind her she's attractive. Objectively speaking, that's a step in the right direction. I should try to diffuse any jealousy before it can become an issue. Not that I plan on cultivating a friendship with Isabella, but Salt Gulch is a small town, and the Mad River faculty forms an insular world. There's plenty of simmering jealousy and tension already; no need to earn an enemy in one of my colleague's wives if I don't have to.

As I'm making my way back down the hall, I spot a door that's slightly ajar. Something about the room beckons. Through the crack, I glimpse dark walls, a sliver of grandfather clock. Feeling furtive, I push the door open just a little wider and step inside. This room couldn't be more different from the rest of the house. It's like an anomaly on a skull, a protuberance or an indentation that catches your eye. There's nothing floral or feminine about it. The walls are painted a rich indigo. Dark wood furniture and tobacco-brown leather dominate the space. Even the green velvet couch looks masculine somehow. Two of the four walls are lined floor to ceiling with books. Weighty velvet curtains block out the afternoon sunlight. A Moroccan lamp casts kaleidoscopic prisms of tangerine on the walls. It's cozy, in a slightly cave-like way. The faint perfume of walnut and old books hangs in the air.

A deep, low chuckle bubbles up from the shadows. There's Lynch, reclined in a worn leather club chair, a book in his lap. His reading glasses sit perched on the end of his nose. He's propped an old paperback on the arm of the chair, under a lozenge of light cast by a small brass apothecary lamp.

I try to back out, embarrassed by my nosiness. Before I can make my escape, though, my foot catches on something behind me. An old-fashioned hat rack tips over, narrowly missing me. It falls with a loud clatter, spilling bowlers and fedoras across the hardwood floor.

Our eyes meet. It's hard to say which of us is more startled.

He recovers first. "Fancy meeting you here, Dr. Bryers."

"I wasn't—I just—sorry to interrupt." I pick up the hat rack, scrabbling to put the hats back on it.

"Do you often wander into private rooms uninvited?" His eyebrows arch.

I respond with instinctive defensiveness. "Do you often host parties while hiding out in private rooms?"

Lynch laughs. It's a rich, full belly laugh. "Touché. Though it doesn't escape my notice that you've answered a question with a question."

"What are you reading?" I venture deeper into the room, not quite meeting his eye.

He holds up the book, its cover facing me. "TC Boyle short stories."

"I love him!" I cross the room, excited. "Which one made you laugh?"

"All of them, so far. I'm halfway through 'Sorry Fugu' right now."

"About the restaurant reviewer? Love that one."

He smirks at me, amused.

"What?" I'm standing just inches from him now, drawn in by talk of Boyle.

"I wouldn't have pegged you as a connoisseur of fiction," he says.

"Because I'm a scientist?" I fold my arms across my chest. "You think I only read scholarly articles and dry, pedantic texts?"

"No, I just—"

"We all contain multitudes."

"Some more than others." There's something wistful in his tone. I wonder what that's about.

I study him. "Why are you in here? This is your housewarming."

He sighs. "I know. Isabella will be furious."

"Don't you like parties?"

"Hate them, to tell you the truth." He looks sheepish. "All the shallow, one-dimensional conversations."

I seat myself on the green couch near him. "How many times can you comment on the delicious canapés and mild spring weather? It's mind-numbing."

He breathes out a chuckle. "So, what are you doing here?"

"Honestly? I felt obligated. Socializing isn't my strong suit, so I force myself to practice. Also, Joe talked me into it."

"Joe?" He looks blank.

"Shepley? You've met him at least twice now." I give him a mock-scolding look.

"The musician. Right. He's your boyfriend?"

"No, just a friend. And he's my tenant."

"That's right." A memory registers in his eyes. "'The dude who lives in your basement.'"

"It's not a basement," I protest.

"So you claim. I suspect you've got him locked up down there. Some kind of twisted human experiment."

I smile. *Sarcasm*. When it's not too subtle, even I can pick up on it.

* * *

Winter

On my way back from the bathroom, I spot Bryers at last; she's in a cozy little tête-à-tête with Lynch in what must be his study. *Naughty, naughty, Dr. B*. Right here in his own home, with his wife passing around cocktail shrimp just outside in the garden.

I consider flattening myself against the wall and eavesdropping from the hallway, but it's too risky. Anyone who has to pee would spot me, and I have no valid reason to be there. Another quick peek inside tells me there's a big window that faces out into the garden.

Two minutes later, I'm in the backyard again. I find the right window and—thank God—it's wide open. Heavy curtains block the view, but their conversation is audible. The rest of the guests are gathered on the other side of the garden. I conceal myself behind a large flowering hedge and stand close to the window.

I hear Lynch's deep, booming bass. "I suspect you've got him locked up down there. Some kind of twisted human experiment."

Hmm. Interesting already. I'm so glad I came. Given Bryers's social freakiness, I was afraid she might not show. That would have been a total drag, given all the trouble I went to. After overhearing a conversation about the housewarming party in the copy room, I went to Lynch's office and finagled an invitation. I had to feign a burning interest in AI. He droned on and on about the latest advances in the technology before I finally worked the conversation around to Salt Gulch. Approximately ten years later, I managed to convince him inviting Cameron and me to this pathetic little gathering was his idea. Men are so easy to manipulate. The only risk is dying of boredom while doing it.

Bryers's voice is quieter, a little harder to make out. I press closer to catch her response. "I leave all the twisted human experiments to you. Or should I say, 'twisted humanoid experiments'?"

"We've established that you don't like parties, you don't like basements, and you don't like what I do."

"I've got nothing against basements, per se, just mislabeling. A perfectly nice ground-floor apartment is not a basement," Dr. B argues.

The word "basement" triggers a series of murky memories, underwater explosives detonating one by one: Ella tied to a chair, her black hair in tangles, a strip of silver duct tape over her mouth; me wobbling my way toward her, tied to my own chair, my mouth straining against duct tape; the sound of footsteps on the stairs.

I push this aside and focus on the conversation. *This is my way to salvation. Do what you came here to do, Winter.*

"What *do* you like?" Again, Lynch's voice, creamy and rich.

"I like talking to you."

I can tell her own boldness surprises her. There's a slight uptick on the last word, a note of disbelief. Like she can't understand why she's saying this.

I understand. Because she's lonely. Because all the lectures and the scholarly articles in the world can't keep her warm at night. Because she longs for a human connection. Like most of us, she doesn't care who gets hurt along the way.

"I like talking to you too." So low I can barely make it out.

"We shouldn't be here." I hear her footsteps. "You should be out there, with your wife."

"My wife will be fine."

"I'm not sure that's true."

Silence.

Lynch's voice breaks it. "What do you mean?"

"She's lonely. Uprooted." Bryers's voice sounds moderated, controlled. "You brought her here. You should show her you're going to stand by her, help her make friends."

"You make me feel like a real shit."

"Well . . ." I can hear the shrug in her voice. "If that's how you feel, maybe you should do something about it."

He sighs. "You're right. I should—"

"What are you doing?" Cameron's suddenly right behind me, watching me with narrowed eyes.

I fumble my phone from my pocket and move a safe distance from the window. "Just checking my texts."

He doesn't look convinced. "Why do you need to come all the way over here to—"

"You know how old people are." I offer an apologetic smile. "If you check your texts, they get that look."

"What look?" He comes closer.

I tuck my phone into my pocket. "Like, *'Oh, right, you're a millennial. Guess everything I read about you is true.'*"

"Everyone checks their phones." Cameron's so rational. It's maddening.

With one hand, I seize his arm. I can just make out Dr. B and Lynch continuing their conversation, but I don't want him to hear it. If he suspects I've been eavesdropping, he might get suspicious. That's something I can't afford.

I lead him away from the window.

"Seriously, what were you doing?" he asks.

I sigh, changing tack. It's unlikely I can do any more spying with Cameron tagging along like a needy puppy. Might as well cut my losses and leave. "I don't feel comfortable here. Everyone's twice our age. If you want to know the truth, I was hiding."

"That's not like you." Cameron's brow furrows as he glances at the open window.

I move to block his view. "Sometimes I'm shy."

"I can't figure you out, Winter." There's an uneasy expression on his face I don't like.

I squeeze his bicep. "Not being able to figure me out is better than boring, right?"

"If you say so."

"What do you say we get out of here?"

"Now?" He looks at me, surprised. We're halfway to the other guests. The sun is warm on my black hair.

"Yeah. Why not?"

"I thought you wanted to come. You seemed really into it."

I run a hand along his back, slipping into my default mode when cornered. Distracting Cameron with sex is always a safe bet. I flash my best come-hither look. "You're saying you can't think of anything you'd rather be doing right now?"

His arm wraps around my waist. "When you put it like that . . ."

"Come on, then. Let's slip out." I hurry toward the door, putting an extra swing in my walk.

"You wicked thing."

I smile over my shoulder at him. "Takes one to know one."

8

Hannah

"DID YOU HAVE a good time?" Joe is sprawled on my living room couch, a bottle of Corona dangling from one hand. He's one of those people who makes himself at home wherever he is. I envy this ability.

I scoff. "Do you really need to ask?"

"I do. Lost track of you for a while," he says.

I open my own beer and squeeze a wedge of lime into the neck. Outside, the March sunset is turning my west windows into a Maxfield Parrish painting. The fog bank on the horizon is neon pink. The sea and the sky are matching shades of morning-glory blue.

"Lost track?" I grab the bowl of guacamole and a bag of chips, carrying it all to the living room. I set the snacks on the coffee table and snuggle into the couch, giving Joe plenty of room to sprawl. It's a familiar ritual. We've sat like this through countless sunsets. I'm not sure why something feels different tonight.

After the stress of the Lynches' "house heating" party, I long to unwind. When Joe followed me inside my place, I didn't protest; he's part of my inner circle, after all. He's one of the two people on the planet I can be unequivocally myself with. That's why it bothers me more than it should, this tight ball of nerves pulsating in my gut, even with him.

"You disappeared for a bit." He takes a swig of beer. I can't quite read his expression. It's somewhere between curious and guarded.

I shove the lime wedge deeper into the bottle and take a sip, biding my time. I'm not sure I want to tell him about my conversation with Lynch. I don't know why. It feels like a secret somehow. I decide to change the subject. "You seemed rather taken with Isabelle."

"Isabella," he corrects. "Are you doing that on purpose?"

"Doing what?"

"Getting her name wrong."

I blink at him, startled. "Of course not. Why would I?"

"I don't know. You're the expert on human behavior. Why *would* you?" Joe reaches over and snags a chip, loading it with guacamole before shoveling it into his mouth.

I drink more beer, staring out the windows. The sky inches toward indigo; the fogbank's neon pink ripens into a fiery plum. My art deco lamps cast a warm glow on the hardwood floors. Shadows from the swaying trees dance on the Persian rug. I try to take this in, to savor the sense of comfort I always feel returning to my haven. I'm home. I'm safe. Somehow, though, my reptilian brain still doesn't get the message.

Joe reaches out and touches my bare foot. I flinch.

"Hey. You okay?" His voice is gentle.

I pull the throw from the back of the couch and drape it over my legs. It feels drafty in here. "Are you saying I'm threatened by Isabel*la*?" I place emphasis on the last syllable.

"*Are* you threatened?"

"She's attractive," I say, my tone noncommittal.

"Very," he affirms.

I look at him.

He grins. "But so are you. Anyway, this town is full of hot women. I've never known you to lose sleep over it."

"I'm not losing sleep over her either."

"So what's going on then?" He puts his hand on my foot again, rubbing the arch through the blanket. "I know something's bugging you. Want to tell me what it is?"

I peel the label from my bottle, avoiding his eyes. My conversation with Lynch felt so intimate. When it turned to his wife, I got confused, flustered, and it's left me feeling befuddled ever since. For some reason, I don't feel like explaining this to Joe.

"I'm okay," I say. "You know me and parties. We're not a good fit."

Joe's hand wanders under the blanket. Strong fingers massage the ball of my foot. Joe's an affectionate guy. Since I'm not used to people touching me, it took at least a year for me to adjust. I used to recoil whenever he pulled me into a bear hug or draped a casual arm over my shoulders. This feels different, though. There's something oddly intimate about someone rubbing your feet. There are close to two hundred thousand nerve endings per sole; I suppose that's part of it.

It feels good. That's undeniable. I can feel the callouses on his fingers from the endless hours spent playing guitar. His skin is warm, soothing. Somehow, though, instead of relaxing me, what's happening right now makes the spiky ball of dread in my belly swell like a porcupine.

I shift position, tucking my feet under me. A brief flash of vexation passes over his features—a quick tensing of the zygomaticus muscles that smooths out almost before I catch it. He's hurt that I've pulled away. Or is he angry? Maybe a little of both.

Why is this so weird? Joe represents fifty percent of my emotional-support network. I can't afford to ostracize him. What's going on here? Why can't I get my bearings?

I tuck myself deeper into my end of the couch, suddenly wishing I'd chosen the chair, even though this would mean turning my back on the sunset.

Our eyes lock. The air in the room feels dense. The pines surrounding the house sing in the evening breeze. My wind chimes clang a mournful tune.

"I feel like something bad is going to happen," I blurt.

"Why do you think that?" He's so still and watchful. It's making me nervous.

I stand, walking to the windows, my body suddenly so restless I can't sit. "I don't know how to explain it."

"Try," Joe implores.

I puff out a small, self-deprecating laugh. "You know me—I don't trust anything I can't analyze. There's this vague dread following me everywhere, though. I feel like the stupid girl in a horror flick walking toward the closet. A part of me is screaming, *No! Don't open the door!* But some other part of me is on autopilot, opening it anyway."

"That sounds scary."

I touch the cool glass with my forehead. "It is."

"Do you think this has anything to do with the big four-o?"

I turn to him, confused. "What do you mean?"

Joe takes a long pull from his beer, wipes his mouth with the back of his hand. "It's a hard age for lots of people. Especially women."

"You think I'm having a midlife crisis?" I can't keep the note of repulsion from my voice.

He laughs, holding up his hands. "Don't look at me like that. I'm just saying . . . maybe the dread you're feeling has something to do with getting older. It's scary shit, aging. Messes with your sense of self."

"You're older than me." It comes out a little pouty.

He smirks. "Only by eight months. That doesn't count."

"Are *you* going through a midlife crisis?"

"Not that I've noticed." He puts his beer down. "Anyway, stop trying to change the subject. We're talking about you."

I turn my back on Joe, pressing my forehead against the window again. The cool glass feels good against my skin. The sunset's gone from a fiery plum to a bruised, faded violet. Hummingbirds dance around the clusters of trumpet vines and passion flowers in my garden. I watch as they fight over the blossoms in the twilight.

Is Joe right? Is the angst I feel just the cliched neurosis of a woman inching inexorably toward menopause? I'm not used to being a mystery to myself. Misunderstood by others? Sure, all the time. But misunderstood by myself? That's a first.

It's annoying.

"It's getting late," I murmur, hugging myself against the chill. Where's that draft coming from? Usually my house feels snug and cozy. Maybe I'm coming down with something. The thought makes me even more peevish. I never get sick.

"You want me to go?" He sounds hurt, but after a moment he adopts a lighter, jokier tone. "Time for Igor to return to his basement?"

I think of Lynch teasing me about my twisted human experiment. Is that what I am to everyone? A mad scientist joke?

I offer a wan smile over my shoulder. "You and your basement fetish."

"Hannah." The serious note in his voice puts me on guard, but I don't turn around. I hear him cross the room, feel him standing right behind me. His hand sweeps my hair over my shoulder, leaving one side of my neck exposed.

Okay, this is definitely more intimate than his usual bear hugs. I'm not adept at gauging the subtle nuances that mark the difference between a platonic gesture and a sexual one. Maybe I'm getting this wrong. Joe and I are friends.

Nothing more. He knows that. *I know that.* If I'm not mistaken, though, there's something different about how close he's standing, the heat radiating from him. I can feel his breath on the back of my neck. His fingers trace my sternocleidomastoid, light as a butterfly.

I turn and look at him, my heart pounding. "Joe? What are you—"

He leans down and presses his mouth to mine.

Okay, definitely not a platonic gesture.

I stand there, frozen. It's not revulsion I feel so much as blind panic. Joe's my friend, and I need him to stay that way. I've heard of the term "friends with benefits," but that would never work for me. I don't do well with ambiguous social situations. The cleaner and sharper the lines, the better I function. Joe lives smack dab in the middle of my friend zone. He's my safe place, my home base, like Amy. When you only have a limited number of comrades, you can't afford to screw things up with half of them.

My brain races; all of my wheels are spinning, trying to find traction, like a truck stranded in the mud. Why would Joe put me in this position? He knows I panic when there's too much information thrown at me. Correction: when there's too much *emotional* information thrown at me. Put me in war-torn Sudan or a malfunctioning prop plane and I can handle excess stimuli like a champ. I'll have the risks analyzed and the procedures planned before most people have stopped screaming. But kiss me without warning before a fading sunset on a Sunday night in my living room? That's a code red.

With as much gentleness as I can manage, I plant my palms on his shoulders and push. Our lips separate. He opens his eyes, a dreamy expression in their hazel depths; it reminds me of how he looks when he's singing one of his plaintive love songs.

I shake my head a little to clear it. Surely he's not in love with me? A craving for physical closeness or sexual release is one thing, but love—the biggest human mystery of all—that's beyond code red. It's nuclear meltdown.

He runs a thumb between my brows as if to smooth the crease I didn't notice forming there. "You're thinking too much. I can always tell."

I try to take a step back but find myself trapped between Joe and the window. "You know I don't do well with surprises."

"You're right. I should have written a formal request, at least two weeks in advance, asking if I could kiss you."

"Don't make fun of me, Joe." I sidestep him, craving more space. "I don't understand what's happening here."

"I've wanted to kiss you for way too long. I figured, what the hell? The worst thing that can happen is she'll freak out." He rubs the back of his neck, embarrassed. "I guess the worst has happened."

"I'm not freaking out," I lie. "I'm just caught off guard."

He reaches for me again, this time cupping my waist with one palm and pulling me closer. "Are you telling me you haven't thought about this? About us, together?"

"That's exactly what I'm telling you." It comes out sharper than I intended.

Joe's face takes on a startled, blank expression, as if I've just slapped him.

"What I mean is, I value you too much as a friend. I'm aware that's a cliché, but in this case it's true. The only people I can relax with are you and Amy. I can't risk losing you. You mean too much to me."

He tilts his head to the side, confused. "You're not going to lose me. We'll be closer than ever."

I guffaw. "Friends who have sex do not get closer. They risk everything for mere physical gratification."

"You think I just want to have sex with you?" His puzzlement deepens. "That's not what this is about."

"What then?"

For a second, we just stand there, held together by our locked eyes.

He grimaces and continues with the air of someone ripping off a Band-Aid. "I think I'm falling in love with you."

On instinct, I cup my hands over my ears. "This can't be happening."

"I'm sorry if that messes with your plans, but it's true."

"Please un-say what you just said," I beg.

"I can't." His smile is sad and a little defiant. "I'm in love with you, Hannah Bryers. Deal with it."

I want to scream. I want to cry. I want to rewind the last five minutes and delete them forever.

Instead, I take a deep breath and exhale, fighting for calm. "I'm sorry, Joe. I don't feel the same. I value you—so much—as a friend, but this"—I wave a hand between us—"can't happen."

He studies me, as if gauging my sincerity. Whatever he sees in my face must convince him. I watch his eyes lose all their warmth at once, like a storm front driving the temperature down. He turns and heads for the door.

"Joe. Don't be angry. Please."

His hand's already on the doorknob. He doesn't look at me when he speaks. "Don't worry. I'll get over it. Right now I just need to be alone."

I open my mouth to say something else, but nothing comes out.

It doesn't matter. He's already gone.

* * *

Winter

Dr. B is distracted this morning.

This works fine for me. Distraction is the mother of cluelessness.

I feel fabulous this morning. It's all I can do to conceal my giddiness. It bubbles like champagne just under my skin, an effervescent shimmer affecting everything I touch. Tonight, the thing I've been planning for weeks will finally happen.

It's Monday, and for once I don't beat Dr. B to the lab. I get there well before eight, but she's already peering into the blackened cavity of John Doe, as I knew she would be from consulting my phone. I go to her, standing in silence near her for a long moment. We both wear white lab coats. In the moody morning light, she looks as crisp and pristine as an angel.

Dr. B lifts a flap of skin with a pair of surgical tweezers, scanning the shriveled organs underneath like a diamond appraiser assessing cut and clarity. When at last she glances up to acknowledge me, I speak.

"Good morning, Dr. Bryers."

"Oh, please." She looks annoyed. "We've worked together for over a year. Call me Hannah."

She's never suggested this before. I give her the required look of awe, even bowing my head a little. "Hannah. How are you?"

Her tweezers drop the skin flap with unceremonious abruptness. "I'm a nervous wreck."

"What? Why?" I provide the expected, wide-eyed "you-could-never-be-anything-but-confident-and-brilliant" look. I understand my role well.

"All warfare is based upon deception."

She straightens and drops the tweezers on a silver tray with a clatter. "This stupid presentation tonight."

"About your Fulbright?" I'm careful not to look at the body splayed between us. I've almost managed to convince myself it really is just any old corpse, not someone I knew, someone I put here. If I stare at it too closely, though, the scene in the forest threatens to overwhelm me, and I can't have that.

Her eyes stay fixed on the ribcage. "Yes. I should be figuring out who this poor guy is, not worrying about dazzling
the board. You know the sheriff's afraid he's one of their own,
right?"

I look at her with doe-eyed wonder. "A sheriff?"

She nods. "Deputy, anyway. Not that it should matter. Everyone who shows up here deserves the same rigorous
examination. Somebody out there misses him, most likely."

"But the cops are putting extra pressure on you because
he's one of them?" I guess.

"*Possibly* one of them." She circles the corpse, studying
it from every angle. Once in a while, her head dips down to
examine it from a fresh vantage point. She's only halfway
present. Most of her brain is running calculations, creating
and discarding hypotheses. I've seen her like this before. She's
intense when she works. Her green eyes shine with visionary
zeal.

"Are they, though?"

She looks up, surprised. I think she forgot I was there.
"Are they what?"

"Pressuring you to figure it out quickly?"

"Oh." She grimaces. "Yes. It's unfortunate, but politics
are inescapable, especially in a small town like this. A deputy
sheriff went missing not too long ago. Basic height and build
matches, from what we can tell. Location makes sense. He
was off-duty when he disappeared, but he was known to hike
in the Salt Gulch Forest on occasion. Chances are this is him,
but I'm struggling to provide a positive ID, given the state of
decomposition."

I turn my gaze to the scalpels on their gleaming tray.
"Have you gleaned anything useful?"

She picks up a scalpel and uses it to pry open the mouth.
"I wish the team who recovered him thought to look for the
teeth. They should have been right there. That was unforgiv-
ably sloppy, tell you the truth."

this morning, seeping through the cracks like sand in the desert. I've blocked out the next few hours to work with a couple graduate students on John Doe's remains. I promised Sheriff Brannigan I'd have some answers as soon as possible. Amy's already done a preliminary inspection, but the sheriff wants me to do a careful study.

As I leave the Anthropology wing and pass through the Computer Science Department, a sudden movement catches my eye. There's a small window on the door of the bioengineering lab, revealing a quick flash of color, a violent jerking motion. I hesitate, peering through the glass. The door flies open, leaving me barely enough time to step back and avoid getting slammed in the face. Two figures burst out into the hallway, elbows and knees flying, obviously in the midst of a physical altercation.

I recognize "Roger," the robot from Lynch's AI demo. He's got his repulsive fake-flesh hands wrapped around Lynch's neck. I gasp, stunned. Roger pushes Lynch against the far wall, pinning him, pressing against Lynch's jugular.

"Stop!" Instinctively, I rush to pull Roger off, yanking hard on his arm. The robot's bicep is steely beneath my fingers, though, impossible to pry off. I hook my arm around Roger's neck, hoping to tip him backward, but my efforts barely register. He remains upright, impervious. I might as well try to knock over a tree with my bare hands.

Lynch makes a strangled sound, his face red.

I'm about to run for help when, all at once, the robot lets go. Panting with effort, I try to make sense of the scene before me.

Lynch leans against the wall, his face still red. It's not vasodilation due to asphyxiation, though. It's laughter turning him the color of a baboon's ass.

He's weak with it. One hand reaches up and wipes away a tear.

The bastard's laughing.

"What the hell was that?" My voice shakes. I can still feel the adrenaline coursing through my veins.

Lynch pats Roger on the back and guides him back toward the lab. One gentle nudge sends him loping through the door without a word. "Go on, buddy. Thanks."

"Is this some kind of joke?" I stare at Lynch, incredulous.

"Don't be mad. I couldn't resist. I saw you coming, and I just . . ." He laughs again, wiping his eyes.

I take a deep breath, willing myself not to take a swing at the arrogant prick. "Not funny."

"If only you could see the look on your face. Priceless!"

"I don't need this." I stalk past him, my spine stiff.

He grabs my arm as I pass. The feel of Lynch's hot fingers on my bare skin makes me jerk away, throwing him off violently; he holds his hands up, as if to defend himself.

"Hey now! It was just a joke. I'm sorry." He gets so close, I'm forced to look him in the eye. His voice goes soft, almost pleading. "Really. My bad. That was tasteless."

"And vile," I spit.

"Vile. Yes. Ask anyone. I'm a vile human being." His blue eyes go from sheepish to warm.

I'm caught off-guard by the warmth. This man has the most expressive face. It's befuddling.

"Believe it or not, that was meant to be a humorous icebreaker."

"Icebreaker?" My heart rate still hasn't returned to normal; my powers of analysis are impaired.

His eyes continue to probe mine. "Yes. I thought I could make you laugh, but obviously I misjudged your sense of humor."

"What do you mean, *icebreaker*?" My tone is incredulous.

"I'm in no position to ask a favor, but my little performance was a prelude to me humbly requesting your help with something very important."

"No doubt," I agree.

"By now, the animals have probably scavenged them. Teeth can be very helpful, especially if we consult with a good forensic odontologist."

Hearing her talk about teeth makes my fizzy mood go flat. Dark memories struggle to resurface, like captives pounding on a locked basement door. I force myself to blank all that out. *"Distraction in your opponent is an opportunity; distraction in one's self is a liability."*

I change the subject. "Any signs of a violent death?"

She shakes her head. "The missing deputy had a history of coronary artery disease. If this is him, it's likely he had a myocardial infarction—a heart attack—with nobody around to call 911."

"That's sad." I try not to be offended that she felt the need to translate myocardial infarction.

Her tone goes philosophical. "There are worse ways to go."

There *are* worse ways to go. I see my beautiful sister, lying still and lifeless in a bathtub filled with blood. Again, I block it out, my stomach roiling with the effort.

She goes on, oblivious to my pain. "I did find a slight chip on one of the ribs, but this was most likely an old injury, nothing to do with cause of death." She levers a flap of skin up with the scalpel, revealing the white curve of an exposed rib bone.

"Is that helpful?" Dr. B needs to be prompted. If you go silent for more than a few seconds, she forgets you're there.

"It might be useful in matching the remains to the missing man. If our deputy experienced trauma to the ninth left rib near the anterior tubercle at any time, that would be too great a coincidence to overlook. It wouldn't be a positive ID, but it would be pretty damn close given the circumstances."

"That's good. Sounds like you've got it figured out, then."

Her brow furrows. "Unless he has no medical records or relatives who recall him suffering an injury there. Then we're left with three possibilities: He sustained the injury without realizing it; he sustained it at the time of death; or he knew about it, but nobody living remembers."

I nod, putting on an earnest "teach-me" face. It occurs to me how hilarious it is that Bryers hates robots. She kind of is one.

"Winter?" She straightens, her tone shifting from brisk to conversational. "Do you understand men?"

It takes me a second to adjust, but I manage. This is an opportunity; I can feel it. "How do you mean?"

"I don't know," she says in a rush, "I shouldn't have said anything. It's inappropriate."

"Guy trouble?" I infuse my question with just the right note of sisterly empathy. *God, I'm good.*

"Yes, but I don't want to—it's unprofessional."

"You can tell me anything, Hannah." I try out the new name, inviting her with my eyes to unburden herself. "I can keep a secret, I swear."

She sighs, setting the scalpel down with an absent frown. "It's just—have you ever had a really good friend decide—out of the blue—that he's in love with you?"

"Once or twice." I smile. She must be talking about Joe, the dude who lives in her basement. "It happens."

"It's so maddening. Why would I jeopardize a perfectly good friendship for a sexual encounter? It's too risky."

Sexual encounter. She's so clinical. I bet she's a total robot in bed. "Good point."

"I'm afraid it will screw everything up." Her forehead crinkles with worry.

I consider this. "Are you attracted to him?"

"I know he's attractive, objectively speaking. Anyone can see that. But no, I'm not specifically attracted to him."

Wow, what a romantic. *I'm not specifically attracted to him.* Print that on a valentine. Jesus, Bryers, what's your heart made of anyway—metal gears and steel spikes?

"The thing is," she continues, gazing at me with intense regret, "I do love him. As a friend. I know it's a cliché, but it's true. The thought of losing him scares me."

I move closer to her and put a hand on her arm. "You won't lose him. He'll be hurt, but he'll come back."

"You think?" For a second, her expression is so childlike, so naive, I want to hug her.

I give her all the calm reassurance she craves. "I don't think; I know."

"That's what I like about you, Winter. You're always so decisive."

I'm not so sure she'd like my decisiveness if she knew what I've decided to do.

9

Winter

BRYERS'S OFFICE DOOR is ajar.

She never leaves her office open. I think of our "girly chat" earlier this morning. She must be distracted by Basement Joe's confession of undying love.

I sidle up and rap with my knuckles, two soft, experimental taps. There's no response. My heart speeds up. I push open the door a little more, poke my head in to be sure. She's not here. I check my app and see she's outside Thorn Hall, near the bookstore. Bryers has left the building.

Fortune favors the brave.

I slip inside, closing it behind me. A quick look around reveals she's stashed her leather messenger bag under her desk. I dart another glance at the door. It's risky, but I'll be quick. I dig around in her bag. She's got a folder filled with papers, a direct deposit pay stub, a tin of breath mints, a tube of French hand cream, a battered leather wallet, and a copy of *The Forensic Examiner*. Just as I'm starting to lose hope, I hit pay dirt: my fingers land on a small, carved Day-of-the-Dead-style skull, and attached to that, a ring of keys. Two silver, one brass. I stash the keys, skull and all, in my jacket pocket and hurry for the door.

I've got my fingers on the knob when I hear brisk footsteps striding down the hall. Whoever it is, they're headed my way. I press my ear to the door. The footfalls sound distinctly female—the tapping of low heels, the light step. I know that gait. It's Bryers.

My throat tightens with fear; a thin sheen of perspiration breaks out all over my body. Shit! What have I done? I've been so careful until now. I can't get complacent. Complacent means sloppy. Sloppy gets you caught.

I can't get caught.

I stand there, paralyzed, not daring to turn the knob. As the footsteps draw near, I see everything I've done, all the planning and preparation that's gone into this moment.

I see myself at sixteen, a razor poised over my wrist. The sudden epiphany, white-hot and sizzling: if I die, she wins. If I die, Ella's death means nothing.

Just like that, a plan formed in the dark basement of my mind. I had to become an undercover operative in her world. I would learn her trade, her craft. Get close to Bryers, teach her to trust me. I would become indispensable. I had to figure out what she values most, what she loves and who she wants. Then, step by careful step, I would destroy her.

Revenge is a dish best served cold.

It's been ten years since Hannah Bryers exploded my life. I spent three of those years self-destructing; I spent the other seven building myself back up, energized by the hunt. I've stalked my prey with the slow, steady steps of a hunter tracking a bear. My revenge is good and cold.

The footsteps continue toward me. My mind races, searching every crevice of my imagination for something to say when she opens the door. No. It won't work. There are no words to explain my presence here. She knows I would never wander into her office uninvited. It goes against every principle I've spent the last year and a half establishing: deference, submissiveness, respect. I'm her best TA ever because I intuit all her boundaries and never cross them. I've studied the invisible trip lines that surround her, the unseen traps that are as treacherous and explosive as land mines.

Finding me in her office would destroy everything.

The footsteps pause just outside the door. I hold my breath. My heart's kicking like a rabbit ensnared in a trap. I spin around and run—in a silent crouch—to the window. Maybe I can get out that way. Bryers's office is on the third floor. The lawn below looks way too far away for comfort. I try to yank the window open anyway. It won't budge. It doesn't matter. There's no fire escape. No ledge. No way out.

I hear the knob rattle behind me. My heart swells to twice its normal size and lodges in my throat. I can't breathe. Any second now, she'll walk in and see me—

The knob rattles again. *Oh, thank Jesus, she can't get in.* The door must have locked automatically. I hear a low curse outside in the hall. I listen for the deadly sound of keys slipping into the lock.

Then I remember; I've got her keys.

I let out my breath slowly, my relief so powerful and overwhelming it's orgasmic.

Her footsteps retreat. I force myself to count to ten. When there's no longer any sound of her presence, I crack open the door and look both ways down the hall. Then I feel for her keys in my pocket and slip out.

* * *

Hannah

I'm furious as I stalk down the hall. I know I left my door ajar. I *know* it.

I'm headed for the Anthro admin office, where the master key hangs on a rusty horseshoe behind the receptionist's desk. It's the key of shame.

But goddammit, I left my door open. It's not like me, I'll admit, but the question remains: Who shut that door, and why?

Who's perceptive enough to realize this kind of prank would drive me wild? Which of my colleagues has already shown a history of practical jokes? Only Lynch.

As if on cue, Mick Lynch steps from his office into the hallway.

"How you doing?" Lynch studies me, his eyes bright and curious.

"Did you pull my door shut?" I blurt.

His curiosity morphs into confusion. "I'm sorry?"

"My door." Even to my ears, I sound petulant. I try to moderate my tone to something approaching professional. "I left it ajar, and somebody's pulled it closed."

He shrugs. "Could happen to anyone."

"I *know* I left it ajar." I say it quietly but with menace.

He studies me for a long time. "I do not know what to make of you."

"Don't make anything of me." I stride past him toward the Anthro office. "Just leave me alone."

* * *

Winter

I make the keys as quickly as possible. The chubby guy at the hardware store is young and gullible and half in love with me by the time I leave. He gives me a fifty percent discount just because I laugh at his jokes and tuck my hair behind my ears.

What do these sad losers think? Because they give us free shit, we'll come back at closing time and offer them a blow job? Or maybe it's enough just to see our eyes light up at their generosity. Maybe it's a fair trade; all they want is a moment basking in our sun.

It's not worth my analysis. I have shit to do.

I drive back to campus, the engine of my ancient MG straining as I climb the final hill. When I tear into the parking lot, I see Bryers's Subaru is still there. I hurry into the social science building, the freshly minted keys in my jeans pocket, Bryers's originals in the pocket of my leather jacket. With breathless hope I survey the building.

Shit. Bryers's office window is glowing a bright gold. I was hoping she'd be in the lab so I could sneak these into her office without being noticed. It's a gray day, the clouds hanging low-bellied and ominous, heavy with rain. The afternoon glowers like a petulant deity sharing his bad news with all the mortals below. I take a deep breath and head for the entrance. The balustrades studded with gargoyles tower over me. The beasts glare down, a look of warning in their fierce little stone faces. I meet their glares with a defiant smirk. *I'm invincible. I have her trust.* She won't suspect me if I work it just right.

I know how to play her. She's my specialty. Over the last year and a half—first as her student, then as her TA—I've learned all I need to know about the Great Hannah Bryers. I could write my doctoral thesis on her moods, her whims, her weaknesses.

Heading for the stairwell, I remind myself with every step that victory will be mine. That was a bad scare earlier, when I was trapped in her office. It shook my confidence, but I can't let the leftover adrenaline from that affect my performance now.

When I reach her door, I find it shut. I knock, my knuckles landing on the wood with just the right volume. Too soft would show hesitancy. She dislikes tentative people. Too loud would sound aggressive, demanding. Bryers doesn't respond well to overbearing. I am Goldilocks, finding just the right volume and cadence.

The keys burn a hole in my pocket. My fingers reach inside, fondling the carved skull. *I can do this,* I remind myself. *When it comes to Bryers, I can do anything.*

The door swings open. She stands there, her shoulders tense, her face wary. There are shadows under her eyes, pale violet smudges. She looks older. More fragile. I breathe in deeply, feeling my own youth and vigor rising like sap in my body. I got in a full nine hours last night. I slept the deep, luxurious sleep of someone who's winning.

When she sees me, her posture relaxes. "Winter. It's you."

"Were you expecting someone?" I duck my head a little, signaling that I respect her schedule. I will defer to her superior demands, slot myself in wherever she can fit me. "I can come back."

She sighs. "No. Come in."

I follow her inside, leaving the door open behind me. "You doing okay?"

"Fine." She collapses into her chair, shoulders slumping. "Just frustrated I haven't made more progress on John Doe."

My expression arranges itself into one of sympathy. "That's tough. You must be under a lot of pressure."

Her hand waves in the air, a dismissive gesture, like she can handle it. Her eyes tell a different story, though. She's under the gun, and the plot twist with Joe's confession has only added to her anxiety. "I wish I wasn't so stressed about this Fulbright presentation tonight."

I beam at her. "It'll be great. Cam and I will be there. We're looking forward to hearing all about your research in Japan. It sounds fascinating."

She looks preoccupied and distracted. Bryers is no stranger to public speaking, but she's not a natural in the limelight. Some professors bask in the attention. Lynch, for example, is a badass in front of a crowd, a gifted performer. Bryers is cut from different cloth. She only wants to convey information and takes no pleasure in taking center stage. It's clear her presentation is weighing on her, making her jumpy. Just wait until she finds out what I've planned for her. I can barely suppress my glee at the thought.

Bryers focuses on me again, visibly pushing aside her troubled thoughts. "Anyway, what did you need?"

"Oh, right." I take out a sheaf of papers. "The copier in the library is on the blink. I was wondering if you could copy this one article for me? I'd like to use it in my discussion section."

She looks at the essay I've handed her. "Not a problem. You can do it yourself, if you like. There's a copier in the workroom right down the hall. The code is one-four-two-two-three."

I hesitate. "The thing is, last time I made copies in there, some of the other faculty gave me serious stink-eye."

"Who?" Her indignation is endearing.

"I don't know." I choose the most ubiquitous description I can think of. "Some old guy in a blazer?"

"Don Simms, probably." She looks disgusted. "I swear, some of the faculty around here are so territorial. They might as well go around pissing on everything."

I giggle. It's just us girls now, talking smack about the stodgy geezers who haunt our hallways.

"Don't let them intimidate you. If anyone gives you trouble, send them straight to me."

I peer up from under my lashes, aiming for just the right look of meek uncertainty. "If you want to know the truth, he kind of . . ." I trail off.

"Kind of what?" She levels her gaze at me.

"Came onto me."

"Are you serious?"

"Not, like, overtly, but the way he looked at me—it made me super uncomfortable." I cast my eyes down at my lap, the demure maiden too shy to cast accusations. "That's why I make all my copies in the library now."

"That's horrible, Winter." She bristles with anger on my behalf.

"Please, don't say anything. It will only make it worse."

"It's unacceptable, though. You shouldn't have to deal with that."

"I didn't want to say anything." I keep my gaze fixed on my shoes.

"Do you want me to talk to—"

"No, please." I give her a beseeching look. "I can't lose my scholarship."

She studies me, her fingers steepled. Finally, to my immense relief, she picks up the article and taps the pages together. "How many copies?"

"Twenty-five should do it."

"I'll be right back."

After she leaves, I make myself count to five. Then I dart behind her desk, open a random drawer, and shove the keys inside. I race back to my seat and try to slow my breathing. In a few minutes, she returns with the copies.

I stand, taking them from her. "Thank you. So much. For everything."

"It's nothing."

"You're so different from the other professors. You're so . . ." I search for the right word, finally landing on "real."

Her eyes scan my face. "Thank you, Winter. That means a lot."

I take a few steps toward the door, backing out into the hall with a tremulous smile. "Good luck with John Doe. And don't worry about your presentation. You'll crush it."

She grimaces. "I'll do my best."

10

Hannah

M Y BOSS, DR. Eli Balderstone, stands at the podium. He's introducing me. I skulk in the wings of the small auditorium, sweating. Though I'm accustomed to addressing crowds, I still get nervous before a big talk.

I peek around the curtain at the assembled audience. The board members take up the first few rows, looking cranky and bored. In the third row, seated on the aisle, I spot Mick Lynch. Next to him is Isabella, and just behind him is Amy. My gaze falls on Winter and Cameron toward the back. Joe is notably absent.

My mouth is dry as a desiccated corpse's. I shake out my hands and pace. The vague dread that's been haunting me for days sharpens into a swirling vertigo.

I know sweating in this situation is normal, but it irks me nonetheless. I remind myself it's nothing more than a signal fired down my spinal cord, triggering the release of acetylcholine. The acetylcholine then moves from the spinal cord, via thousands of nerves, to the four million-plus eccrine glands. Then it filters fluid from my bloodstream, releasing sweat through millions of pores. Simple, really, and ingenious—if you're in a desert and need a built-in cooling system. Not as convenient if you're about to present before a crowd of two hundred in a pressed silk blouse and don't want to look like you've been fire-hosed. Still, visualizing the physiological process calms me.

A little.

I try to concentrate on Eli's introduction.

"Dr. Bryers is the author of the groundbreaking textbook *Forensic Anthropology in Theory and Practice* as well as the award-winning memoir *Dead Men Do Tell Tales.* She's here to talk to you about her recent trip to Japan, where she conducted research on a Fulbright grant at the world-renowned Kyoto University. Without further ado, I give you one of our most beloved and accomplished professors, Dr. Hannah Bryers."

A polite round of applause signals it's go-time. My pulse skyrockets. I cling to the curtains, fighting the childish urge to flee. Then I paste on a confident smile and stride to the podium.

"Thank you, Dean Balderstone, for that gracious introduction. As the dean says, I had the pleasure of living in Kyoto for a month over winter break, working with some amazing colleagues at Kyoto University. Tonight, I'd like to tell you a little about that journey and how it has affected my work both as a professor and as a forensic anthropologist. Most of all, though, I would like to paint a picture for you of the lovely, ancient city of Kyoto and its many wonderful people."

The opening is always the hardest part for me as a speaker. I know you're meant to connect with the audience—share a humorous anecdote, a pithy quote, or a provocative question. It warms them up, lays the groundwork for the talk to come. Inevitably, I skip this step, even if I have an attention-getting hook rehearsed. Blind panic drives me straight into the main points. I've had enough attempts at humor fall flat to know that endearing myself to the audience in this way isn't an option for me.

With sweaty palms, I seize the clicker from the podium and advance to the first slide in my presentation. A photo of KU's iconic clock tower fills the screen. "Kyoto University was established in 1887—pretty humbling, coming from a school established a mere ten years ago." This gets a scattered chuckle.

I make eye contact with Malcolm Cummings, chairman of the Board. He's also one of the most intimidating men in Salt Gulch. He was the president of Stanford before he retired and moved up here to build a sprawling clifftop mansion and raise goats. He stares back at me, his expression as cryptic and impassive as a sphinx's.

"I went to Kyoto primarily to collaborate with this man." I press the clicker and a new slide pops up. "Dr. Ichiro Matsumoto. He's the world's foremost expert in forensic entomology. Some of you may be wondering, 'What exactly is forensic entomology?' In a nutshell, it's the scientific study of arthropods—otherwise known as insects, spiders, and crustaceans—found on decomposed cadavers during legal investigations. Dr. Matsumoto is the author of various cutting-edge books on the subject, as well as the lead consultant on virtually all of Japan's high-profile cases requiring a forensic entomologist."

I'm starting to relax now. The acetylcholine flooding my spinal cord just seconds earlier begins to assimilate and normalize. My body is starting to get the memo: I'm on home turf. This is where I live. I can talk about Dr. Matsumoto and his arthropods all day.

Less frightened than when I began, I step out from behind the podium and stroll downstage a few steps, addressing my audience with what I hope comes off as jaunty aplomb. "In other words, this guy knows a whole lot about bugs."

To my immense relief, this gets a proper laugh.

I change slides, not looking at the screen. I've worked on this presentation for weeks. I know every image like the back of my hand. "This is Dr. Matsumoto's lab at Kyoto University. As you can see, it looks like any forensics lab anywhere in the world. But if you look closer, you'll see a few differences."

I click to the next slide, a close-up of Matsumoto's groundbreaking diagnostic tool. That's when I feel something shift in the room. As anyone will tell you, I'm not the most astute at determining subtle social cues, yet even I can sense something is very, very wrong.

There are gasps. Eyes go wide. Nervous titters, chortles, and guffaws explode throughout the auditorium like bursts of fireworks.

At first I think I've had an extreme wardrobe malfunction. I look down at my charcoal pencil skirt, my green silk blouse. Nothing seems to be amiss. I touch my face, wondering if bodily secretions are pouring from some visible orifice—a nosebleed, maybe. Nothing. Then I glance over my shoulder at the screen.

Instead of the expected diagnostic tool, an embedded video is playing. Not just any video. A pornographic one. It shows a naked woman bent over an autopsy table. She's being enthusiastically penetrated from behind by a man in a white lab coat. He's of Asian descent, extremely short but strikingly well-endowed. She's moaning with pleasure; her cries increase in volume as she nears climax. When she turns her face to the camera, I see with a pang of deep shock and revulsion that the woman is me.

What in the name of God is happening?

I'm paralyzed. The image is mesmerizing. It's me, but it's not me. The face is mine, but the body isn't. She has much larger breasts, a more pronounced posterior. She is—ever so slightly—the wrong color, an olive-toned hue rather than my own Irish alabaster. My whole system floods with adrenaline. I can't breathe.

The room starts to blur. For a few seconds, my body shuts down. I lose all sense of time.

Suddenly, Mick Lynch is standing next to me on stage. The screen behind him has gone dark, though the moans and grunts of copulation continue. He gestures to Toby in the booth, yanking a finger across his throat. The sound cuts out, and there's a deep, chilling silence.

"One of the hazards of working at a cutting-edge university is that sometimes our students are too smart for their own good," Lynch says.

More nervous laughter.

"It would seem Dr. Bryers is the victim of a practical joke. I assure you we'll get to the bottom of it." There are a few snorts at the double entendre. Lynch cringes a little but soldiers on. "In the meantime, I'm going to assist my esteemed colleague in her presentation."

I gaze at him, wide-eyed, too numb with shock to utter a sound.

"You were about to tell us what makes Dr. Matsumoto's lab unique." His eyes hold mine, willing me to snap out of it. "Can you elaborate?"

I swallow hard. My mouth is so dry my tongue sticks to the roof of my mouth. I dislodge it with effort.

"Take your time." He's soothing, solid. Everything in him wills me to recover. He's like a brave fireman coaxing a frightened kitten from a tree.

"Dr. Matsu—" My voice breaks. I start again. "Dr. Matsumoto has developed a diagnostic tool the likes of which the world has never seen."

"Interesting. What is it that sets this tool apart?"

I clear my throat. I can do this. "He's refined a technique called direct analysis in real-time with high-resolution mass spectrometry, or DART-MS for short."

"Fascinating." Lynch really does look intrigued. "Tell us more."

I glance at the audience. Though a few people continue to whisper behind cupped hands, most of them seem to have regained their composure. I risk a look at my boss, Eli Balderstone. He's watching Lynch with undisguised admiration. I'm torn between pure, unadulterated relief that Lynch is saving my ass and resentment about needing to be saved.

"Matsumoto has demonstrated that entomologists can now instantly differentiate between various fly species, based on the amino acid profiles of the eggs."

"What specifically allows him to accomplish this?"

Just like that, we're off and running. Lynch interviews me for the better part of an hour. Though I hate to admit it, the interactive element makes it a more engaging presentation than I could have managed on my own. He forces me to bring it down to a human level when I get too technical. He even manages to coax humor from me. A skilled straight man, he never lets the audience laugh at me; he simply sets the comedic moments up for me, leading me toward the punchline.

When we finally wrap up, the audience seems to have forgotten about that mortifying video.

But I know they haven't.

And I never will either, as long as I live.

*   *   *

Winter

As Cameron and I leave the auditorium, he's visibly shaken.

"Well, *that* was interesting." I keep my tone neutral, not wanting to set him off.

Cameron is protective of Bryers. When my masterpiece came up on the screen, I saw how his jaw tightened. His knuckles went white as he gripped the arms of the chair like a passenger in a plane that's going down.

"That was seriously messed up," he corrects.

I bite my lip. This is my least favorite side of Cameron. He's so damn fond of her. So worshipful. I was afraid he'd react like this—like a kid who's just seen his favorite superhero humiliated.

"I mean, who would *do* that?" He's beyond indignant; he's enraged.

I tread carefully. "Not everybody loves Bryers, you know."

"But to sabotage her like that? In front of her bosses? In front of everyone?" We pass under one of the old-fashioned lampposts. Lit from above, Cameron's eyes are cast in shadow, making it hard to read his expression. "That's insane. I can't imagine what kind of monster thinks that's funny."

For a second, I almost lose it. I have to dig my nails into the tender flesh of my arm to keep from screaming. To slow my pounding heart, I remind myself of four important points.

1. Cameron doesn't know Bryers, not really.
2. He has no idea what she did to me, what she did to Ella.
3. If he did know, he'd want to see her suffer as badly as I do.
4. He can't know; that would ruin everything.

I say nothing. We walk in silence for a few minutes. I'm acutely aware that if I open my mouth right now, a tirade will come spilling out. I've been looking forward to this all day— my hour of triumph. For weeks, I've been planning it. I had to scour the dark web for somebody skilled enough at deepfake and seedy enough to do what I wanted without asking too many questions. I had to provide him with enough video footage of Bryers to make a passable three-minute clip. Then I had to plot how to access Bryers's laptop at just the right moment. The app I installed on her phone helped with this. I knew she'd been preparing her presentation for weeks, so it was crucial that I embed the video at the last possible second, or she might rehearse and spot it. I've plotted this move with the skill and finesse of a master chess player.

And now Cameron is shitting all over my victory.

"You sure are quiet." Cameron glances at me. It's not suspicion in his face so much as confusion. He wants me to seethe with him.

I realize I have to deliver. "I'm just so furious about this. She must be mortified."

"I know." He exhales, his breath steaming in the cold night air. "It's disgusting. In this day and age, for a woman of Dr. Bryers's standing to be objectified like that."

"You don't think it was really her, do you?"

He scoffs. "No way. Are you kidding? Some kind of bullshit photoshop thing. Have you heard of deepfake?"

I widen my eyes, all innocence. "No. What's that?"

"I don't know much about it. I read an article online, though—it's basically photoshop for moving images. Some douchebags on Reddit were making celebrity porn that way. There's an app for it. Most sites are officially banning it, but some are conveniently slipshod about enforcing their own restrictions. I mean, you've got Scarlett Johansson in a three-way with aliens or whatever the hell these mouth breathers want to watch. It's going to get hits. Hits mean money."

"How do they do it, though?" I need to know how much Cameron understands about the process.

"Something to do with AI creating the seamless integration of images."

"AI?" I seize on this. "You don't think Lynch . . .?"

"No way. Never. You saw how he stepped in. Maybe one of his students, though."

I pretend to consider this. "If he did do it, hopping on stage to save her ass would be an excellent way to deflect."

"That's ridiculous. Why would Lynch want to mess with her like that? They're colleagues."

"Come on, Cam." I give him a sidelong look meant to convey how naive he's being. "Academia's cutthroat. I hear faculty bashing faculty all the time. They're petty and competitive as high school cheerleaders."

"I don't see it." His tone is flat. He's not buying what I'm selling.

I shrug. I can't afford to push this agenda too hard; it will look like I'm invested. "Maybe not."

He shakes his head. "Poor Dr. Bryers. She froze. You could tell she was totally freaked out."

"Had to be a shocker." I turn away to hide my smile. Some of the delicious thrill comes back to me, skittering along my skin like champagne bubbles.

Cameron doesn't notice my pleasure. He keeps talking, oblivious. "They better launch a full-scale investigation. Whoever did this has to be expelled. They should be banned from attending any university anywhere. It's bullshit to let this kind of violation slide."

I say nothing. A hot ember of fury smolders inside my ribcage. I should get a goddamn medal for what I did tonight. Exposing Bryers, step by step, is a noble endeavor. It's my life's mission, in fact—my raison d'être. It's no coincidence I've focused on Bryers and not the handful of others involved in the case: the detectives, the social workers, the lawyers. If it weren't for Bryers, Ella and I would have gotten away with our attempt to balance the scales of justice. We had every right to do what we did. Nobody should have to put up with the abuse we endured with Nana. We had everyone else fooled. Bryers was just starting her career back then, but she breezed in and uncovered the one piece of evidence that sealed my sister's fate.

Ella and I were prisoners in our grandmother's creaky, antebellum home, stuck in her sadistic web. Nana Jones was a terrifying woman, a victim of her own mood swings and dark impulses. She possessed a bizarre need to see other people suffer—even, or maybe especially, the people she loved. No doubt, if psychologists had ever gotten their hands on her, she would have been diagnosed with several personality disorders. In the south, though, Nana Jones was just a quirky old woman from a fine family that had fallen from grace. We still had the grand old mansion in Apalachicola, but we'd long since lost the ability to fight its alarming decay. The town accepted us as disgraced nobility, politely looking the other way while Nana got crazier and crazier.

In my dreams, I'm always following Ella. She leads me through the rotting rooms of our childhood home, where the mildew blooms like dark flowers across the ceilings. Her face is always turned away from me, and she can never hear me calling for her. No matter how loudly I yell her name, she's forever slipping away from me, flitting like a ghost around corners, up stairwells, through doorways. She leads me into scenes we survived together, past the men Nana brought there, into the basement where we suffered the ugliest indignities any human can expect to endure. Somehow, though, I'm left to face these horrors alone, denied even the comfort of my sister's hand in mine.

Cam knows nothing about any of this. It galls me to think the guy I'm sleeping with is so deeply ignorant. And okay, yes, I work to keep him in the dark, but that's no excuse. If he had even an inkling of intuition, he would see right through Bryers and her holier than thou Margaret Mead persona.

He'd see her for what she is: a murderer.

CHAPTER

11

Hannah

THE MORNING AFTER my Fulbright presentation, I'm in the lab by seven. I didn't sleep, of course. Humiliation had me tossing and turning all night, replaying the horror of watching that sickening video fill the screen. Who would go to such great lengths to make me a laughing stock? Fresh suspicion is gaining strength in me, as inexorable as a hand closing around my throat: someone is out to get me.

I'm not falling prey to wild conspiracy theories. Last night's debacle proved it beyond a shadow of doubt. The dread, sitting like silt in the pit of my stomach the other night with Joe? That wasn't indigestion. It was premonition, pure and simple. Somebody wants to humiliate me, to drag my name through the mud. First there was the incident with my office door, now this.

In all my years working here, I've never felt so vulnerable. What's changed? We have new students every year, so that cast of characters is constantly in flux, but that doesn't explain it. Surely if this were the work of some demented, angry student, I'd have noticed their bad attitude in class. I mentally scan the sea of student faces, some of them familiar, some little more than shadowy figures at the back of a large lecture hall. Would any of them go to this much trouble to humiliate me? It seems unlikely.

The only real change since last year is the newly formed Artificial Intelligence Department, spearheaded by Lynch. This type of thing never happened before he arrived last semester. I recall the little prank he played with his "killer robot." He's obviously got a proclivity for practical jokes. And okay, yes, he did step in and save me when I froze on stage last night, but isn't that the sort of thing a narcissist might do just to make himself look good? What a brilliant plan: sabotage me, then save me. I saw the look of hero worship on Eli Balderstone's face when Lynch jumped up on stage and seized control of the situation.

I try to ignore these inconvenient distractions and concentrate on John Doe.

The lab is only a few degrees warmer than the frosty morning air outside. Turning on the lights, the sterile white space with its gleaming silver autopsy tables springs to life under a flood of fluorescents. I breathe in the comforting smell of disinfectant and pull on my lab coat. The cool, distant analysis required for my work is my only weapon against the swarm of suspicions and paranoid second guesses crowding for space inside my mind.

Taking a deep breath, I locate John Doe's cadaver storage cabinet, type in my code, and open the door. The tray comes sliding out soundlessly. Using tweezers, I pull away the blackened flesh to examine the spine more closely. The five lowest vertebrae are fused, so that tells me he was probably at least twenty-three. By that age, the vertebrae that form the sacrum have become a single unit. Analysis of the cranial suture closures indicates he was most likely between the ages of twenty-three and forty when he died. Since the missing deputy was thirty-eight, it's not out of the question that these remains are his.

Something's nagging at me, though. My instincts tell me John Doe was on the younger side of the range I've established. I grab a magnifying glass and peer more closely at the pubic symphysis, a secondary cartilaginous joint between the left and right superior rami of the hip bones. In early adults, the pubic symphysis is usually rugged in texture, traversed by horizontal ridges and intervening grooves. By the time someone reaches their mid-thirties, these bones get smoother and are bound by a rim. They continue to deteriorate as the person matures. In John Doe's case, there's still plenty of roughness on the surface of the pubic symphysis, indicating he probably died in his mid-twenties.

Armed with this information as well as the discovery I made yesterday when examining the ribs, I grab my phone and call Sheriff Brannigan to give him an update. He picks up after just one ring, jumping right in without any chitchat.

"What have you got for me, Dr. Bryers?" His voice is terse and a little distracted, as if he's in the middle of something.

I appreciate the lack of small talk, so I follow suit. "I found a chipped area on one of the ribs. It looks like an old injury. Do you know if your deputy was ever wounded on—"

I haven't even finished the question when he cuts me off. "I'll be right over."

Before I can answer, he's hung up. I sigh, annoyed. He'll assume I'm in my office, which means now I have to leave the lab and meet him there. Humans make things so complicated.

He must have been nearby, because by the time I lock up and walk down the hall to my office, he's already waiting by my door. Brannigan's a little younger than me, I'd guess. His dark hair is threaded with silver, but it's thick and healthy looking. He stands about six feet tall, his khaki uniform pressed and crisp. His brown eyes study me, searching my face for information. He clutches a couple to-go cups from Magnolia Café.

"Good morning, Sheriff." I unlock my office door and gesture for him to go in.

"Dr. Bryers." He walks inside and offers me one of the cups. "I was getting coffee. Figured I might as well bring you some. Black okay?"

I take it from him. "Thanks."

Brannigan's good-looking in a conventional way. He has the swagger of a high school quarterback, a man who's used to charming people without trying. His body is still strong and lean, but there's a slight softening around the edges—the jock going to seed in slow motion. It's not very generous, but I can't help thinking he probably peaked in high school. There's something a little bitter about the curve of his lips, like life hasn't panned out the way he thought it would.

"Really hoping you've got some answers for me." His orbital palpebral muscles push his brows into a hopeful triangle. "We're all on pins and needles about Dan."

"I understand," I say. "You're emotionally involved."

He takes a sip of his coffee. "You could say that."

I sip my coffee to be polite. It's dark roast, something I abhor. Though I try to hide it, the disgust must register on my face.

"Everything okay?" He throws me a concerned look.

"Sure. Fine." I put the coffee on my desk.

Brannigan takes a long swig of his and tosses the cup in the trash. I remind myself how essential it is to get my head back into work. All of this mulling over who's trying to ruin me has to stop. One of the sheriff's men is missing. It's my job to tell him if the decaying corpse in there is the one he's looking for. It's a serious task. My answer will dictate the people he notifies and what he tells them. If my calculations are off, somebody could be told their son or husband, or father or brother, is dead, perhaps erroneously. I know I come off as cold, but I do think about these things. It's part of what gives my work meaning.

"As I said on the phone, there's a small, chipped area on one of the ribs. It looks like an old injury. Do you know if your deputy was ever wounded on his left side—perhaps a bullet grazed his ribcage, right about here?" I gesture to the relevant area on my own torso.

His lips tense as he considers. "I don't think so. But he hasn't been with us for long. Could've happened back in Texas."

"The teeth weren't recovered at the scene, which makes my job harder. My guess is he died a month ago, maybe more."

Brannigan doesn't say anything. The distant look in his eyes tells me he's running this against the timeline of his missing deputy.

"So you think it could be him?" Brannigan says at last, his eyes meeting mine.

"Could be, but I have reason to believe this man was younger than the one you're looking for. You said he was thirty-eight, correct?" I flip through my notes.

He rubs his stubbled jaw. "Yeah, that's right."

"Try to get your deputy's medical records," I say. "Find out about any past injuries he sustained. Could even be from childhood. It's the ninth left rib near the anterior tubercle, if that helps."

"His name is Dan Fowler."

"I'm sorry?" I blink at him, distracted.

"Dan Fowler. You keep calling him 'my deputy.'" The masseter muscle twitches in his jaw. "He's a person, okay? A friend."

"Yes. Of course." *Damn my clinical distance.* I need to work on that. "Dan Fowler. I understand."

* * *

Not long after the sheriff's departure, Lynch pokes his head into my lab, his face full of curiosity, his trademark look. I continue to examine John Doe, barely looking up.

"Morning, Hannah." His tone is gentle. "Mind if I come in?"

"I'm quite busy," I say, my words brisk and perfunctory.

He takes a few steps inside the lab anyway. "I just wanted to check in after last night."

In the most neutral tone I can manage, I say, "I'm fine."

"Really?" He takes another step in my direction. His blue eyes are bright, his pale yellow sweater bringing out the gold surrounding his pupils. For a second, our eyes lock. His expression is so compassionate and caring, I can't help but doubt my suspicions. Then I remind myself, an estimated four percent of the population is sociopathic. These people have no conscience, often possess above-average intelligence, are deeply manipulative, and are often just as deeply charismatic. Is Lynch one of them? I had him pegged as a narcissist, but I'm no expert in psychology. Perhaps he is precisely the sort of person who can stab you in the back and then offer to staunch the blood with kindness and sympathy.

I tilt my chin up, ready for a fight. "Actually, if you want to know the truth, I got no sleep last night, and I'm furious. But I think that's your intent—to make sure I'm completely and utterly humiliated."

"Humiliated?" His forehead creases with bafflement. "Why would I want to—"

"I did a little research into this 'deepfake' process." I watch him, searching his face for signs of guilt or glee. "It's made possible by AI. Did you know that?"

Lynch's puzzlement only increases, if his face is to be believed. He stares at me in wonder. "You think I did this?"

Again, my conviction wavers. I have to look at the evidence, though. Before Lynch arrived on campus, none of these disturbing pranks ever took place. For him, it was probably just a quirky practical joke. A way to keep things fun in the stuffy halls of academia. Maybe he's putting me in my place, showing me that, even if a woman gets a top-notch education, writes a mountain of scholarly articles and textbooks, she's still—at the end of the day—just an object.

I ignore the wounded note in his voice. Injured tones can be faked, just like pornographic videos. "It wasn't all that good, by the way. I knew right away it wasn't me. That woman's body looked nothing like mine."

"Hannah, please, I would never—"

"Don't tell me what you would *never*," I spit. "This sort of thing never happened before you came here."

"Post hoc ergo proctor hoc." The hurt bewilderment lingers in his eyes. "After it, therefore because of it."

"I know what post hoc is," I hiss.

His hand goes to his heart. The sunlight slanting through the windows glints on his forehead, highlighting the furrows there. "I have so much respect for you."

I snort, unable to contain myself. "You're saying you had nothing to do with this?"

"I swear to you." His eyebrows arch.

"I know you're fond of practical jokes."

"Answer me this." He leans against the wall. "If I wanted to see you suffer, why would I step in and save you?"

"So you could look like my savior to everyone in that room." I can feel my face going ugly with rage, but I don't care.

He jerks his head back as if I've slapped him. "You think I went to great lengths to objectify you so I could play the hero?"

"I don't know," I admit. "All I'm saying is, all signs point to you."

"You must think I'm a real misogynist bastard." He's getting angry now. Fire lights up his eyes. He looks away, as if searching for patience.

"My opinion about you is beside the point." My tone is terse, crisp. "I'm looking at evidence."

His eyes find mine again. He stands up taller, his barrel chest inflating. "I went up there because I hate that somebody would do such a thing to you. I wanted to hear what you had to say, and I despise that some punk turned you into Paris Hilton, just because they could."

"Not just anybody could," I correct. "That prank took skills. You're one of the only people around here who could pull it off."

All the fight seems to go out of him. His smile is sad and bitter. "If you say so."

My phone lights up with a text from Eli Balderstone, requesting I meet him in his office as soon as possible. "If you'll excuse me, I need to wrap up here."

"I saved your ass," he says over his shoulder as he stalks out. "Glad to see it's appreciated."

"In the future, don't do me any favors," I call after him.

*   *   *

Eli stares at me over his reading glasses, his expression somber. "I want you to know, Hannah, we take this sort of thing very seriously."

I nod. It's not even nine, and already my day feels like a treacherous obstacle course. After my encounter with Lynch, my cortisol levels are off the charts. My throat feels thick with emotion, so I don't risk a reply.

"Do you have any idea who could have tampered with your presentation?" Eli asks.

I clear my throat. "It was stored on my laptop, which is password protected."

Eli takes his glasses off and polishes them with a handkerchief he pulls from his pocket. "Is there anyone who might have seen you type in this password?"

I shrug. "Not that I can think of. I'm quite security conscious, as you know, but I frequently use my laptop in class and in labs. It's possible one of my students observed me typing it in, but it seems highly unlikely."

"I see." Eli nods, his dark eyes thoughtful. "Rest assured, we plan to launch a full-scale investigation. This type of incident cannot be tolerated."

A long, uncomfortable silence fills the room. What neither of us mentions is that I'm up for tenure this semester. Everything about me is under a microscope. Though he's framing this meeting as a chance to reassure me the matter will be investigated, I'm far from comforted. The fact that somebody hacked into my computer could call into question my vigilance about network security, which is never a good thing. I'm not afraid of technology, but I'm far from an expert in the many ways hackers can access information. The thought only adds to my sense of vulnerability, something I find profoundly uncomfortable.

"If it's any consolation, your presentation was well received, in spite of . . ." He trails off, color rising in his cheeks. "Your research in Kyoto is impressive. You managed to convey that quite effectively, in spite of everything. Dr. Lynch did an admirable job stepping in."

"I didn't need him to *step in*." This comes out more vehemently than I intended.

Eli studies me. "Of course not."

"I was perfectly capable of continuing." Not strictly true—I was the proverbial deer in the headlights—but my pride won't allow me to admit this. I refuse to join Eli in his hero worship of Lynch.

"Understood." Eli's gaze remains fixed on me, his expression unreadable.

I know I shouldn't, but I can't help adding, "Nothing like this ever happened before we started pouring money into the AI Department."

One bushy eyebrow lifts slightly. "Are you suggesting . . .?"

"Deepfake video is a specialized skill." I swallow hard, fighting to get words past the lump in my throat. "One that's inextricably interwound with artificial intelligence."

"Do you have evidence that someone in the AI Department is responsible for—"

"It just happened last night," I spit, unable to control my anger and frustration. "Of course I don't have evidence. I'm just using common sense."

Another long silence, this one even more uncomfortable than the last. I fear I've handled this meeting poorly, but backpedaling will only weaken my position further. I force myself to say nothing.

"Hannah, I know this must be very hard on you." Eli's tone is gentle, but beneath the compassion I hear a note of pity. Nothing makes me more furious than being the object of pity.

I stand, my jaw clenching. "I have to prepare for class."

Eli stands as well, looking relieved to have an excuse to end our stilted meeting. "Of course. I'll be in touch."

I can't even meet his eye as I hurry from the room.

12

Winter

THE CLOUDS OVERHEAD are serrated; spindly knobs of spine and curved ribs glow white against the purpling blue. I park my MG on Navarro Ridge and hike through the woods. I know where she lives. I've mapped it a hundred times. I've never been here, though. I wanted to go see it so many times, but I made myself promise I wouldn't risk it until I had a good reason.

The keys in my pocket are reason enough.

The afternoon breeze whips through the woods, making the pines and cypress sing. The earth under my feet is spongey, thick with needles. When I look up I catch the shadow of a blue heron gliding on silent wings through the forest. Its long neck is thin and graceful. My boots make no sound as I scamper down the hillside.

I breathe in deeply as I walk; the perfume of mushrooms and redwood fills the air. Wisps of salt and brine drift up from the sea. In the distance, the crash of the surf murmurs. The ground is thick with ferns. They spill from shaggy stumps and mounds of earth. I walk in hairpin turns down the steep ravine. When I have the house in sight, I stop for a moment to take it in.

It's a perfect gem of a home. The second-story porch surrounds the whole perimeter, and large windows face in every direction, both upstairs and down. At the center of the peaked roof, a square skylight apex pokes out like a diminutive lookout tower. There is something pagoda-like in the simple square shape, the bold red rails of the porch, the way the top story mirrors the bottom like a layered cake. The redwood-shingled siding and the stylized windows feel modern. The effect is art deco, tidy and eccentric all at once. The home sits perched above the sweep of forest, a treehouse temple. Through the veil of cypress and pine, the sea shines beneath the whale bone–patterned sky. The clean breeze caresses my face.

I'm winning. I know it now. Yesterday, trapped in her office, I wasn't so sure. I could feel it all slipping through my fingers. My hard work seemed about to crumble, fragile as a sandcastle in a rising tide. I didn't let it break me, though. I'm stronger than ever.

I double-check there are no cars anywhere in sight. Bryers has class, and so does her downstairs tenant, Joe Shepley. I parked on the ridge as an extra precaution. Neither of them will be home for at least two hours. The nearest neighbor is miles away. I have time.

When I get to the winding path that leads from the hillside to the porch, I can feel my breath coming faster. It's excitement more than effort that has me almost panting. I approach the ornate front door, thinking of all the years leading up to this. They give my exhilaration weight—the satisfaction of delayed gratification.

Patience isn't something I was born with. It sure as hell isn't something my elders instilled in me. If my mom and dad had it, I wasn't around to observe. They died before I was lucid enough to notice. Nana knew nothing about patience. She was all impulse and cover-up. Her life was one sadistic act after another, strung together by a chain of remorse.

Ella knew how to wait. She must have leeched all the patience from our mother's womb, hoarding the serenity and the introspection. Every Halloween, we'd dress up as matching sets: Tweedledee and Tweedledum, Thing One and Thing Two, Mary-Kate and Ashley. After trick-or-treating, we'd sit on our matching twin beds, the light from our pink ruffled lamp casting a soft rose haze on the striped wallpaper. I'd gorge for hours, systematically working through my candy until my bedspread was a wasteland of wrappers, my fingers sticky with chocolate and caramel and the garish colored residue of Jolly Ranchers. Ella would choose three treats, eating each one in tiny, birdlike bites. That was her idea of binging. She'd allow herself one piece a day after that, hiding her stash in a big Ziploc baggie stuffed inside our father's old briefcase, her prize possession. It had a combination lock on each of the brass latches. At night she'd pop a single Sweet Tart into her mouth and see how long she could keep it there, dissolving it on her tongue, never chewing. She was the queen of delayed gratification. That candy lasted until Easter.

I've had to teach myself this skill. Sometimes, when the Nana-like impulses rise inside me, dark and slippery, I have to breathe and count and think of Ella. So many times I've wanted to lash out—fling all my carefully laid plans aside and let my simmering rage boil over into something explosive, consequences be damned. Ella's with me, though, tucked inside my DNA, urging me to slow down, think it through. When your twin is gone and it's your fault, you have to do what you can to keep her alive.

Of course, it's not *all* my fault. Most of the blame goes to Bryers.

I slot the key into the lock. There are three to choose from, but I guess right on the first try. The teeth slide into the slit in one smooth movement. It's impossible to ignore Ella's presence, a whispering figure just behind me, urging me forward. Even though she's the patient one, I can feel her rising excitement, her pride in all the work I've done to arrive at this moment.

I push the door open. The smell that hits me is crisp and clean—furniture polish and lemons. I step into the hush of the entryway, taking in the open floorplan. Evening light bathes the whole space, turning the hardwood floors a buttery gold. The silence, broken only by the distant barking of sea lions, feels thick and solemn as a temple.

Sanctum sanctorum.

It's so pristine in here. No dirty dishes teeter in the sink; no books or papers lie strewn across the dining room table or granite countertops. It's orderly as a furniture showroom. Checking my boots to make sure I won't trail pine needles or dirt, I take a few more steps inside, gazing around in wonder.

A quick survey of the living room, dining room, and kitchen tells me there's little to glean here. It's all too spotless. I make my way to the bedroom. As I enter, goosebumps rise along my arms. The thrill of penetrating her haven is better than sex. I understand at last what Ella understood all along: The longer you wait, the greater the thrill.

Large, framed botanical prints hang on the walls. There's a queen-sized sleigh bed with a fluffy white duvet and a riot of bright throw pillows. The bedside bureau catches my eye. Secrets live inside nightstands. I go to it and open the top drawer. A zippered cloth pouch with zigzagging designs sits atop a jumble of scholarly journals. It looks vaguely African, no doubt purchased at a market stall in Kenya or Zimbabwe during one of her many globetrotting adventures. It's about the same size as a paperback book. Inside, a stash of Trojans and a vibrator nestle together.

Bryers, you devil. So you do have an actual vajayjay tucked inside those sporty wool slacks. Autoerotic sex life with the hope of something more? Are you getting some from Joe the Basement Dweller? I pluck one of the condoms from the collection and check the expiration date. May of this year. Not quite expired, but the clock is ticking. These suckers usually last at least a few years, so it's safe to deduce she doesn't get serviced very often— or at least not here, unless Joe brings his own party favors.

I put the sad little pouch back where I found it and go to the shelves, which cover most of one wall. Predictably, they're packed with books—everything from psychological thrillers to the expected dry tomes. The shelf at eye level displays four framed photos. I pick up the first one. It shows Bryers as a much younger woman surrounded by three strapping men. They're all in formal wear, the guys in tuxes and Bryers in an emerald-green satin dress. The dude with his arm around Bryers must be her dad. He's handsome, an aging Harrison Ford with a twinkle in his eye. The other two are younger; one of them is hot in a jockish, boring way; the other one is edgier, with a face prematurely aged by hard living. He's looking at something outside the frame, distracted, and his cynical smirk implies he doesn't often pose for family photos. It's clear they're just that, though—family. Not a super tight clan, from the awkward tilt of their smiles, but related nonetheless. They resemble one another too deeply for anything else to make sense. They have matching auburn hair and green eyes. The way the men crowd around Bryers gives the impression of protectiveness, a pack of wolves guarding their cub.

I think of Bryers's tomboyish aversion to girly chats. She rarely wears skirts or dresses. I've seen her grit her teeth at sorority girls—not that MRU has actual sororities, but we've got our share of basic bitches with their eyelash extensions and push-up bras. Maybe some of Bryers's hardness, her awkwardness with women, comes from growing up in an all-male world. Where's the mom in this picture?

I pick up a photo in a tarnished silver frame; it's tucked a little behind the others. A long-haired beauty with laughing blue eyes holds a baby on her hip. The colors are faded;

the woman's bright orange bellbottoms and flowered top have dulled to muted shades. This must be Mommy. Since this is the only picture of her, I'm guessing either she's dead or she abandoned the family early on. Poor little motherless Bryers.

A quick stab of resentment twinges in my gut. We may both be motherless, but this doesn't make us members of the same tribe. She made me sisterless, and for that she'll pay. There is no room for compassion in my plan. She will always be the enemy.

The next frame contains a photo of Bryers and a buxom blonde chick I've seen her with around town. They're tight, from what I've gathered. It's a selfie taken on a beach somewhere. The blonde is laughing, her head thrown back, her generous mouth stretched wide in what looks like genuine happiness. Bryers wears an amused smirk, her eyes going sideways in the direction of her friend, indulging her this once.

I set this one down and reach for the final photo. It features Joe Shepley and Bryers. They're sitting on a lawn somewhere, a striped picnic blanket beneath them. A couple empty beer bottles linger at one edge of the frame. A guitar case crowds the opposite corner. Neither one is looking at the photographer. This time, Bryers is the one who's laughing, caught off guard, while Joe nudges in close to her, one shoulder bumping against hers, his eyes drinking her in.

So Basement Joe can make you laugh, huh? I recall the odd little chats we've had, last Monday at the pub and then yesterday in lab. My suspicion that Joe is the friend who wants more crystalizes into conviction. Bryers doesn't let a lot of people in. I hold the photo closer, studying the look on his face. There's hunger there, as well as affection. At the Lynches' housewarming party, I saw the way he looked around for Bryers when she went missing. He made conversation with the women who darted around him like bees swarming honey. All the while, though, he kept glancing over his shoulder, consternation etched beneath the easy smile.

He's got it bad.

An idea hits me. I haven't known—until now—what I'm looking for, but holding this photo, I realize how I can use it. *"In the midst of chaos, there is opportunity."* Sun Tzu's immortal words drift through my mind. Bryers is in chaos right now. Joe's recent confession of love, the presentation-debacle, even the small annoyance of finding her office door locked—all of these irritations add to my perfect storm. *"Let your plans be dark and impenetrable as night, and when you move, fall like a thunderbolt."*

I stride toward her bed. I'm falling like a thunderbolt, bitch.

*   *   *

Hannah

As soon as I walk through the door, I notice the smell. It's musky. The air around me feels thick. I pause in the doorway, slipping off my shoes, listening hard. The wind outside clangs the wind chimes, rustles through the pines. In the distance, the surf murmurs. I stand motionless, sniffing the air, alive to the slightest sound. I'm a wary native, testing the jungle for predators.

Am I crazy, or has someone been here?

I kneel, studying the floor. A tiny smudge of mud is smeared into the oak planks. I didn't leave that smear. I always take off my shoes, and I would have noticed if it was there when I left the house this morning.

Somebody has definitely been here.

Wearing only socks, I tiptoe over to the living room and grab a large Turkish vase. It's got enough heft to do real damage before it breaks. I'm not a violent person, but I've had to defend myself before. I'm not afraid to knock someone out, if that's what needs to happen. I threatened to cut a cabbie's throat once in a taxi outside Istanbul. In Alaska, I had to point a gun at someone—never mind that it wasn't loaded. In Cairo I avoided being raped by breaking my assailant's nose. You don't travel like I do without encountering a few dangerous situations. I've taught myself to live in the moment, to sense the threat before it becomes unmanageable.

It sickens me, resorting to violence, but there is power in knowing you can defend yourself.

I've never had this feeling in my own home before. In spite of my isolation, and the improbability of someone breaking in, I always lock the doors and windows before I leave. This far north of Salt Gulch, I have few neighbors. It's mostly pot growers up here, and they keep to themselves. There was no sign of forced entry when I let myself in.

Moving through the house, a niggling sense of absurdity starts to gnaw at me. Everything appears unchanged. I check the back door; again, nothing amiss. Maybe all the trouble at work is messing with my head. Then I recall the smear of mud, the smell, and I know I'm right. It's something my travels have taught me: what we call intuition is actually a complex amalgam of the senses, internal and external, working together to protect us against danger. I've learned to trust my senses.

I creep toward the bedroom. My fingers tighten their grip on the vase. I hold it like a baseball bat, ready to swing. The door is ajar. I inch toward it, soundless in my socks, and push it open. The room is empty. I check the closet. All clear.

Then I turn to the bed, and my heart stops.

There on the pillow is the photo Amy took of Joe and me last summer. We're sitting on a picnic blanket at Mercy Springs Park. I remember the day—a balmy Sunday in June. The three of us gathered there in the afternoon. Joe brought his guitar, and he played us a few songs. We ate tacos and drank beer and laughed. For me, it was a rare moment among friends, a carefree reprieve from responsibility and social awkwardness. When I framed it, Amy took this as further proof that I'm secretly pining for Joe. She was wrong, though. What I saw when I looked at that photo was proof I'm not alone. I have friends I can be myself with. For most people, that's probably a given; for me, it's precious.

I trace my finger over the glass. It's shattered. A spider-web pattern fractures outward, a violent hole at its center. Coldness rushes over me.

In a desperate attempt to stave off the sinking pain of betrayal, I try to reason this out. Someone has been here. I knew that from the moment I walked in. Joe's the only person with a key; I gave him a spare when he moved in so he could water my plants when I'm out of town. Joe and I haven't talked since his ill-fated pass two days ago.

Ergo, Joe's a lunatic.

My brain races through the humiliating events unleashed since he stalked out of here Sunday night: the office door pulled closed, the Fulbright presentation debacle. That first stunt could only be done by someone who knows me. Joe understands how tiny derailments can set me off. For someone else, a locked office door would be no big deal. Joe knows I hate humbling myself before office staff, though, asking for the master key and getting ribbed about being the absent-minded professor. I don't roll with the punches very well. And the presentation? Joe's no computer genius, but he could easily hire a student to pull off the deepfake footage. What better way to put a woman in her place after she's rejected you than to objectify her sexually in her workplace?

The old adage had it wrong: Hell hath no fury like a guitar player scorned.

Now, with this photo, it's obvious that humiliating me isn't enough. He wants me to know it's him. He's reminding me he can violate my space whenever he likes.

As if on cue, Joe's pickup pulls into the drive. His truck door slams. I stand motionless as I listen to him entering his apartment downstairs. He had class this afternoon, but he was still here when I left for work this morning. Plenty of time to let himself in and leave me this twisted valentine.

I go to the kitchen, pull a dusty bottle of Patron from the back of the pantry, and pour myself a shot. I don't often resort to alcohol to steady my nerves, but my hands are shaking. I need a little something to take the edge off.

With deep chagrin, I remember confronting Lynch today in the hallway. *God, I feel like such a drama queen. Why did I accuse him without evidence?* It was reckless—childish. You can't go around flinging accusations at colleagues. It's the prime example of shitting where you eat. So what if Lynch played a practical joke on me? That was a very different kind of prank, one performed out in the open, where the only witnesses to my gullibility were him and me. The presentation sabotage was another animal entirely. It involved plotting and scheming behind the scenes with one aim in mind—to hit me where it hurts. Joe knows work is my life. He knows nothing could pierce my sense of self like literally being fucked in front of the board of trustees.

The tequila isn't working. I pour another shot and throw it back. The sense of betrayal runs so deep, an ocean of Patron can't touch it. Joe was part of my inner circle. He was fifty percent of my acquired family. My biological relations are strangers compared to Joe and Amy. Now I have to face the startling realization that I never knew Joe the way I thought I did.

I slam my palm down on the counter. *Enough.* There's nothing else to do but face this head-on. If Joe's going to undermine me, to degrade me and bait me and sign his name to it all, I've got no choice but to confront him.

With my hands still trembling, I storm out of my house and down to Joe's door. I knock three times. The cherrywood reverberates under my knuckles, sending sharp sounds out into the pulsing crickets. I'm incensed. My whole life, I've never been this furious with someone I considered a friend.

He opens the door. His flannel shirt is unbuttoned to reveal the T-shirt beneath. He raises his eyebrows at me. "To what do I owe this pleasure?"

I jab him with the frame, our picture distorted beneath the shattered glass. "What the hell, Joe?"

"What's this?" His face goes from arch to befuddled.

"How could you?" To my intense annoyance, I hear my voice wobble. "I thought we were friends."

"What are you talking about?" He takes the picture from me, his brow so furrowed it looks painful.

A bitter, mirthless laugh erupts from my throat. "You can't be serious."

"I swear, I don't—"

"You cannot lie to me right now, Joe." I run my hands through my hair. "I can't take it."

He scans my face. The confusion looks authentic. He's a performer, though. Bewilderment can be performed.

"I found that on my pillow just now." I stare at him, willing him to deny it.

His expression doesn't waver. He holds the picture up and studies it, like the answer lies there.

"Are you saying you had nothing to do with that?" My voice wobbles again. I throw my hands out. "You're the only one with a key."

"I swear to you, I don't know who did this."

I shake my head. "I want to believe you—"

"Jesus, Hannah, you know me. I would never . . ." He hands me back the ruined frame, his mouth turning down at the corners in a wounded frown. "This hurts enough as it is. Please don't insult me with accusations."

I study him, trying to find some clue about what's happening here. Logic says Joe's the only suspect, but his face tells me he's speaking truth. I throw my head back and look at the stars. This is too much. My system's overloaded.

"I tell you what, though." He shifts gears, going from injured to protective. "If somebody left that on your pillow, you've got to watch your back."

My silence is pure speechlessness, but he takes it as agreement.

"I heard about the presentation," he continues. "Somebody's got it in for you."

I bite my lip. A part of me longs to break down. The presentation, my argument with Mick, even my stupid office door—it's all conspiring to bring me to my knees. I know if I start to cry right now, Joe will fold me into his arms, pull me inside, pour me a stiff drink. He'll look after me.

I can't do that, though. I can't afford to take comfort in the arms of potential enemies.

"We should change the locks. Like, immediately." He squints at me in the porch light. "You want me to take care of it?"

"No." I breathe out a sigh. "I'll do it. Thanks."

"Look, I know this is a tough time for us, but . . ." He gives me a pained look as he trails off. "I just need a few days to get my head on straight."

I back away from him. "Sure. Take all the time you need."

"I don't mean it like—shit. You want to come inside?"

"No. I'll let you have your space." I turn toward the stairs. "Hannah?"

"Yeah?" I don't turn around.

Joe speaks to my back. "I don't want it to be this way."

"Neither do I." I walk up the stairs, each footstep echoing through the dense forest like a gunshot.

13

Winter

LYING NEXT TO Cameron that night, a single thought pulses through me. *"Opportunities multiply as they are seized."*

I can't stop this mantra. Shadows dance on the ceiling; cars growl through the streets. Students stumble from the one pub in town, laughing and calling out to one another, their voices pitched high and loud. It's a Tuesday night. The party is brief.

After one, the streets go quiet. A thick, sinister fog rolls in. Wrapped in mist, the old-fashioned streetlamps of Salt Gulch evoke turn-of-the-century London. I lie on my side, staring out the floor-to-ceiling windows. Cameron snores beside me, oblivious.

"Opportunities multiply. Opportunities multiply." I can't sleep; there are too many opportunities to seize.

I flip over and study Cam. In the yellowish glow from the streetlights, his face is as peaceful and innocent as a child's. What's it like moving through life as Cameron Copeland? He's so earnest, so hardworking. His motives are never shrouded. He's as guileless and transparent as a puppy. I trace a finger down the side of his face. His lips curve into a dreaming smile.

It's clear what I have to do. It wasn't part of my plan, but now I understand the depth of Sun Tzu's wisdom. When you're on a roll, there can be no hesitation. When you move, fall like a motherfucking thunderbolt.

I climb out of bed, careful not to wake Cam. It's unlikely. He can sleep through anything. He's one of those lucky bastards who turns off like a flipped switch at eleven or twelve every night and sleeps like the dead for a solid eight hours. His idea of insomnia is a little restlessness in the middle of the night after getting up to pee. He's got no idea what real sleeplessness is—the hours that stretch in surreal silence, stirring ghosts. The deafening hammer of a bedside clock ticking the seconds away. Cam is blissfully ignorant about all that.

Grabbing my phone from the nightstand, I tiptoe to the living room and pace in the dark. *I need to think this through.* It can't be half-assed, this seizing of opportunity. It has to be strategic. On the other hand, I can't dither. It's got to be tonight.

I pull on my jeans and sweater, moving as quietly as I can. Then I silence Cam's phone and send him a text:

> *Sorry, didn't want to wake you. Family emergency. Uncle in bad accident. Have to go to San Francisco. Be home as soon as I can.*

I stuff a few pairs of underwear, an extra shirt and socks, and my toothbrush into my backpack. Then I slip out the door, down the musty stairwell, and out into the night.

The fog feels good against my face—clean and cold, bracing. I pull on my jacket and climb into my MG. I put it in neutral and let it roll a little ways down the hill before I start the engine. I can't risk the wheeze and cough of the engine waking Cam.

When I get to campus, I park over by my dorm. For now, it's the least conspicuous place, hiding in plain sight. Sitting in my car, I call Bryers's office and leave a message, letting her know I won't be around in the morning, that I'm in San Francisco dealing with a family emergency. This done, I pull my hood over my head and walk at a brisk pace. With one hand in my pocket, I fondle the keys I made yesterday, tracing my fingers over the jagged teeth. *Keys to the kingdom.* There's something exhilarating and right about slinking through the shadows at—I check my phone—3:14 AM. I feel powerful, invincible. The stone buildings tower over me, their windows dark, opaque. It's just me and the gargoyles now; they know how to keep my secrets.

Inside the lab, the smells of formaldehyde and putrid flesh mingle. I pull a tiny Maglite from my pocket and use it to navigate the stainless-steel tables. When I reach the cadaver storage cabinets, I type in my code and open the door. The tray comes sliding out soundlessly. I move my flashlight over the blackened remains of John Doe.

A slow smile spreads over my face in the darkness.

* * *

Hannah

Wednesday morning, I'm still struggling to get my mind around everything that happened yesterday. The conversation with Joe continues to haunt me. I keep seeing his furrowed brow, the look of hurt disbelief in his eyes. From there, it's an easy hop sideways to my argument with Lynch and his incredulity. *"If I wanted to see you suffer, why would I step in and save you?"* In less than twenty-four hours, I've managed to alienate one of my best friends and one of my most prestigious colleagues. They can't both be guilty. Is it possible neither one of them did anything? Maybe whoever's after me wanted to put me in this position, off-balance and suspicious of everyone.

There's a knock at my door. I know it's Brannigan, since we've arranged to meet, but I'm feeling paranoid, so I don't just call out, "Come in," as I usually would. I step out from behind my desk and open the door. The sheriff stands there, his stance wide, his mirrored aviators propped on top of his head.

"Morning, Dr. Bryers." Brannigan cuts right to the chase. "Listen, I looked into Dan's medical records. There's no reason to think he ever suffered an injury to his ribs."

I frown. "Did you check with his family members?"

He nods, wincing a little at the memory. "Yeah. That was fun. They're more worried than ever. Missing person cases are the worst."

Though I'm not an investigator, the pain of asking loved ones for information to determine if a corpse could be their missing person is something I've experienced myself. I hope my empathy shows in my expression, because I'm terrible at putting such complexities into words.

Brannigan clears his throat, blinking hard. "I was hoping you could walk me through your findings. The more I know, the more I can start cross-checking that information with missing person lists."

"Certainly." I sort through a pile on my desk, locating my notes on John Doe. "As I mentioned yesterday, the left rib injury is our strongest lead. It's unusual and could result in a positive ID. With the teeth missing, age is hard to determine, but my examination of the secondary cartilaginous joint between the left and right superior rami—"

He holds up a hand to stop me. "I barely made it through basic anatomy. It might be easier if we look at the body together, and you show me what you found."

"Of course." I grab my keys and walk him down the hall to my lab. As we walk, I try to manage his expectations.

Fed on a steady stream of *CSI*, people often assume forensics experts can work miracles. I like to remind them there are limits. "The next time you find a body you need identified, it would be better if your office called me immediately. It's important, in my line of work, to examine the context."

"Context?" He sounds wary.

"Identification is a process," I remind him. "We have clues, and those may lead to answers, but seeing the corpse in its original context helps yield important information. It would also give me a chance to recover essential identifiers such as hair and teeth, which tend to fall out during the decomposition process."

His tone goes from wary to defensive. "Don't know if you've noticed, but we don't have bodies popping up right and left in this town. My guys don't have much experience with this sort of thing."

"Of course." I soften my tone. "I'm just making a suggestion, should the situation ever arise again."

"Understood."

We've reached the lab, so I unlock the door and lead him inside. Crossing the room, I punch in my code and pull John Doe from the storage cabinet. The stainless-steel tray slides out. I catch my breath when I get a good look.

Somebody's doused this corpse with destructive chemicals. The stink of hydrochloric acid fills my nostrils. I cough, caught off-guard. Everything—the tissue, skin, organs, even bone—are reduced to a gelatinous mess.

Brannigan recoils.

I shove the tray back inside the cabinet and close the door. "Something's happened."

"What in God's name was that?" His eyebrows slant to a peak.

"Somebody has contaminated the evidence." I feel sick. "I have no idea how this happened."

He heaves a deep sigh. "This doesn't inspire confidence."

"This has never happened." I'm too shocked to pretend otherwise. "It's unheard of."

"Let me get this straight." He moves his gaze to the ceiling, like the answer is written there. "You're scolding me about negligence—"

"I wasn't scolding you," I correct. "Just trying to clarify the proper procedure."

He looks at me like I'm trying his patience. "And now you're saying someone snuck in here and basically dissolved the body? Is that what you're telling me?"

I don't know what to say. My hands shoot out to my sides. "That's what it looks like, yes."

Brannigan grimaces in disgust. "Jesus. What kind of place are you running here, Dr. Bryers?"

I have to admit, his question is valid. I never would have thought such a thing possible. My sense of security slips another notch. Whoever's undermining me really knows me. They know what sets me off, what injures my pride, what humiliates me. They're more perceptive than I would have thought possible. I feel exposed and shamed on a level I've never experienced before. More importantly, they must have access to everything—my lab, my home, my computer.

Brannigan shakes his head and watches me from under his prominent frontal bone. "This is unacceptable."

I have a feeling groveling and apologizing will only make this worse. I lead him toward the exit. "I promise I'll find out what happened here."

"What's your security setup?"

"We're extremely secure here. This is a fluke. Like I said, I'll get to the bottom of this."

"You better."

I ignore the rudeness of his tone. "You have my word."

He doesn't look appeased. "We're not through here."

"For now, I think we are." I give him a tight smile. "I promise, this is not up to our standards. Something anomalous has happened here. I'll find out what's going on."

Brannigan gives me a long, searching look. "There's no room for sloppy work on this. It's important."

"I understand. Now, if you'll excuse me, I have a mystery to solve."

CHAPTER

14

Winter

I CAN'T BE SEEN in Salt Gulch today. My emergency has to get me out of the way during the time someone could have sabotaged the body. I drive south, buy some pastries and a cup of coffee at a bakery in Arcata. Then I park at Moonstone Beach and eat them on a slab of driftwood. The spring sunshine and wisps of fog mix together. I watch a family frolic with their puppy along the water's edge—a young mom and her two little boys. They look obscenely happy. The puppy's oversized paws plow through the froth strewn in foamy mounds along the waterline. Normally such a heartwarming tableau would irritate me, but today I'm feeling generous.

I'm winning, after all.

A little after noon, I text Cam and then leave another message on Bryers's office phone. I tell them my uncle's stable, but I'm sticking around to make sure he's not alone. Even though I'm operating on only a couple hours sleep, I feel invigorated, ready to take on the world, my senses hyper-alert. The pounding surf, the clean air, the shrill cries of seagulls, even the puppy's cuteness all funnel into me.

It felt good dousing John Doe with acid, dissolving Bry-ers's chances at figuring out his true identity. Only I know the answer to that question: Jake Applebaum.

Jake and I grew up together. I knew him well in Apalachicola—as well as I knew anyone back then, out-side of Ella and Nana. When he showed up in Salt Gulch, I panicked. He knew everything about me. He was here for grad school, majoring in computer science. When he started showing up, trying to insert himself into my life, wanting to reminisce about Apalachicola, I knew I had to get rid of him. He could ruin everything. I couldn't have anyone around who could point out the connection between Bryers and me.

He had to go.

Jake had a severe peanut allergy. Once, in the third grade, he ate a cookie he didn't know had peanuts and almost died. The idea was so simple, yet so elegant. Nobody knew we'd ever had a conversation. Both times he'd approached me, I was alone, once in an isolated corner of the library and another time in the lab. He lived off cam-pus, had no friends to speak of, and was estranged from his family. Jake's mom was dead, and his dad was an alcoholic he'd lost touch with, so I knew his family wouldn't miss him. I asked him to go on a hike with me—face to face, so there'd be no electronic footprint—and he agreed all too eagerly. He'd always had a crush on me. We met at the community forest, I slipped ground peanuts into the sand-wich I offered him, and voilà.

Except it wasn't so voilà. I expected a simple, uncompli-cated death, maybe some coughing followed by unconscious-ness, but it turns out death by peanuts is pretty gruesome. Constriction of the lungs causes bronchospasms. The face swells, and then there's vomiting. "Anaphylactic shock" always sounded sterile to me, a frozen moment before a quick collapse. It's not like that at all. It's visceral and dark and dirty. The sight of Jake convulsing on the forest floor—his eyes rolling back in his head—is carved into my brain like a scar. It wasn't the most terrifying thing I've ever witnessed, but it comes close. I made him suffer alone with no hope of salvation. It was my hand that smeared those ground peanuts all over the sandwich. It was me who snatched the EpiPen from his desperate, clawing fingers.

I wanted to walk away, avert my gaze from the horror, but something wouldn't let me. I stood in that forest, transfixed, watching the light drain out of his face until his eyes went glassy.

It was a relief when Jake finally stopped struggling and surrendered. It took way too long. I'll never forget the way he looked at me, an expression of mute betrayal in his eyes. I even felt a pang of what I guess was guilt. It's not an emotion I'm familiar with, so I wasn't sure, but a black shadow swept over me, and I shivered.

Once it was done, I texted his roommate from his phone. "Jake" wrote that he couldn't handle school anymore and decided to go home for a while to "figure things out." I hoped this was at once specific enough to avoid anyone reporting Jake missing and vague enough to discourage more digging. Knowing what a loner Jake was and how little his family cared about him, I hoped this would do the trick. Since I haven't heard any rumors of a missing student, it must have worked.

Jake didn't deserve to die, but I did what needed to be done. There's nothing to be gained by combing over the wreckage once a decision's been made. I know my path is righteous, and that absolves me. I don't feel great about what happened to Jake—okay, yes, what *I did* to him—but I couldn't let a guy like him ruin everything. He wasn't my enemy, but he was in the way. He's collateral damage. I get

that he was innocent in all this, but we all have to go some-
time. It just so happens Jake Appelbaum's time was up.

* * *

That evening, when I'm heading back toward town, I spot
the sheriff's car outside the Lucky Penny. It's a dive bar on the
south side, a little crusty, with filthy bathrooms and sticky
floors. It's got an old-fashioned jukebox, three dart boards,
and two pool tables. It's a favorite among law enforcement
and criminals alike. They serve burgers that are decent and
steak fries that are thick and hot. Cam and I go there now
and then when we're tired of the pub. I've seen Sheriff Brannigan belly up to this bar more than once.

Instinct tells me this is a chance to work more magic.
My car pulls into the parking lot before I can second-guess
myself.

Once I've parked, I ask myself if this is a good idea. I
can't do anything that might throw suspicion on me. After
this latest attack, Bryers will be out for blood. It's hard to say
how long she'll suspect Joe, if she ever did. When she saw
the photo, she must have accused him; at the very least, she
talked to him about it. Whether or not he persuaded her he's
innocent, I have no way of knowing. Bryers can be stubborn,
though. If she believes it was him, she'll be hard to convince.

This doesn't mean I'm beyond reproach. I can't get too
cocky. She has no reason to suspect me, but I can't go flaunt-
ing my advantage. I know she had a meeting with Sheriff
Brannigan this morning to discuss her findings. No doubt
they'll talk again soon. On the one hand, the temptation to
make nice with Brannigan—test his mood, maybe even slip
in some extra doubt about Bryers—is almost too strong to
resist. On the other hand, if he happens to tell Bryers about
our conversation, that could come back to bite me.

I don't have to talk to him about Bryers, though. I can
make breezy conversation. It never hurts to make friends with

the sheriff. We've met before, but only briefly. Last time I was here, about two months ago, he and I both walked over to the jukebox at the same time. He let me go first, but hovered over my shoulder, commenting on my choices. He seemed a little buzzed. We had some definite chemistry. He's hot, in a fortyish way. Flirting with him will be a pleasure.

That's it, then. I'll just talk to the guy. No Bryers, nothing but frivolous banter. If we hit it off, so much the better. Who knows? All this could be moot. He might be on a date or something. I heard he got divorced last year. I doubt he'd bring a woman here, but maybe I'm wrong. I'll just go in, check it out, see if there's an opportunity. I can't afford to get sloppy, but I can't pass up a lucky coincidence either.

Walking in the door, my eyes struggle to adjust to the dim shadows. The smell of stale beer and charred meat slaps me in the face. I've only been here late at night before now. The happy hour crowd is sizable; at least thirty people fill the booths and hunch over burgers at the smattering of tables. I hear the crack of pool balls, and Shania Twain croons from the jukebox. I spot Sheriff Brannigan at the end of the bar, finishing the last of his burger and swigging the remains of a Budweiser.

He's alone. I take a seat near him, leaving one empty stool between us.

The bartender sidles over. He's got bloodshot eyes and a belly that spills over his belt buckle. "What can I get you?"

I order a pint of Stella and watch Brannigan in the mirror behind the bar. He's checking me out. I can feel his gaze moving over me as he trails a fry through a puddle of ketchup. I wait. It doesn't do to make the first move with guys like Brannigan. They like to think they're calling the shots.

"Nirvana," he says.

"Sorry?" I spare him a glance.

He moves to the stool next to mine. "You chose Nirvana last time you were here. On the jukebox."

I raise an eyebrow. "Good memory."

"Some things are hard to forget." He shakes his head. "I hate Nirvana."

"So . . . memorable in a bad way."

"I could have forgiven you for that. It was the Beyoncé I really took issue with."

"Everybody's a critic."

The bartender delivers my beer. Brannigan pays for it before I have a chance. When I look at him, he shrugs. "I like what I like."

"And what is it you like?" I take a sip of beer.

He shakes his head. "So many things. Too many, really. I'm a big fan of inner tubes, for example."

"Never heard of them. What is that, ska?"

He laughs. "We're done with music, moving on to pastimes. I love to float down the river on a big fat inner tube, a cooler of beer trailing behind me."

"Sounds boring."

"Sacrilege! Nirvana, Beyoncé, and now you're attacking my favorite hobby?"

I tilt my head to the side. "Is that really your favorite hobby?"

His grin is slow and boyish. "A close second, anyway."

"I'm Winter," I say, returning his grin.

"Shane." He holds out a big, suntanned hand. We shake. His grip is firm and dry. "Though I feel like I already know you, since we've traded insults."

"So much more revealing than compliments."

He studies me. "What do you do when you're not polluting the world with terrible music?"

"I'm a student at MRU."

His eyebrows arch. "Should you be drinking beer?"

"Graduate student." I take a healthy swig. "So, yes. Definitely."

"Really? What are you studying?"

I hesitate. Lying is riskier than telling the truth. "Forensic anthro."

"Yeah?" He leans back, considering. "That's a coincidence."

I give him a blank stare. "How so?"

"I was just in your neck of the woods. Had a meeting with Dr. Bryers this morning."

It's my turn to arch my eyebrows. "Really? About what?"

He searches my face. I turn my attention back to my beer, watching him in the mirror again. I can't look too eager.

"I probably shouldn't say." Brannigan pops another fry in his mouth, his jaw working, the muscles flexing as he chews. His flirtation's eclipsed by something darker. He's pissed, and he wants to talk about it, but he knows it's unprofessional.

"Bryers has a great reputation." I keep my tone neutral, detached. "People come from all over the world to study with her."

Brannigan broods over his fries, saying nothing.

"Sometimes I wonder, though . . ." I let this hang between us. My finger traces the rim of my pint glass, lost in my own thoughts.

He perks up. "You wonder what?"

"Oh, nothing." I paste on a polite smile. "She's my mentor. I'm so grateful for everything she's done for me."

"But . . . ?" he prompts.

I give him a chiding look. "If you think I'm going to talk shit about my professor, you can forget it. I never would have gotten my scholarship without her. She's amazing."

Somebody breaks at one of the pool tables. The balls make a sharp, explosive sound as they collide. Johnny Cash starts up on the jukebox.

Brannigan leans in closer, his tone confiding. "Nobody's perfect. What were you going to say?"

"Just . . . I don't know." I rotate my glass, pensive. "Sometimes I question her methods. Lab security is kind of lax. I mean, we deal with some high-profile cases. It's a classroom, but it's also a forensics facility."

He nods, sympathetic. "Exactly."

"And, even if they're not high-profile cases, every body we examine deserves complete professionalism. There's somebody out there with a missing person, and we have the power to give them answers." I flash him a quick, earnest look. He doesn't need to know I'm using Bryers's favorite rhetoric. "That's an awesome responsibility."

His eyes lock onto mine. "It's good to know somebody in the department sees that."

I backpedal. "Don't get me wrong. Bryers is brilliant. She taught me everything I know."

"But brilliant doesn't always equal careful. Or respectful."

"God, I shouldn't have said anything." I run a hand through my hair, distressed. "If she heard me questioning her work, Bryers would yank my scholarship in a heartbeat."

"Sounds like a tyrant."

"Not at all. She's just used to getting her way."

"You've got nothing to worry about." Brannigan pushes his basket of fries away and stands, swiping at his mouth with a napkin and yanking his wallet from his pocket. "This conversation never happened."

"You promise?" I look at him, all dewy eyes, the damsel in distress.

"I can be very discreet," he assures me.

I let my eyes linger on his broad chest before sliding back up to meet his gaze. "So can I."

* * *

Hannah

"I don't understand how this could have happened." I'm with Amy, letting down my guard for the first time all day. We're at the little Thai place downtown, Eye of the Thai-ger.

The waitress has tucked us into a booth at the back, and we've got an array of our favorite dishes spread out between us. The yam nua is fragrant with spices; the pad krapow moo saap looks delicious. In spite of the orgy of color and aromas steaming between us, I haven't had a bite. I still feel too wrung out from the day's events to stomach anything but tea.

Amy puts a slice of beef in her mouth and chews thoughtfully. "You need to eat."

"I know." I obey, shoveling a mound of rice and a portion of pork onto my plate. Once it's there, though, I stare at it, mournful.

"You didn't do anything wrong." Amy levels her gaze at me, trying to get through. "Somebody's messing with you. We just have to figure out who it is."

"And once we do?"

"We make him pay. Big time." Her blue eyes go wide, like this is obvious. "Nobody puts baby in a corner."

I stare at her blankly. "What?"

"Shit, sorry, I forgot you're pop culture illiterate. What I mean is, I've got your back." She smirks. "It's a colloquial expression meaning 'I'll watch out for—'"

"I know what having someone's back means." I try some rice. It tastes like paste. "I'm not sure I've conveyed just how ghastly it was—the sheriff glaring at me while I stared dumbly at this gelatinous mess. It was literally a scene from my nightmares."

Amy's brows pull together. "You reported this to your boss, right?"

"Of course. I had to." I cringe, recalling Eli's face when I told him. "This is the worst possible timing. I'm up for tenure, so everything I do is under scrutiny."

"I guess you don't have to file a report with the cops, since the sheriff was right there." Amy takes a swig of beer.

I rub my forehead. "He had front-row seats to my disaster."

"This isn't 'your' disaster, Hannah. You did nothing wrong. Somebody's after you. They're committing crimes against you, and those crimes are escalating."

A new thought occurs to me. "Maybe John Doe is the key to this whole thing."

"What do you mean?" she asks.

"Let's say he was murdered, and whoever killed him knew I was supposed to ID the body." I pause, thinking it through. "If the killer undermines my reputation and destroys my chance at identifying the victim, his chances of getting away with it increase exponentially."

"Good point." Amy's voice goes soft and thoughtful. "But it can't just be a random criminal. This person has access to your house, your laptop, your lab. Whoever it is, they know you well."

"Yes." I bang the table with the flat of my hand. Our yam nua and pad krapow moo saap jump. A woman with a toddler at the next table startles and shoots me a dirty look. I lower my voice. "I think so too."

"Which is good, in that it narrows the playing field."

"Considerably." I think of how few people truly know me.

She twists her mouth to the side, chewing.

"What?" I can tell Amy's thinking something she's not sure she should say.

"It's just," she trails her chopsticks through a smear of sauce, "more of a dick punch."

"A dick punch?" I echo.

Her chopsticks rise and skewer a slice of mango. "Because it's got to be somebody close to you. In a way, that makes it worse."

"Yeah." I blink, wondering why I haven't fully grasped this until now. "It does."

Amy shrugs and sips her beer. "But let's stick with the positive—at least we know it's not some random creeper stalking you from afar."

"No, it's a creeper stalking me from up close." I can hear the waver in my voice. The overwhelming reality of what Amy's saying washes over me. Somebody in my life, my inner circle, hates me. Also, they might be a murderer. A shiver runs through me. I sip the lukewarm tea, trying to fight the chill.

"Let's be systematic about this," Amy says, around a bite of pork. "Sometimes, when the stakes are high, you've got to compartmentalize."

"I agree." I pull a tiny moleskin notebook from my purse and click my ballpoint pen. "Let's make a list."

"Great idea, but don't forget to eat." She waves at the feast before us with her chopsticks.

I'm not sure I can swallow a bite until we make progress on this. The lack of control I've felt all day sits in my gut like a lead weight. "So, who knows me well enough to torture me like this?"

"Me," Amy says, without hesitation.

"Dear God, tell me it's not you."

She gives me her "bitch, please" look. We move on.

"Does Lynch know you well enough?" She stares into space. "I know you accused him of ruining your presentation, but would he even be capable of the rest?"

"I don't know." I consider the various incidents and whether Lynch is a likely suspect.

As if reading my mind, Amy waves a palm through the air as though she's clearing a blackboard. "We should back up. Let's list the crimes against you, one by one."

I nod, pen poised over the paper. "Number one, the door."

"Yeah, I'm not so sure that's a crime," she says, dubious.

I shake my head. "Anyone who knows me would realize how much little detours throw me. I know it's petty, but I thrive on order. Locking myself out of my office makes me feel stupid. You know me—I hate feeling stupid."

"So true." She flashes me a fond smile.

I scribble another note. "Number two, the presentation."

"God, that was crazy," She cringes.

"Number three, the break-in and photo vandalism."

She shakes her head in wonder. "That had to be off the charts creepy. Tell me you called the cops."

"I thought it was Joe at the time." I wince. "Maybe I should have."

"You definitely should." She waves her chopsticks. "You need a paper trail. What else?"

I bend over my notebook again. "The vandalism of John Doe. Full hydrochloric acid dousing. The guy is the consistency of tapioca pudding."

"Ew." She gives me a scolding look. "I'm eating."

"Sorry." I study the list. Though a part of me would love to take a break from obsessing over this, it feels good to get things down on paper, to reason things out. "That's our incident report. Now, on to suspects."

"Joe knows you well enough, but he'd never—I mean, right?" She looks distressed at the very thought.

I feel sick doing it, but I jot his name down anyway. "I don't want to believe he'd stoop so low, but he's definitely on the list. Opportunity, motive—potentially, he's got both."

She shakes her head and takes a long pull from her beer. "Can't picture it, but you're right. We've got to look at the facts. So far we've got Joe and maybe Lynch. What about your students? Could you have a mentally unstable devotee who's disgruntled about a grade or something?"

"Not many of them know me well enough," I say.

"Anyone observing you closely might guess these things are going to mess with your head."

"Wait." I hold a hand up. "I thought we ruled out random creepers stalking me from afar?"

"Not so random and not so far. I'm talking about people with a chance to observe you who might not be on your radar. To you, they're just a face in the crowd."

I try another bite of rice and consider. "It's possible. But that would open the pool to just about anyone I've dealt with who felt slighted or pissed off. That's a big pool. You know I'm not a people person. I don't even notice I've offended people half the time."

"Agreed. Let's call that 'unknown person with grudge.'"

I add "UPG" under Joe and Lynch. "Are we assuming the same person is behind all four incidents?"

Amy tilts her head back and forth. "Not necessarily. It's a strong possibility, but not an established fact."

"I keep thinking about access," I say. "Joe had access to my home, Lynch could probably get access to the lab and my presentation, and anyone could access my door and pull it closed. I can't think of one person who has access to all four, though."

"Joe's faculty. Could he sweet-talk a janitor into unlocking the lab or get a hold of a master key?"

"Even if he did, once you're inside, there's an access code for the body storage cabinets." I try to imagine Joe finding a work-around for that. It doesn't seem likely.

"So even Lynch would have trouble with that, right?"

I nod. "Though Lynch seems more capable of cracking a code. Who knows? Maybe he has some sort of high-tech AI gadget that knows how to bypass keypads."

She pulls a face. "Maybe. Who has the code, besides you?"

"A couple grad students."

"Which ones?"

"Just Winter and Cameron. They have the code, but not the keys."

"Add them to the list."

An ugly feeling slithers through the pit of my belly. I write their names in slots four and five, but my fingers twitch with the desire to cross them off. They're my star students, my protégés. The thought of being betrayed by them is almost worse than Joe and Lynch. If it's Joe, that hurts, but at least my romantic rejection helps explain why he's lashing out. Lynch and I have butted heads since we met. There's a competitive edge to our relationship that makes cutthroat sabotage unsavory but not unimaginable. With Winter and Cameron, I can think of no such explanation to soften the blow. They worship me. What if that's all an act? If it is, then my role as mentor and teacher is a complete sham. If my best students feign allegiance but secretly want me to fail, then I don't have any idea whom I can trust.

I remember something that makes me feel a little better. "Winter was out of town on a family emergency late last night. She was in San Francisco when John Doe was vandalized."

"People can fake emergencies."

"Maybe. But Cameron said she left his place in the middle of the night."

"These two a couple or just roommates?" Amy squints, thinking hard.

"A couple."

"So they could be in it together?"

"I doubt it. But yes, it's possible." My pen hovers over Winter's name. I ache to cross her off. For some reason, she's the worst possibility. I see so much of myself in her; it's akin to being stabbed in the back by a little sister.

"This Cameron guy. Does he have motive and opportunity?"

I try to picture serious, earnest Cameron sneaking around behind my back, pushing me toward failure. "I did choose Winter as my TA over him."

"Big blow to his ego, huh?" Amy drinks more beer, her expression cynical and knowing.

"Maybe." I lean back in my chair, staring at the ceiling as I try to make the pieces fit. "Now that I think about it, Cameron does have more opportunity than most."

"How so?" She looks intrigued.

"He's good with computers. I've seen him in Lynch's office, so he must be interested in AI. That makes the deep-fake video possible. Also, he's taking Joe's guitar class. He could have gotten wind of Joe's feelings for me. You know Joe. He's not big on boundaries. What if he said something to Cameron, who saw it as an opportunity to mess with my head by pulling that stunt with the photo?"

"How would he get into your house, though?"

I continue staring at the ceiling, trying to visualize the scenario. "Joe's forgetful. Maybe Cameron snuck his keys during class, faked some urgent business, made copies, and slipped them back into Joe's bag without anyone noticing."

Amy nods. "You've got an ambitious grad student who's pissed because you've given his girlfriend more accolades than him. He gets his revenge by humiliating you in front of colleagues, throwing suspicion on Joe, and undermining your credibility with the sheriff."

I scratch off Winter's name and circle Cameron's. *The pieces fit.*

"It's far from conclusive," she says, watching as I circle his name over and over. "But I'd keep an eye on him. Lynch and Joe too, but especially this Cameron guy."

I skewer a piece of pork and put it in my mouth, chewing experimentally. As much as I hate the idea of Cameron being our culprit, I can't deny the process of analyzing the suspects has done me good. I feel more in control. The pork tastes spicy and tender, less paste-like than my previous bites. It's not much, but it's progress. I long to feel normal, in control, master of my own universe.

Amy's gaze falls to my list again. I look down. A nimbus of red sauce has dripped onto Cameron's name, a bloody-looking splatter that makes my stomach churn with warning. I put down my chopsticks.

I don't believe in omens. Even after I blot the paper with my napkin, though, the stain looks ominous.

15

Hannah

AFTER WE'VE PAID for dinner and boxed up the leftovers, Amy has to leave. She's driving to Eureka for a Tinder date with a guy who owns a shoe store. She said he looks like Stanley Tucci in his photo and sounded like Alan Arkin on the phone. I don't know who either of those people are, so her comparisons do nothing to explain the allure. It's a mystery to me, her willingness to face date after hopeless date. Her boundless optimism and spirit of adventure never cease to amaze.

Walking through the dark parking lot, I take a moment to look up at the stars. Eye of the Thai-ger, like most of Salt Gulch, sits on a bluff above the sea. The stars are sharp and bright; they spread in all directions in the black March sky. With so little light pollution, they're as vast and visible as a fistful of gems flung across velvet. A cold, salty breeze tries to reach under my scarf. I cinch it tighter around my throat and zip up my coat. The pampas grass whispers in the wind; there's something sinister and foreboding about the sound.

Eye of the Thai-ger and Yamada's pub share a back parking lot. The sound of live music and drunk people radiates from the dark wooden walls. A low bass beat thumps from the steamy interior. I walk toward my Subaru, keys clenched in one fist. The grass goes on swishing in the breeze. An owl screeches in the trees above, making me jump. I watch its shadow take flight from the upper branches of a cypress and dive into the grassy meadow of the bluff. The hapless prey lets out a squeal, then goes silent as the owl lifts again, flapping toward the forest, a creature twisting in its talons. I watch, thinking again of omens.

A sound behind me makes me spin around. There's a shadow there, a tall silhouette on the back porch of the pub. I grip my keys tighter and hurry toward my car. I'm surprised at my own skittishness. It's probably just a pub patron who's stepped outside for a smoke. I wonder if it's paranoia or intuition making me jittery and superstitious.

I hear footsteps crossing the porch, coming down the steps. I don't look back as they move across the gravel of the parking lot. With one hand, I fumble for my key fob. It slips from my hands and falls to the ground. I scrabble in the gravel, cursing under my breath. What's wrong with me? I've bluffed and fought my way out of sketchy situations around the globe. Still, the footsteps continue toward me, and my heart hammers harder inside my chest.

Seizing my key fob at last, I spin around to confront my would-be attacker. It's impossible to decipher any details, but I can just make out a bald head glinting in the moonlight.

"Dr. Bryers." Mick Lynch's deep bass emerges from the shadows. "Sorry—didn't mean to startle you."

I put my hand to my chest, feeling the rise and fall of my sternum. It's embarrassing, admitting that he not only startled me but scared the shit out of me. I try to catch my breath, not trusting myself to speak.

"I saw you and I just—wanted to talk, if you have a second. God, I scared you. I'm so sorry. I should have let you know it was me."

I pocket my key fob, struggling to compose myself. Adrenaline continues surging through me. My fight-or-flight receptors refuse to get the memo—not an attacker. A colleague. Of course, the two aren't mutually exclusive. Nothing about his tone or body language is threatening, though. I need to get a grip.

"I'm fine. A little jumpy, that's all."

Neither of us says anything for a moment. The murmur of the waves rolling in and out blends with the music from the pub. Lynch turns his head, and the moonlight catches his profile. He looks tired and sad.

"Is everything okay?" I ask.

He shoves his hands into the pockets of his leather jacket. "Not really, if you want to know the truth."

I wait for him to go on. The silence stretches, growing more awkward every second.

His posture looks defeated, something I've never seen in him before. "I feel shitty about our argument. I don't want to be at odds with you. I've been worried about it ever since."

My brain races to analyze his motives. Is this a calculated move on Lynch's part or a sincere effort at reconciliation? If he's done nothing, I'm eager to bury the hatchet. It's never wise to be combative with colleagues, especially rising stars like Lynch. If he's not guilty, I'm the one who owes him an apology—a huge one. Then I picture his name on my list, a top suspect. Which is more dangerous, making peace with him or continuing to treat him like a criminal? As soon as the question forms, I realize there's a third option: make peace but remain wary. It's the most strategic approach, especially if I want answers.

Treat him as you would a Sentinelese warrior: give him a wide berth and watch for weapons.

I sigh. Humbling myself has never been my strong suit. "It's possible I jumped to conclusions."

He raises his eyebrows. "You? The imminently logical Dr. Bryers?"

"Are you going to make this difficult?" I glare.

"Not at all." His expression brightens. "In fact, you know what I'm going to do?"

"What?" I watch him, unsure of where he's going with this.

"I'm going to buy you a beer."

I smirk. "What makes you so sure I want a beer?"

"Honestly? Don't take this the wrong way, but from the looks of you, your day sucked almost as hard as mine. It's my duty to insist we pour some alcohol on our wounds."

"You do know alcohol's a depressant, right?" I'm trying not to smile, but his out-of-nowhere enthusiasm is infectious.

"That's a myth." A burst of laughter escapes from the pub's backdoor as it swings open, and a couple stumbles out. "You hear that? Do those people sound depressed?"

"Fine. My day *has* 'sucked hard,' as you say."

"Yeah?"

"Yeah." I meet his gaze. "Lead the way."

*   *   *

Winter

"Harder—yeah! Like that." I'm on all fours, slick with sweat. The sheriff's ceiling fan wafts cool air over my damp skin.

I can feel his fingers tightening their grip on my hipbones. He's strong. And a little rough. I like that. Cameron treats me like fine china. This is a refreshing change from all that tenderness.

He growls, giving one last thrust before he lets out a sound like a wounded bear. I feel his body shudder, then his torso folds over mine. He bites my shoulder, then my neck.

With a happy sigh, he pulls out, disposes of the condom, and collapses onto the bed beside me, staring at the ceiling, dazed.

I do love that expression. They always look so helpless after sex, like little boys.

"God, that was fantastic." He grins, goofy and shy all of a sudden.

I flop onto my back beside him. "Totally."

"Did you . . .?"

"Are you kidding?" I stretch my arms over my head. "Like four or five times."

This is a lie, of course. He doesn't question it. Guys like him never do.

"Didn't want to assume."

"Couldn't you tell?" I flex my toes, enjoying the soft caress of the ceiling fan.

"I thought so, but . . . you know. First time. Hard to be sure." I can already hear the narcotic heaviness in his voice. His naked body sprawls across the bed like a starfish.

I lie there, listening as his breathing deepens. Within five minutes, he's out, snoring at such volume I wince at the cacophony. It's deafening. No wonder he's getting a divorce. His soon-to-be ex-wife probably never slept.

When I'm positive he's too far gone to notice, I slip from the bed and dress in the fading light. Then I hurry out to my car and drive to campus with a smile on my face. *"Opportunities multiply as they are seized."*

I can feel them multiplying. It's dizzying, watching the doors open one after another.

Ella's with me. That's all there is to it. I asked for her help, and she's here. She's got me.

Sometimes I think that's why I'm doing all of this. To keep Ella close. She lingers in the kiss of salty air streaming through my cracked-open window. Her smell, warm and familiar, surrounds me in the tiny capsule of my car. I always feel close to her when I'm taking steps to ensure justice is served. She understands why I need to do this. She gets it. She knows I do it all for her.

I never had to explain myself to Ella. It's the magic of twins. You just know. Maybe it's the nine months we spent together in the warm, murky world of our mother's womb. We never knew our mom beyond the hazy footage of babyhood. She died before we could register her presence as more than a half-remembered dream. Ella was always the realest person for me, the one who proved other people do exist, that they feel things as deeply as I do. Everyone else was background noise, flitting shapes in the fog.

When I get to campus, I follow the same pattern I established yesterday. I park near my dorm, and after a quick detour to my room for a bottle of Wite-Out, I walk to the lab. A security guard strolls down the corridor, engrossed in his phone screen. Once he's turned the corner, I let myself in with my contraband keys. This time, I walk past the body storage cabinets and go straight to the chemical storage area.

I focus on the cans and bottles containing peroxidizable compounds. Peroxide-forming chemicals have a limited shelf life. Most lab accidents occur when these babies sit too long; they become unstable and can cause explosions. If you add an out-of-date solvent and evaporate it—say, in a rotovap—you've got a perfect storm brewing. It will concentrate in the bottom of the glass reaction vessel. Once that happens, the slightest movement can cause the dry, shock-sensitive peroxides crystals to explode. Because of this, Bryers insists all peroxidizable compounds be labeled with the date they're received and opened. It's standard operating procedure for labs, but she's especially vigilant about it, devoting entire lectures to the importance of proper storage and labeling.

I seek out the most unstable compounds: butadiene, chloroprene, divinylacetylene, isopropyl ether, tetrafluoroethylene, vinylidene, and chloride. I find the ones with expiration dates looming. Opening my bottle of Wite-Out, I erase all of the dates on these. Whispering each compound like a lover's name, I work with meticulous attention to detail, dabbing on the white liquid with the tiniest possible strokes. When all the White-out is dry, I disguise my handwriting, trying to match it perfectly to the other labels. With careful forgery, I set the clock forward by several months. It's enough time to render them dangerous, but not enough to alert anyone to my sabotage.

When I'm finished, I survey my work. Hardly the Sistine Chapel, but it will do.

I'm playing the chemical equivalent of Russian roulette. Nobody can guess who will use the out-of-date compounds, or in what capacity. If I know undergrads, though, this will be enough to cause an accident, probably soon. I feel the secret thrill of a gardener sowing seeds. You may not know when, or if, your efforts will bear fruit, but the promise of germination stirring beneath the soil is enough to sustain you.

*   *   *

Hannah

Mick Lynch sits across from me, golden light gleaming on the skin stretched tight across his well-formed cranium. The basket of fries between us is mostly demolished. We've long ago finished our pitcher of beer. It's very late—I can't bring myself to pull out my phone and confirm just how late. The band stopped playing long ago. Yamada and his staff have started cleaning up. The pub is winding down, the smells of cleaning fluid gradually eclipsing the muskier perfume of sweaty dancers. The scraping of chairs and clatter of dishes replaces the bursts of laughter and drunken mating calls.

We've talked about so many things: semantics, ancient Greek texts, a robot in London detecting eye disease, anime, my trip to Somalia. In spite of my earlier determination to give Lynch a wide berth, I've found myself drawing closer and closer. I keep forgetting that his name is printed neatly in slot number two of my suspect list. It's appalling, but instead of remaining wary, I've found myself revealing sides of myself I barely even acknowledge. There is something undeniably magnetic about this man. All my social awkwardness has slipped from me tonight, a magical reprieve for a few hours. For days, I've been perseverating nonstop about my ruined presentation and the growing list of crimes against me. In the fuggy warmth of the pub, sipping pints of Scrimshaw, I forget about all of that.

He makes me laugh. This is something I never knew about myself—that I could laugh until tears stream down my face. It's the most wonderful feeling, like shaking off gravity, like flying. After the heaviness of the last few days, I relish this vacation from my train wreck of a life.

When Yamada-san starts shooting us apologetic looks, we both know we have to leave. The trouble is, I feel like there's so much more to talk about.

Reluctantly, I pull my phone from my pocket and check the time. "Oh my God! It's almost two."

"You have class in the morning?"

"Not until noon. You?" I can't believe how the time evaporated. We've been sitting here talking for close to six hours. How is that possible?

"No lectures tomorrow, just lab." He hesitates, like he wants to say something else.

I look at him sideways. "What?"

He gazes down at his enormous hands. I recall my awkward commentary on their size that day at the coffeeshop and feel myself start to blush.

His eyes find mine, a bashful curve to his lips. "I know it sounds crazy, but I'm not ready to call it a night."

I open my mouth to say something, realize I have no idea what, and shut it again.

"But, of course, I understand if you want to get home." He backtracks. "I've already taken up so much of your time."

"Honestly? I was thinking the same thing," I admit.

"That I've taken up so much of your time?"

"No. That I want to keep talking."

His grin is warm. "How about a nightcap at my place?"

I can't hide my surprise. What about his wife? If the time hadn't disappeared so effortlessly, it would have crossed my mind before now. If I'm being honest, it has. The looming specter of Isabella has flitted in and out of my consciousness, though I've managed to keep her at bay. What does she think of her husband staying out so late with another woman?

I clear my throat. "Won't we wake your wife?"

A shadow passes across his features, a storm cloud drifting over sunlit fields. "She's not there."

"Oh. Is she out of town?" A growing discomfort gains traction inside me. *Is that what this is about? Is he looking for a quick fling while his wife's away?* The idea evokes an uncomfortable mixture of anger and excitement.

He winces, like my question causes him physical pain. "She's in LA."

Yamada-san begins turning off lights. We stand, taking the hint. As we head for the back door, calling out *"Oyasumi nasai"* to Yamada-san, I try to process what's going on. Together we make our way down the steps of the back porch. We hesitate in the dark parking lot. It occurs to me that we've come full circle, that we're standing in the same spot where he scared me six hours ago. It feels like so much has changed since then; it feels like everything has changed.

"Isabella and I . . ." He runs a hand over his head, looking pained. "We've split up."

"What? Why?"

"She hates it here." He sighs, looking out toward the sea. The wine-dark waves glint in the moonlight, and a buttery half-moon hangs suspended above the horizon. "I can't understand it. For me, Salt Gulch is a wonderland."

"Is it too isolated for her?"

He shrugs. "That's part of it. Tell you the truth, this has been in the works for years."

I can feel myself growing unsure again. My reprieve from social awkwardness seems to be ending. I'm like Cinderella watching her coach turn into a pumpkin. "What's been in the works?"

"The disintegration of our marriage." The sadness in Lynch's voice makes me want to hug him. I remind myself to keep my distance.

"I'm so sorry." It's a lame platitude, but I don't know what else to say.

He shakes his head and changes the subject. "Anyway, I should let you get home."

The invitation for a nightcap isn't reissued. I'm disappointed and relieved in equal measures. It's a terrible idea for so many reasons. He's still one of my suspects, after all. I may not be a relationship expert, but even I'm aware of the hazards involved in drinking with a man after two AM, especially one recently abandoned by his wife.

I need to quit while I'm ahead. "I had a great time."

"So did I." He reaches out and brushes a strand of hair from my eyes. "I love talking to you."

"I haven't laughed that hard since—forever." I can't quite bring myself to admit that nobody's ever made me laugh like that, not even Amy. The revelation feels too new. My body is still buzzing with the sweet release of it.

"I hope the next time I run into you at work you won't accost me."

"Is that what you're after?" I imitate the teasing lilt in his voice. "A free pass at work?"

"I don't know what I'm after." His tone goes serious. "I just really want to see you again. Soon."

"I'd say the statistical probability of that is high."

His hands cup my face, drawing me close. I feel his lips on mine, voluptuous, warm, and full of confidence. My body presses against his, drinking in his warmth. The kiss lasts a long time. It's dizzying, intoxicating. Everything in me cries out for more.

With great effort, I peel myself away from him. As his arms drop to his sides, I ache to feel them around me again. I'm a mess.

"Goodnight, Lynch."

"Night, Bryers. Promise me you'll think about that kiss all night."

"The statistical probability is high." I smile like a crazy woman and force myself to walk the remaining steps to my car.

CHAPTER

16

Hannah

ON FRIDAY, A little after six in the evening, I finally pick up my office phone and call the sheriff. His is the last voice I want to hear—I've heard it echoing through my dreams, and not in a good way—but I need to make the call. I've got to bite the bullet before the weekend, get this unpleasant task checked off the to-do list.

When he answers, he sounds distracted. "Brannigan," he barks, each syllable clipped.

"Hi, it's Hannah Bryers from MRU."

"Right. Hi." He moves away from a pounding source of noise—it sounds like a jackhammer. "Anything new?"

I pause, a little startled. How can I have something new? The body is the consistency of pudding. The sheriff's the one who was supposed to do his homework.

I modulate my voice so it doesn't come out bitchy. I can't afford to antagonize this man any more than I already have. "I just wanted to check in and see if you've found any missing person reports that match what we were able to deduce about John Doe."

"Wellll. . ." He draws out the word. "As I recall, John Doe got liquefied before you could tell me anything very useful."

"I understand. That was unacceptable." I try to maintain a tone that's dignified yet humble. "But we still know what we know."

"And what is that exactly?"

"The injury to the left rib, the approximate date of death, and the likelihood that the deceased was in his mid to late twenties."

The sheriff stays silent so long, I wonder if he's hung up. When at last he speaks, the jackhammer starts up again in the background. "As I said, nobody's shown up on my missing persons list to match that description, but I'll keep working on it. In the meantime, I'd suggest you stay in your lane. I know how to do my job, Bryers. Lately, I'm not so sure we can say the same about you."

Brannigan hangs up, leaving me gaping at the phone.

A knock at my door startles me from my thoughts. I replace the phone in its cradle, my hand trembling. "Come in."

Lynch appears in the doorway. He fills it, towering inside the frame. "What's wrong?"

"Nothing." My hands fly to my face, as if to rearrange whatever expression lingers there.

He takes a step inside. The door shuts behind him. "What is it?"

"Nothing," I repeat, shaking my head to clear it. "It's complicated. How are you?"

Lynch takes a seat in the chair across from my desk. Ignoring my question, he says, "You don't have to do that."

"Do what?"

"Put on a brave face." He leans a little closer. "You can be real with me."

"I'm fine."

He doesn't look convinced. "What is it, Hannah? I'm a good listener. You can tell me."

I think of his name on my suspect list. Then, with reckless abandon, I decide there's nothing to lose by telling him what happened. If he's behind any of it, maybe a flicker of guilt will appear in his eyes. Lynch does have a remarkably expressive face, after all.

"I've had a number of things happen, one after another, within the last week." I squint at him, trying to read his expression.

He leans forward, his elbows resting on his knees. Nothing changes in his eyes except a deepening curiosity. "Like what?"

"It started with someone pulling my office door closed, locking my keys inside. I know it doesn't sound like much, but it bothered me. Then there was the presentation Monday night." I clear my throat, remembering how I accused him of sabotage.

He nods. "Which was terrible, but you recovered nicely."

"The next day, when I got home, somebody had been in my house."

His expression does darken, but it's not guilt written across his features. It looks more like protectiveness. "A break-in?"

"No signs of forced entry. Whoever did it had to have a key."

"How did you know someone had been there?" Lynch's brow furrows; I wonder if he's assessing me for delusional tendencies.

"There was a photo on my pillow. In a frame. The glass was shattered." Before he can ask me more about this, I move on. I don't want to get distracted by the Joe issue. "The next day, when I met with the sheriff to discuss my findings on a missing person case, I discovered the corpse had been mutilated."

"Whoa." Lynch's eyes widen. Again, I search for the slightest hint that his surprise is inauthentic. Either he's an excellent actor, in control of his own body language, voice modulation, and even physiological responses, or he's honestly hearing this for the first time.

"Yes. Whoa." I run my hands through my hair, feeling the distress of that experience afresh. "Nothing like this has ever happened in my lab. I'm very conscious of all the risks in a facility like mine."

"A series of unfortunate events." Lynch looks out the window, then back at me, his gaze piercing. "You think they're connected?"

I cradle my face in my hands, the beginnings of a headache blossoming at my temples. "Maybe. Probably."

"Somebody's out to get you."

"It seems that way."

"Do you have any suspects?"

This conversation needs to stop here. It's one thing to lay out the events for him, but telling Lynch my theories about who could be behind it is going too far. You don't share your suspect list with a suspect.

With my usual tact and finesse, I change the subject. "Can we talk about something else?"

He looks confused. "If you want, but maybe it would help to—"

"I need a break from it." I swipe my hand through the air, clearing an imaginary slate. "Tell me something good."

"Something good? Okay." His brow furrows in concentration, shifting gears. Then his face lights up with animation. "We just got a grant for almost a million dollars for AI research."

"No way."

"For real." He nods, his expression happy as a child. Something occurs to him, and he frowns. "Though, given your feelings about AI, that might not be a good thing in your book."

I shrug. "Maybe you'll toss some of the cash our way when you get tired of spending it."

"Not likely." He claps his hands together. "Here's something good: I saw a fox last night."

"Really? Where?"

"In my yard. Made the most godawful racket, like a demon with a head cold."

I smile. "They sound horrifying, but they're cute."

"I know. I'm smitten." His eyes linger on mine, the words taking on new layers the longer I hold his gaze.

I look away. "Have you heard from Isabella?"

"Yes." His shoulders deflate. For a second I'm sorry I asked. "She's staying with an old friend of ours."

"Oh?"

There's something loaded about this, something important. I'm about to pose another question when he breaks the silence with a torrent of words. "She's moved in with my ex-colleague, a fellow professor at UCLA. Mike McGaffin. We used to be tight. They always had a thing for each other, which was—whatever. I mean, I didn't want to make it worse by getting possessive, but now—" He breaks off, looking lost. "Now they're living together. Just like that. Twelve years of marriage and—poof—it's like we never happened."

"Shit. I'm sorry."

"You know what? It's okay." Lynch gives me a look equal parts despairing and brave. "It sounds crazy, but this will help me get over her a hell of a lot faster."

"So you're definitely splitting up?" I try to infuse the question with the appropriate notes of sympathy and regret, but a tiny spark of glee worms its way in without my permission.

"Definitely." His eyes search my face.

I have no idea what to do with my hands. They're suddenly problematic appendages, aimless and extra. I sit on them.

"I have an idea." A sly twinkle in his eye alerts me to a shift in mood.

I give him side-eye. "What?"

"You busy right now?"

I glance at my clock. It's late on a Friday. Amy's on her way to Shasta to spend the weekend with her parents. Joe and I haven't talked since Tuesday night. My plans for the weekend are as blank and desolate as a midwestern prairie.

"Not really," I say, still skeptical but unable to hide a hint of a smile.

Lynch stands, slapping his thighs. "Come on. I want to show you something."

*   *   *

Winter

"You are not going to believe these. God, I haven't had these things in so long." The girl holds out a large plastic bowl filled with neon-orange Cheetos. She has white-blonde hair cut pixie-short, blunt bangs hanging in her hazel eyes. "Try one."

I reach out and pluck a single Cheeto from the bowl. When I put it on my tongue, artificial cheese flavor fills my mouth. I chew and swallow.

The girl watches this process with undisguised fascination. "Amazing, right?"

We're at an Ides of March party. It's in a big, creaky Victorian outside of town—a rickety, run-down, grande dame of a house that was no doubt breathtaking a hundred years ago. Now it's home to seven or eight grad students, a gaggle of theoretical physics majors who like to get high and talk about dark matter.

Why, exactly, they're hosting an Ides of March party I have no idea. Nothing sets it apart from all the other MRU parties I've been to, aside from the fact that it's the fifteenth of March, a Friday. Cameron is friends with Tim, or maybe Todd—I can never remember. That's why we're here. Cam's in the living room, talking to said Tim or Todd. I can't stop thinking about how useless this whole scene is, how I'd rather be doing a thousand other things. Sipping lukewarm beer in a dirty kitchen with a girl who thinks Cheetos are the height of culinary achievement is not my idea of a good time.

"I'm Laila, by the way." The girl sets the bowl on the counter and holds out her hand. Her arms are covered in tattoos—full sleeves, from what I can tell, with an underwater theme. A jellyfish hangs suspended near her elbow. A seahorse curves around her bicep. Her fingertips are stained orange.

I shake her hand, trying not to cringe. "Winter."

"Winter," she coos, her voice caressing the syllables. "What a cool name."

"Are you part of the physics clan?" I zip up my hoodie, feeling cold in spite of the crowded kitchen. The house is drafty as a meat locker.

Laila laughs like I've said something hilarious. "God, no. I'm in journalism."

"Yeah?" I feign interest. "Like, you're a working journalist? Or a student?"

"Both. I'm a reporter for the *Salt Gulch Bulletin*, and I freelance for the *Press Democrat* when they need someone this far north. I'm working on my master's in media studies."

This gets my attention. "Really? That must be interesting."

Laila rolls her eyes. "Half the time I'm stuck writing about city council meetings or the Pumpkin Fest or some other soul-sucking small-town bullshit."

"And the other half?"

"If it bleeds, it leads." Laila pops a Cheeto into her mouth, consuming it with slow, deliberate relish. "Murder, suicide, car crashes. Mostly drug related, but not all. We get our share of random tragedy. That's my thing. I like to be first on the scene. I'm a full-on adrenaline junkie."

"Ambulance chaser with a heart of gold?" I say.

Her mossy eyes light up. She roars like I'm the wittiest person ever. "I love that! I should have that tattooed on my butt."

We talk for a while. She's sharp and ambitious, feisty and unapologetic. A refreshing change from all the earnest, idealistic save-the-spotted-owl MRU students full of outrage over how "The Man" and corporate greed are cooking the planet to a crisp. Those people bore the shit out of me. Laila has an edge to her, a gleam in her eye that's half feral. Her laugh is annoying—loud, enthusiastic bursts that turn heads—but aside from that, I don't hate her.

While we talk, I think hard about the best way to work this. As usual, I have to play my cards right. Having the sheriff in my back pocket will prove useful—I'm sure of that. Building rapport with an enterprising young reporter hungry to break a story could be even better. *"Opportunities multiply as they are seized."*

When she fetches her jacket from a nearby chair, pulls out a slim wooden pipe, and asks if I want to go outside, I don't hesitate. The kitchen's getting so crowded and loud it's giving me a headache. There's a dankness to the air, a whiff of mold and sweat. I pull on my coat. We slink through the jungle of gangly physics dudes and escape into the cool evening.

On the back deck, a chorus of crickets greets us. The sound reminds me of buggy nights in Florida. There's no cicada's chirrup here, but in the wet, rain-soaked hills folded around the house I hear a vast symphony of frogs. Above us, the trees sway in the cool evening wind. Fog tinges the breeze, a kiss of dew.

"You smoke?" she asks. The sound of the muted party pulses from the windows.

"No, thanks."

Laila's movements are fluid and focused. With a flick of the wrist, she opens an Altoids tin. Her small, pale hands pluck the tips of green buds and pack them into her wooden pipe. She tucks the stray tendrils snugly into the bowl, then retrieves a silver Zippo from her pocket and lights up.

"You're interesting, Winter."

I don't bother to point out we've been talking exclusively about her. That's fine with me. The less she knows about me, the better. People always like you best if you shut up and listen. Most of us have an endless capacity to talk about our own lives. If somebody listens—or seems to listen—we think they're fascinating. It's the reflection of ourselves we crave, the perfect mirror. I'm happy to be Laila's compact. It means I'm opaque, invisible.

I shake my head, watching a ribbon of smoke unfurl from her lips. "I'm not that interesting."

"You are. You're like me."

I just raise my eyebrows. Laila holds the pipe to her mouth again. Her lips are plush and pink. She inhales, then blows smoke rings. They float in weightless circles before they drift into nothing.

I know she wants me to ask how we're alike, but I resist.

She likes my resistance. Her smirk is one of grudging admiration. "You and me, we're both ruthless. We take no prisoners."

"You just met me," I remind her.

She waves this away. "That doesn't matter. I recognize one of my own."

"And what clan do we belong to, exactly?" I infuse my tone with a light, teasing air, but deep down something's stirring. I haven't felt real kinship with anyone since Ella. I sense the truth of what she's saying. We are alike. This strange girl covered in underwater tattoos is like me. We're both relentless about getting what we want. I can tell by the way she talks about her writing, the aggressive way she's taking ownership of me now, pulling me into her circle.

"The cutthroat clan." She grins, tries to hand me the pipe.

"I'm good." I keep my hands in my pockets.

With a teasing smile in place, she says, "You don't give much away, but even that's revealing."

My eyes widen a little. "Oh yeah?"

She nods, her eyes never leaving mine. "You don't like people to see the real you. That much is clear."

"I'm an open book." I know my face is calm, unreadable, but my heart skips a beat.

"You're from the south." She squints at me, tapping her lighter against the porch railing. "You've tried to lose your accent, but I can still hear it in the vowels, like a secret hiding just beneath the surface. Not Alabama or Mississippi, though. Not that sort of south. Someplace farther east. From the faded tan lines, I'm going with Florida."

Now my pulse is racing. "Good guess."

"You're not that into the guy you came here with." She grins, smug now, in her element. "You're sleeping with him, but you're not in love. Not even close. My guess is, you don't *do* love. You just do convenience."

"Harsh," I say on a breathy laugh.

"You're not the kind of person who's naturally attracted to the small-town charms of Salt Gulch." She tilts her head, studying me. "No, you had a specific reason for coming here."

I give her a slow clap. "Very perceptive."

She shrugs. "I was a psych minor. It comes in handy now and then."

You don't let your guard down with someone like Laila. She's calculating. It will take maximum acuity to ensure I come out of this even half a point ahead. I just have to hope she thinks my plan is mutually beneficial. It is, but she has to believe it's her idea. "So, how do you find your stories?" I ask.

She looks puzzled. "Police scanner, mostly."

"You ever do investigative pieces?"

"Sure." She nods. A light dawns in her eyes, that feral gleam again. "Why? You got a lead on something good?"

I shake my head. "Not really."

Is it my imagination, or does Laila see right through this ruse? Maybe I'm losing my touch. Her smile is so slow and knowing, it makes something in the pit of my belly flip over.

"What is it? I know you want to tell." She takes one more hit, then taps out the pipe and tucks it in the pocket of her jacket. "I never reveal my sources."

I make a show of looking reluctant, though it feels like a thin charade.

She bumps her hip against mine. "What do you got, Winter? Give it up."

"I really shouldn't."

"You should."

"It's my professor. Dr. Bryers? I work for her."

"TA?"

I nod. Nibbling my lip, I hesitate.

"She sleeping with her students?" Laila asks.

My hand goes to my mouth.

She tilts her head; her looks says, *Don't bullshit a bullshitter.*

I back off the shocked innocent routine. It's always such a hit with guys, but with her it falls flat. She sees right through me. I can't decide if this is exciting or alarming.

"What then?" There's a touch of impatience in Laila's question.

I decide to play it straight—or, at least, straighter. "She's been screwing up."

"How so?"

"Mistakes in the lab. A pretty big one this week."

"I'm not sure sloppy lab work is all that intriguing to the general public." She's playing me, making me want to prove myself relevant.

I shrug, turning the tactic back on her. "If you're not interested . . ."

Her attention shifts to the place where our hands rest close to one another on the porch railing. She runs the tips of her fingers along my fingers, her touch as light as a hummingbird's wing. "I'm interested."

It takes me a second to adjust. I've been wondering if the chemistry between us is merely the crackle of like minds or something more. Now I see the look in her eyes, the hunger there.

I can work with this. Nothing's stopping me from playing this to my advantage. I glance at the windows, the wavy glass glowing with the light of the party. I can see Cam in the living room, discussing something intently with Tim/Todd, their heads bent close together. When Cam talked me into coming here, he'd said, *"You never know, Winter. You might make some new friends."* At the time, I resented the condescension in his tone. Now I think he might be right.

The porch is full of lengthening shadows. They can't see us out here. We're just silhouettes, indistinguishable from the gathering darkness.

An illicit thrill shivers up my spine. I'm so glad I came here. This could be good. Really good.

I can feel Ella's hand at work here, guiding me toward victory.

Laila leans closer, her face inches from mine. I can smell whiskey and weed on her breath. "You have something you want to say? Just say it."

"I'm scared." I infuse my voice with a tremulous wobble. "I don't want to get her in trouble."

She shakes her head, a barely perceptible movement. "Bullshit."

"You don't believe me?"

"Not for a second."

I smile. There's something exciting about this girl— something fierce and liberating. "Okay, fine. I kind of do want to get her in trouble, but I don't want to get caught."

"Now *that* I believe." Her nails trace my knuckles. She works her way between my fingers, moving with slow, deliberate certainty to the tender flesh between each digit.

"My scholarship depends on not getting caught."

"Got it." Laila inches even closer. Her pink, full lips hover near mine. "What about 'I never reveal my sources' did you not understand?"

"I just met you," I hedge. "How do I know I can trust you?"

"Do you trust your instincts?"

I breathe out a laugh. "Most of the time."

"What do they tell you right now?" She slides her hand under mine, tracing shapes against my palm.

"I think you're a master manipulator."

She licks her lips. "You know the etymology of manipulation?"

I shake my head, mesmerized by the proximity of her mouth.

"It comes from the Latin *manipulus*, meaning 'handful.'" Laila slips her hand inside my jacket, skimming my waist. Her thumb hooks into the belt loop of my jeans, tugging me closer.

"You're a handful." I let my gaze slip over Laila's cleavage before meeting her gaze again. "That's pretty clear."

"So, what is it you want to tell me, Winter?" She tilts her head like she's going to kiss me, stops before our lips touch.

"We've got a corpse in the lab. Bryers was supposed to identify it. The sheriff was worried it might be his missing deputy."

"Now we're getting somewhere." She pulls away a little. Light dawns in the hazel depths of her eyes.

I lean forward only enough to let my bottom lip graze hers. I pull back, assessing the effect. Her lids flutter closed, a narcotic dreaminess suffusing her pretty face.

"Bryers screwed it up," I whisper. "Security's loose in her lab. Somebody destroyed the corpse."

Laila's eyes pop open. "Destroyed it?"

"Doused it with hydrochloric acid." I make a face, indicating how serious this is.

"Like in *Breaking Bad*? Seriously?" She looks intrigued. "You're right. That's a good story. I could use that. You know this for sure?"

I nod.

She tugs me closer again. This time her lips land squarely on mine. I feel her mouth parting, the fullness of her lips, the impossible softness of her tongue. She is all warmth and silk, like falling into a vat of peaches. I lose myself in the kiss, my surroundings going vague and hazy for a long, elastic moment.

Somebody stumbles out the back door, burping loudly. We pull away. For two seconds, I'm scared it might be Cam. That's ridiculous, though. He's not the kind of guy who belches in public. It's Tim/Todd, followed by Cam. By the time Cam comes into view, I've stepped away from Laila, hands shoved into the pockets of my coat.

Cam peers into the shadows. "Winter? Is that you?"

I cross to him and grab his hand. "Hey, babe."

"It's cold as a witch's tit out here," Tim/Todd declares. He sounds drunk. "Hey, Laila. What's up?"

"Nothing much." She sounds amused.

"You want to head home?" Cam whispers into my ear. "This party's kind of boring."

"Sure," I tell him. "Just two seconds and I'll be ready." I turn back to Laila. "Give me your phone."

"What?" Her tone's tart, but not angry. Good. Tart I can work with.

"Your phone." I hold my hand out, imperious.

She obliges.

I punch my number into her contacts and hand it back. "Text me. We'll continue this conversation some other time."

"Whatever you say." She slips her phone back into her pocket and gives me a mock salute.

I nod goodbye to Tim/Todd, lace my fingers with Cam's, and lead him toward the door.

* * *

Hannah

"This is unbelievable." I gape at the view, twirling slowly to see it from every angle.

His voice is gleeful. "Isn't it?"

"How did you know about this place?"

"President Foley brought me here when I interviewed."

I spin to glare at him, irked. "Why didn't they bring *me* here?"

He shrugs. "I guess they wanted me pretty badly."

"Ouch." I join Lynch at the stone wall. We're in the most ridiculous rooftop turret you can imagine. It's the western-most building on campus, a gothic tower clinging to the cliff face. It's called Mad River Tower. It's made of stone, a circular, three-story, fairy-tale castle with a rooftop turret flanked by four spires. The sea spreads out on three sides. Right now the bay is painted in colors fading from rich indigo to juicy peach. The sun sinks with great dignity into the sea, like a legendary actress making a grand exit. Fiery yellow spreads around her as she descends. Seagulls swoop, cawing in delight. The air is so clean and fresh, I keep breathing it in, greedy lungfuls of salty cold.

I've been to Mad River Tower before now, but only the bottom floor. Everything else is off limits—or so I thought. Mick has the keys to the stairwell, knows how to work the latch on the crazy oak trapdoor that releases you into the parapet. I'm only kind of kidding about feeling stung. I thought I was respected around here. Why would Lynch have access to something kept secret from the likes of me?

It's a little like stumbling on a fabulous party you weren't invited to.

"I'm sure they wanted you too." He leans his elbows on the stone parapet. "Who wouldn't?"

"Not badly enough to bring me here, apparently."

A smile spreads across his face. "Good. So you haven't seen it? I was worried."

"I'm not part of the hip crowd," I grouse.

He grabs the stone rail with his big hands, leaning into it. "You're very hip."

"Not really." I tell myself to stop pouting, but the more I think about this, the more it bothers me. It taps into childhood scars—the girl not invited to parties because she had no social filters. Years of this can wear you down.

"Don't be mad." His eyes study my face, trying to detect my mood.

I meet his gaze. It's stupid to get worked up over this. Lynch's blue eyes hold mine, streaks of gold catching the light.

"You're the most accomplished woman I've ever known." He smiles at me, his eyes dancing. "You have to know that."

"It's not the same as being liked." It's out of my mouth before I know I'm going to say it.

His smile is soaked in tenderness. "Being liked is for the mundane. You're worshipped."

"Not this week." I stare out at the setting sun. The clouds have caught fire now, burning with tangerine light. "I've been a laughingstock lately."

"You're being undermined." He toys with a strand of my hair. "You haven't done anything wrong."

For a terrible moment, I can feel tears burning behind my eyes. I stare at the water again, my heart hammering—with what emotion I'm not sure. Fear? Excitement? Absolution? The balm of his words is undeniable. I hadn't realized, but I've been carrying around a secret shame. I know I didn't cause these humiliating events, but unconsciously I've been blaming myself. I'm not accustomed to feeling inept. My normal mode is total control over my environment. I can't help but assume, deep down, that any slip from perfection must be my fault.

Lynch reaches out and pulls me into his arms. For a long moment, I curl into him, feeling safe and warm for the first time in ages. He smells good—woodsy, clean. A little citrusy, with hints of eucalyptus. His chest is broad and strong. The bulk of his pectoralis major flexes under my fingers. I feel like a child. It's not the most empowering pose, but for a few moments I relish my own smallness. After so many years of being strong, this tiny slice of protection feels luxurious. I don't ever want to leave.

Eventually, though, I pull away, embarrassed.

He crooks a finger under my chin, forcing me to look up at him. "We're going to figure out who's doing this. Mother-fucker's going to pay."

I can't help but smile. "Damn straight."

"That's the spirit." He nods approvingly. "Nobody puts baby in a corner."

"Oh, Jesus," I say, laughing. "You sound like my friend Amy."

"Why?"

"She said the exact same thing."

"The same *Dirty Dancing* reference?"

I nod. "Though I have no idea what that is. She had to explain it to me."

"You've never seen *Dirty Dancing*?"

"I've seen a couple dozen movies my whole life," I admit. "That doesn't happen to be one of them."

"Oh, wow. You're joking, right?"

I shake my head. "Amy says I'm pop-culture illiterate."

His fingers find my face again, this time tracing the line of my jaw with his knuckles. "Let me guess. You were raised by hyper-intellectuals who allowed no TV and had you reading Latin texts before you could crawl."

"Not at all." I close my eyes, savoring the feel of his fingers on my skin. "My dad and brothers had a TV. I preferred to sit down by the creek with a book."

"Down by the creek with a book," he echoes, like this is something wondrous. "You're one of those drop-dead smart girls."

"Drop-dead smart?" I repeat.

His hands move down to my waist, encircling me with his strong, oversized phalanges. Once again, I feel small compared to him. Considering he's one of my suspects, this should alarm me. Instead, it sends sunbeams of heat radiating through me.

I try to retain my composure, though inside I'm melting like chocolate in the sun. "As opposed to drop-dead gorgeous?"

"The two are not mutually exclusive. You should know that, Dr. Bryers. You happen to be both." He presses me against the stone wall and kisses me.

His mouth is heat and cinnamon. I close my eyes, wrapping my hands around his neck. His fingers slip under the hem of my shirt, making contact with my bare skin. The sensation makes me moan against his mouth. It's so unlike me, I pull away, embarrassed. My head's spinning.

Lynch studies me. "You okay?"

"I don't want to be your bad pancake," I blurt.

"My bad pancake?" He looks mystified.

I nod. "It's a term my friend Amy uses."

"Go on." His expression never loses its note of amused wonder, like I might be a genius or a lunatic, he hasn't decided which.

I put my hands on his chest, feeling the muscles there but trying not to get distracted. "The first relationship after a major breakup. It's like the first pancake in a batch."

"How so?"

"It's either undercooked or burnt; you haven't got the settings dialed in yet, so it's destined to be discarded as inferior."

She explained it better. I don't know why I'm talking about this. It's so unlike me. My brain feels staticky, like a radio station that's lost its signal.

In spite of my mangled explanation, a look of understanding lights his eyes. "Like a rebound thing."

"Yes. Your wife just left you. You're not thinking clearly. I'm a useful distraction from the pain, but once I've served my purpose . . ." I trail off, unsure of how to finish this sentence.

He steps away, giving me space. One hand goes to his face, rubbing at his forehead. I miss those hands on me already. In spite of this, I continue to babble.

"And we work together. Work is my haven. If I *am* your bad pancake, we'll both have to be reminded of it day after day. It could be awkward."

Lynch's elbows rest on the parapet, his attention turning to the water, the setting sun. His face is gilded in apricot light. I've never seen anyone so beautiful. For reasons unknown to me, I'm pushing him away—this man I'm more attracted to than anyone I've ever met. At least I can admit this to myself. Is my resistance really about his recent breakup, or is something more basic to blame? The desire spiraling through me is so intense. Maybe I'm going on about bad pancakes because I've never felt so out of control in my life.

I stand beside him, both of us staring at the sunset. The sun is just a rim of gold now, a melting lozenge of light. The sea is tangerine.

After a long moment, he says, "I see your point."

"So I *am* your bad pancake?"

"No." He looks at me sharply. "You're not. You can't be. You're too important."

"But . . .?" I prompt.

"I understand if you want to give it some time." He flicks another look at me. "It's sudden. I must look like damaged goods. I get that. I'm coming on too strong."

I want to correct him, tell him he's perfect, how kissing him is the peak experience in a life filled with adventure. I want to order him to put his strong, warm hands on me again, to devour me, and so what if I moan with raw, naked longing? Who cares? I'm ready to fling myself into that abyss, no matter the cost.

Instead, I stand beside him and stare as the last remnants of sunlight slip into the darkening sea.

CHAPTER

17

Hannah

FIVE DAYS LATER, on the spring equinox, I'm standing in the lab, watching my undergrads. There are twenty of them, working in pairs, each of them huddled around their beakers. Their white lab coats and safety goggles lend them a professional air, but I'm not fooled. I know which ones are clumsy, which ones are sloppy, which ones are reckless. Notebooks are spread across the work surfaces as they scribble down the chemical reactions. It's a basic experiment, one I've overseen a thousand times, so the temptation to slip into autopilot is acute, but I resist. Though my saboteur hasn't struck for a full week now, I've been on guard. My nerves are taut as piano wires, singing with tension. I want to believe the trouble has passed, but I know better. Something in my gut remains clenched tight, braced for the next disaster.

"We're working with several peroxidizable chemicals here. What's the rule with these?" I pace between their stations.

"Always check the dates." Kim Matheson, the daughter of one of my colleagues in the engineering department, speaks up. She's got the best grade in the class.

"Exactly. And why is that?"

Her lab partner, José Llamas, answers. "PECs might explode if they're subjected to heat, light, friction, or mechanical shock."

"Exactly." I nod. "And PEC stands for?"

"Potentially explosive chemicals," Kim answers, squinting as she studies the dates on her canister of chloroprene.

"Excellent." I notice someone watching me through the window in the lab door. It's Lynch. Without my consent, a goofy smile takes hold of my face. With a distracted air, I say to the class, "Any questions?"

Nobody raises their hand. They're mostly ignoring me by now anyway, intent on their work. I sidle as casually as possible to the door. I haven't seen Lynch since our complicated encounter last Friday. I've tried not to obsess. It's hard, though. I've been dreaming about him—long, complicated dreams full of lust and longing. It's impossible to know if the silence between us indicates he's giving me space or fleeing after my ridiculous bad pancake analogy.

"I'll be right back," I mumble to nobody in particular. I open the door and slip out.

In the hush of the hallway, I gaze up at him. Seeing Lynch in the flesh, after spending hours with him in my dreams, feels surreal. "Hey."

"Look at you, shaping young minds. How's it going?" His gaze drinks me in, searching every inch of my face like he plans to memorize it. He's wearing a blue shirt that sets off his eyes.

To my great annoyance, I feel a flutter in my belly like there's a fish trapped there. The memory of curling into his arms makes me long to do it again—step into the warm envelope of his body heat, feel him wrapping around me, keeping me safe. I can't decide if this is weakness or a new kind of strength.

I shrug. "I'm fine."

We both start to speak at the same time, then stop.

"You go," he says.

"No, you." I laugh. "I don't even know what I was going to say."

"I need to see you." Lynch looks down at his shoes, then back up again. There's a vulnerability in his expression that makes him appear ten years younger. "I didn't want to crowd you, but I can't stay away."

I can't keep the smile off my face. "That's good."

"Good that I didn't want to crowd you, or good that I can't stay away?"

"I want to see you too." *Keep it simple, Bryers. Jesus, this man.* Is it possible I'm falling in love for the first time at forty? I thought I understood love before this, that I'd experienced it, but this is something else entirely. Maybe I'm undergoing a hormonal shift, some kind of perimenopausal shake-up that's flooding my system with the last of my declining estrogen.

"Good." He huffs out a relieved breath. "How about tonight?"

A sudden explosion rattles the windows of the lab. I hear a scream and spin around. Kim Matheson is clutching her neck, blood spurting through her fingers. Heart pounding, I yank open the door and rush to her.

In the confusion, it takes me a moment to understand what's happened. The students are all standing like statues, frozen, eyes wide under their safety goggles. José's lab coat is splattered with blood, but aside from a small cut on his forehead, he appears unharmed. Kim and José's beaker must have exploded, sending shards of glass flying.

As I rush toward Kim, she falls to the floor, still clutching at her neck. Her dark eyes dart around the room in a panic. I kneel beside her and pull her hands away. A shard of glass about the size and sharpness of a razor blade is lodged in her throat. It seems to have missed the carotid artery, from what I can see—thank God. If it severed that, she would bleed out in a matter of minutes. Though the amount of blood is alarming, I think the glass must have nicked the anterior jugular. It's bad, but not as bad as it could be.

"Somebody call 911!" I shout, trying for calm and authoritative but landing much closer to hysterical. José scrambles for his phone, punching in the numbers, his fingers shaking.

I help Kim lie all the way back on the floor. Breathing steadily to calm my nerves, I yank my lab coat off. Then I realize it's polyester, not ideal for soaking up blood.

Lynch is there, kneeling on the other side of Kim.

"Give me your shirt," I order.

He looks shocked for a moment, but doesn't hesitate. He yanks it over his head. Meanwhile, I concentrate on Kim's injury. The glass is sticking out of her throat at an angle. I recall from my first-aid training that impaled objects shouldn't be removed, since they can do more damage to nerves and blood vessels on the way out. I grab Lynch's cotton T-shirt with one hand and wrap it around the wound, trying to keep her blood loss minimal. Vaguely, I'm aware of gasps and cries of alarm from the students all around me. I press Lynch's shirt to the wound, applying pressure, mindful not to compress the carotid arteries.

José, still holding his phone, says, "They're on their way."

"Is anybody else injured?" I glance at Lynch. Shirtless, he looks like a lifeguard—toned and brown.

"I'll check." He stands, surveying the room. Lynch puts on his booming professorial voice. "Okay, everyone, let's stay calm. Is anybody else hurt?"

"I'm bleeding," José says, indicating his forehead wound. "It's not bad, though."

Lynch investigates the cut.

"There's a washing station and a first aid kit over there," I say. "Anyone else with minor abrasions, line up and wash them out. There could be chemicals in the cuts, so you need to get them sterilized right away."

Lynch leads them over to the station and helps them clean up. Three of the students have minor cuts—luckily nothing serious.

I turn my attention back to Kim. Her eyes are glassy. She's staring up at the ceiling with a faraway expression.

"Stay with me, Kim. You're going to be fine. Everything's going to be fine—just hang in there." I can hear the sirens, thank God. Salt Gulch is a small town. *Please. Let them get here in time,* I think. She's lost so much blood already.

"Professor Bryers?" Kim's voice is small, like a little girl's, tentative and dreamy.

"Don't talk, sweetheart." I never call anyone sweetheart, least of all my students. It just seems like the right thing to say.

The paramedics bustle in then, and I step back, so grateful for their arrival I could kiss them. They load Kim onto a stretcher and whisk her away. I look around, dazed. After a brief conversation with José about the explosion, followed by an even briefer examination of my students, I decide that getting to the hospital is the top priority. I dismiss the shaken class and turn to see Lynch staring down at me, still shirtless.

"I'll grab a shirt from my office," he says. "Meet you at the hospital?"

I nod, grateful that he's read my mind, and rush outside to my car.

* * *

Winter

I run into Bryers in the parking lot. She's white-faced, her skin glazed with sweat. There's blood splatter on her forehead and all over her pale green blouse. She looks like an actress in a horror film.

Though we've never hugged before, I open my arms on instinct, and she falls into them. We stand there under the cloudy sky, the air thick with coming rain. She's like a child in my embrace, her body small and trembling.

When Bryers pulls away, she looks at me, her brow furrowed. "You heard?"

"No. What is it? What's happened?"

"An accident. In the lab." The wind whips her hair into her face. She pushes it away, impatient. "A beaker exploded. Kim Matheson was injured."

"Shit. Is it serious?"

She nods, swallowing hard. I wonder if she might be sick. I hope not. I don't deal well with vomit.

"It's bad. Maybe the jugular." She pauses, searching the clouds for words. "There was so much blood."

"You going to the hospital?"

She nods again, this time holding out her shaking hands. "I don't know if I should drive. I'm still so full of adrenaline."

"Let me," I say, pulling her toward my car.

Bryers follows, a new meekness to her. When she straps herself into the passenger seat, she looks odd and out of place, like a character stuck in the wrong movie. We drive to the hospital, and all the while I'm quizzing her about the accident. I feel a tightness in my gut, knowing Kim almost bled to death because of what I did. She might die. That's on me.

Then I think about the damage a lethal lab accident will do to Bryers's reputation.

I never liked Kim much.

This could be the thing that pushes Bryers over the edge.

It's the edge I've been working toward, the abyss. I keep nudging her closer and closer to the cliff. I've spent the last seven years positioning myself to herd her toward this very spot. In spite of slight pangs of conscience, I'm glad this has happened. It's the quickest route to where I hope to go.

When we get to the hospital, I let Bryers out near the entrance and wish her luck. I may not like Kim Matheson, but I'm not going to watch her suffer. I do have my limits.

On my way back through town, I stop at Misty Cove and text Laila.

Big news on thing we talked about. I'm careful not to get too specific. There's no reason to believe I'll ever be linked to any of this, but best to cover my tracks.

I watch the blue dots chase one another . . .

Where are you?

I text, *Misty Cove*, and she responds with *Be right there.* I get out of my car and pull on a sweater. With one eye on the turnoff to the parking lot, I watch the pounding surf. The storm clouds are thick over the slate-colored sea. Little brown birds chase the froth of the waterline while gulls churn overhead, hunting for scraps.

I know I should feel bad about Kim, but I just don't. It's something Ella never understood about me. Her heart was so open and vast. That's what killed her. I'm sorry, but it did. It's only because my heart is hard as an uncooked potato that I can do all of this.

Laila pulls into the lot in an early model BMW, a deep scarlet with peeling paint. Her long legs emerge first, followed by the rest of her. In spite of myself, I feel a flutter of nerves. This girl has me on pins and needles. I've never met anyone who is more my match.

She's wearing a dark green bomber jacket, black boots, skinny jeans, and a faded yellow T-shirt. Her face is alive with excitement, the bloodhound who's picked up a scent.

I can't help but admire her ambition.

"There you are," she says, like we lost track of one another for a minute at a party. "I was hoping you'd get in touch."

I've been avoiding Laila's texts since we met. I wanted to wait until I had something good. You can't squander sizzling chemistry like this on a series of meaningless texts. You have to store up the energy, let it fizz, only releasing it when you stand to gain something tangible.

"I have something."

"All business," she chides. "You want a beer?"

"Sure, why not?" I don't want to scare her off with naked ambition, even though that's what I see in her. Some people can't handle the truth.

Laila goes back to her car and returns with a couple Pacíficos. From her jacket pocket she extracts an opener and deftly pries off their lids. She hands one to me, her smile dazzling in the stormy gray light.

We clink bottles and drink.

"You've been avoiding me," she says.

"Not really." I shrug. "I'm just busy."

"Sure. If you say so." Her smirk is sly and knowing.

I sigh. "Are you pissed?"

"Not at all." She looks surprised. Her lips fasten around the bottle, and she takes another long drink.

"So, I have something to add to that story I mentioned."

"The Great Lab Caper?"

I turn to her, my patience wearing thin. "Look, if you don't want the information, I'll turn it over to somebody else."

"I want it." She says it simply, without a hint of desperation.

I appreciate a woman who won't beg.

"It's about Bryers. Something else has happened. Something big."

"Do tell."

"Right now, there's a student in the ER. A beaker exploded during Bryers's class today. The girl almost died."

"Wait, she almost *died*?" Laila looks at me, all pretense of coyness gone. She recognizes a big story when she hears one. "Because of a broken beaker?"

I fix her with my stare. "A piece of glass impaled this girl in the jugular. She's not out of the woods yet. She lost a lot of blood."

"Oh my God. She really might die?" There's that feral gleam again, the ambulance chaser.

I nod. "When I left the hospital, it was touch-and-go."

"God," she repeats.

"Plus," I add, "she's Professor Matheson's daughter. You know, that weird guy in engineering? The one with the comb-over?"

"Seriously? That's crazy." Her enthusiasm is gratifying. "This is going to shake up the whole community."

"Exactly."

We stare out at the water, leaning on the wooden fence.

"Why do you want Bryers to go down?" She doesn't look at me when she asks it. There's gentle curiosity there—no judgment, just an interest so neutral it's almost clinical.

I think about my answer. This has to be just right. Laila, more than anyone I've met for years, seems to know instinctively how I think. If I'm going to keep my plans from her—and that's essential—I need to hit just the right note.

"If she's doing sloppy work and students are in danger, I think the community should know." I don't lay it on too thick. The reporter in her won't buy it if I do. "People around here trust her. Maybe they should think twice. That's all I'm saying."

She flashes a dubious smile. It's a look that says, *"I know there's more to it, but fine—be that way, don't tell me."*

"Do you have enough to write the story?" I change the subject.

Laila gives me a calculating look. "It's a little sketchy to write an entire article based on one source I just met."

"I don't know if the sheriff will talk, but I can ask him." I push my hair away from my face.

"You're in with the sheriff?"

"Yeah." I decide to leave it at that.

She bumps a hip against mine. "Aren't you full of surprises."

"Am I?" I flash her a winning smile.

"So, about your boyfriend—"

"Don't worry about Cam." I lean over and kiss her on the mouth. She has the most voluptuous, pillowy lips. My fingers reach up to fondle her throat.

"He's not your—"

"He's nobody."

She raises an eyebrow. "Does he know that?"

"Let's just focus on this." I lean in and taste the sweetness of Laila's mouth again, losing myself in her softness.

* * *

Hannah

Gil Matheson stares at me, his nostrils flared. "I don't understand how you could let this happen."

I shake my head. "I'm meticulous about checking dates."

"Not meticulous enough, apparently."

Gil's wife, Charlene, puts a hand on her husband's arm. "Honey, this isn't helping."

"I don't care." He's red-faced, so furious the rage is like a wall of heat coming off of him. "Our daughter could die because of this woman's gross negligence."

Lynch comes around the corner, carrying two coffees from the hospital cafeteria. I called Kim's dad as soon as I'd learned from the doctors she was in surgery. We don't know much more than that. She's been in there at least twenty minutes. The Mathesons showed up while Lynch was fetching caffeine. Gil hasn't stopped heaping abuse on me since he arrived.

I'm more inclined to fall on my knees and beg their forgiveness than try to defend myself. Kim's accident has me racked with guilt. Now that the adrenaline has ebbed, I'm cocooned in a terrible sadness. *Kim could die. These people might lose their only daughter.* I stepped out to talk to Lynch right before the explosion. I wasn't even in the room. His accusations are spot-on. It's because of my negligence this happened.

Or is it? Even if I hadn't slipped into the hallway at the crucial moment, this accident probably would have occurred. Not probably—definitely. It had nothing to do with a lack of supervision; it's all about the compounds themselves. As usual, I checked the dates on all the PECs before the experiment. I lectured the students on the importance of examining their own labels—it's an endless refrain I repeat every time we work with peroxidizable compounds—but I never leave that inspection up to them.

Could somebody have tampered with the dates? The thought keeps haunting me. I know what this will sound like if I bring it up, though. It will look like I'm desperate to deflect, trying to cast blame on an unseen villain rather than accept responsibility. I don't dare mention this to Gil or Charlene. Anything I say at this point will only work against me.

Gil isn't finished with me yet. He turns away from his wife and gets right up in my face, his skin still flushed with fury. "I will do everything in my power to make sure you pay for this. I hope you know that."

"Hey, buddy, why don't you back up?" Lynch inserts himself between us, gently cupping Gil's shoulders as I take the opportunity to retreat a few steps.

Gil blinks up at Lynch. "What business is this of yours?"

"I was there when the accident happened." Lynch's voice is calm, steady, unruffled by Gil's hostility. "I can assure you Hannah wasn't to blame."

"Oh, you can *assure* me, huh?" I'm not always adept at recognizing sarcasm, but Gil's tone fairly drips with it. "We'll see about that."

"You're upset. That's natural." Lynch drops his tone to a confiding, soothing register. "It's your daughter in there. You want someone to blame. I know I would. But . . . I promise you . . . turning on a colleague isn't the answer."

Gil looks at him with undisguised loathing. "I don't give a shit about your promises. I don't even know what you're doing here. Like I said, this is none of your goddamn business."

"If you're going to hurl accusations at Dr. Bryers, it's my business." A new hardness creeps into Lynch's tone now, a low note of warning.

As much as I'd like to let Lynch handle this, I know I can't. It's never been my style to let a man defend me. After weeks of feeling victimized by shadow forces, I can't help but savor Lynch's willingness to jump to my defense. That's no excuse to wilt into the shadows, though, staying silent while the men battle it out.

"Gil, you have every right to be angry at me."

Gil whips around, fixing me with his beady eyes. He says nothing, breathing hard through his nose like a bull about to charge.

"The important thing now is to focus on Kim," I say, my voice trembling. "She's in there fighting for her life—"

"Don't tell me about my daughter," Gil explodes. "If you weren't so damn negligent, my little girl would be just fine."

"See, that's where you're wrong." Lynch's warning tone ratchets up a notch. He's still steady, calm, but I can hear the tension coiling inside his words.

"Are you a lab safety expert?" Gil transfers his ire back to Lynch again, spittle flying from his lips.

"I've spent plenty of time in labs, sure, but more importantly, I know Hannah." Lynch throws me a fleeting look of such searing warmth I feel it in my bones. "She's got too much integrity to put her students in danger."

Logically, I can't help thinking how Lynch *doesn't* know me, not really. He happens to be right on this, but he hasn't known me long enough to vouch for my character. Even with my social handicaps, I do realize mentioning this would be unwise.

We all turn at the sound of footsteps striding down the white linoleum toward us. It's Dr. Perkowsky, the physician I talked to earlier. She's a tall, gray-haired woman in her fifties. Her lithe figure cuts through the gurneys and wheelchairs with confidence.

Charlene reaches her first, wringing her hands, her face white.

Dr. Perkowsky's long-boned face is lined with a lifetime of smiles. "I take it you're Kim's parents?"

Gil and Charlene nod, their shoulders so tense they're halfway to their ears.

"Your daughter's in the ICU. She's stable, but we want to keep an eye on her."

A tiny sob escapes from Charlene's pursed lips. Gil runs his hands over his face like a man trying to wake up from a nightmare.

"The glass nicked her jugular. Luckily, the people on the scene reacted quickly enough to minimize the damage." She glances at Lynch and me with a quick nod of approval. "We've stopped the bleeding, and we have every reason to believe she'll pull through with no lasting damage."

"Oh my God." Charlene cups her mouth with her hands, eyes streaming with joyful tears. She pulls the doctor into a hug. "Thank you."

When Dr. Perkowsky extracts herself from the hug, she looks back at me. "Don't thank me. Thank Dr. Bryers. She's the one who saved your daughter's life."

Charlene spins on her heel and wraps me in a fierce hug. "Thank you, Dr. Bryers. God, thank you."

I catch a glimpse of Gil's expression. His lip curls in disgust. He doesn't share his wife's unadulterated joy. It's clear he still considers me the enemy.

"Can we see her?" Charlene asks the doctor.

"Sure. She's sleeping—she needs her rest—but you're welcome to sit with her for a bit. Just give the team a few minutes to get her set up. She should be in . . ." The doctor consults a clipboard. "Room 243. She'll look a little rough, so prepare yourselves for that. But she's going to be fine."

"God bless you." Charlene tugs at her cardigan, pulling it tighter around her as if for warmth. "We can never thank you enough."

The doctor smiles and strides back down the hallway, her shoes squeaking against the white linoleum.

Charlene turns back around to face me. The tender gratitude in her eyes is overwhelming. "You saved her life."

"I just reacted to an emergency."

"She almost killed her." Gil spits the words out. "Don't forget that."

"Gil, I'm so sorry for—" I begin, but he cuts me off.

"No." He holds up a hand. "I cannot listen to another word of your shit."

With that, he stalks off, his wife trailing unsteadily in his wake.

18

Winter

Laila's place is wild. She rents a room on the third floor of a damp, teetering house, with dark walls and so many shelves full of books it looks like a library. In the living room, we pass a woman in her forties, toking on a bong, her leathery breasts half falling out of her stretched-out camisole. An orange cat winds its way around our legs as we climb the stairs. On the third floor, Laila leads me toward a bright blue door at the end of a hallway.

Inside her bedroom, the atmosphere shifts dramatically. It's like walking into a hothouse filled with exotic blossoms. There are red Chinese lanterns everywhere. The walls are completely covered in a colorful collage—a smattering of ads from the forties, film noir stills, comic book covers and maps. The walls breathe with life. Mobiles of strange objects dangle from the rafters—twisted spoons, animal skulls, colorful glass bottles brimming with dried flowers. It's a claustrophobic womb of ideas and images. A rolltop desk sits in one corner. A pretty picture window surrounded by ferns and orchids looks out on the gray-green sea. Near the window, a queen-sized bed, covered in a gold satin quilt and piled high with exotic throw pillows, sits on a brass frame.

She kisses me, her breath hot and her mouth hotter. When at last she leads me toward the bed, I don't resist. I've never been with a woman. The prospect is both exciting and terrifying. I wonder if I'll even know what to do.

Her finger tucks under my chin, studying me. "You're new to this."

I nod, grateful and also freaked out that she's read my mind.

"It's not that different. Just follow your instincts." She grins, nipping at my bottom lip. "You're a natural. I can tell."

"What does that mean?" I can't decide if it's a compliment.

She lifts one shoulder before tearing off her jacket. "It means don't worry. You'll love it."

She's right. I do love it. There's so much softness every-where, like drowning in silk. The feel of her mouth on mine is pure plush velvet. She tastes like vanilla and tangerines. She's playful and feisty, uninhibited in a way that makes me drop my own inhibitions. It's exhilarating and scary, being with Laila—a huge, uncharted continent I explore with eyes wide open.

Later, we lie side by side, tangled in her sheets, staring at the shadows playing on the ceiling. A cool ribbon of breeze unfurls from the open window, spreading gooseflesh along our bare skin. I can hear the sea lions in the distance, barking and moaning in time with the pounding surf.

"Tell me the truth." She runs one finger up my sweaty thigh. "Why do you hate Bryers?"

I sit up. "Is that why you brought me here? To ask me that?"

"Relax." She rolls into a seated position, pulls a joint from a glass box by the bed. With languid fingers, she snatches up a Zippo and lights it. After a cinematic exhale of smoke, she looks at me, loosely hugging her knees. "I brought you here to do what we just did, you idiot."

"You swear?"

She smirks. "Better than that. I pinkie-swear." She holds out a pinkie.

I link mine with hers, meeting her eyes. "I don't hate Bryers."

"Liar."

"Shut up!" I bat her with a pillow.

She struggles to keep the joint aloft and out of harm's way.

Out of nowhere, a violent need to leave comes over me, so complete and overwhelming I have to fight the urge to bolt from the room.

Laila hugs her knees tighter, offering me the joint. I pluck it from her fingers, pretend to take a hit, but don't pull the smoke all the way into my lungs. I'm not sure I can handle the added pressure of an altered state right now. I need to keep a clear head. I have to get out of here without alienating Laila.

I have no idea why I feel this sudden impulse to flee. Maybe it's intuition. Maybe it's the nakedness, literal and figurative, that plagues me. I haven't felt this visible since Ella. Laila pierces my practiced facade, sees right through my layers of camouflage. In a way, it's a huge relief. It's also over-whelming, a level of exposure I'm not prepared for. I'm start-ing to wonder if coming here was a terrible miscalculation.

I fish my shirt from the tangle of sheets and pull it on, not bothering with my bra. "I should get going."

"Need to get back to your boyfriend?" I catch a glimpse of hardness in her face, something flinty in her eyes.

I ignore the boyfriend question and go for vague. "Work to do."

She pulls on a white camisole and picks up her phone, dismissing me. With her other hand, she puts the joint to her lips and takes another long drag, the muscles in her face tense with concentration.

I find the rest of my clothes and pull them on, sensing I've mishandled the situation but unsure how to fix it. When I open the door, the cat is there, blinking up at me with disapproval. "Is the cat allowed in your room?"

"What?" Laila sounds annoyed and a little surprised, like she'd already forgotten I was there.

The cat slips past me, stalking toward the bed, haughty and indignant. I don't repeat the question. It leaps onto the bed and begins kneading the rumpled sheets with a proprietary air. Laila pets the animal absently, scratching between its ears.

I pull on my sweater and wrap my scarf around my neck, searching for the right words. Minutes ago, we were so raw and intimate. Now we might as well be on different continents. I know I initiated the distance, but the wall has gone up so quickly and with such force, it's disorienting. Laila's arctic stillness feels like a slap. Cam is always complaining that I shut him out. I wonder if this is what he's talking about.

"You seem mad." I sit on the edge of her bed, trying to catch Laila's eye.

She doesn't even look up from her phone. "You going to call the sheriff?"

I hesitate.

Her eyes finally deign to meet mine. "I can't run the story without him."

"I've given you plenty."

She leans back against the pillows, resting the joint on the lip of a glass ashtray beside her bed. Smoke winds its way through the afternoon sunlight, mingling with dust motes. "I'm not going to stake my reputation on the word of some disgruntled TA."

I bristle at this. "Fine. I'll take it to somebody else."

Her eyes are cold and hard as stone. "So that was bullshit, about knowing the sheriff?"

"No." It comes out defensive, angry. I dial back the defensiveness, going instead for bravado. "You want me to phone him right now?"

She calls my bluff. "Go for it."

I raise an eyebrow. My gaze falls on the joint smoldering in the ashtray. "You want to interview him right this second?"

Her smile is slow. She takes another defiant drag off the joint and nods. "Ready when you are."

I fish my phone from my pocket and bring up Brannigan's number. This could blow up in my face, but I refuse to back down from Laila's challenge. She's pissed me off now; there's no turning back. I hit the "Call" button and wait while it rings, my mouth going dry with nerves. Laila reaches across the bed and jabs the "Speaker" icon on my screen, which annoys me, but I let it slide, holding the phone between us.

"Hey." He answers with a smile in his voice.

My confidence spikes. I give Laila a triumphant look. "Hey, yourself."

"What's going on?"

"Nothing much," I purr.

"You still polluting your brain with Beyoncé?"

I let out a deep, husky laugh, intimate and warm. "Every chance I get."

"Naughty girl."

Laila shakes her head and rolls her eyes, but I recognize the flicker of grudging respect in her smirk.

"Listen, Shane, I have a question." I drop my tone to a low, confiding one. "You remember that conversation we had about Dr. Bryers?"

He hesitates, thrown by the change in subject. "Sure."

"Well, something else happened today. An accident in the lab. A student's been seriously injured. She might die."

His tone is wary. "Okay."

"This reporter's been hounding me." I flick Laila a quick look. "She's writing a story about Bryers. You know I would never want to hurt Bryers's reputation, but I'm starting to think the community needs to know about what's going on in that lab."

There's a long, loaded silence.

Fighting flurries of panic, I press on. "I wouldn't ask under normal circumstances, but this girl in the hospital— she's a friend. It breaks my heart, what's happening at MRU. I'm scared." I let a little wobble enter my voice. Brannigan responds to the helpless-kitten-up-a-tree thing.

Predictably, his tone becomes protective. "Has Bryers threatened you?"

"No, nothing like that. I just—I can't go on record with what I know. But if you could say something . . ." I trail off, letting this dangle.

"Who's this reporter work for?"

"*Salt Gulch Bulletin* mostly, sometimes the *PD*. She's solid." I look at Laila again. Her expression's become alert, watchful. She sits up straighter, listening intently.

"Huh." Noncommittal, more a grunt than a word.

"Would you talk to her? I can get her on the phone right now, if you're willing." I hold my breath.

He's silent.

On instinct, I backpedal. He has to believe this is his idea. "You know what? I shouldn't have called. I'm just really freaked out. I mean, students are dying. I thought if we warned people—but forget it. I don't want to put you in an awkward—"

"Put her on." He's gruff and determined now.

"Are you—"

"I deal with reporters all the time. Don't worry. Let me talk to her."

I smile, handing the phone to Laila with a gallant lit-tle bow. She shakes her head, her expression amused, and snatches the phone from my outstretched hand.

Ten points for Winter.

* * *

Hannah

By the time we leave the hospital, it's raining. The storm clouds blowing off the sea all day unleash their pent-up fury. Lynch and I huddle under the awning outside the ER. We survey the storm, listening to the rain hammering against the metal roof. An ambulance pulls up, and paramedics leap from the back. They rush a stretcher through the automatic glass doors. As they pass, the man in their care catches my eye. His expression is so desolate, something in my chest tightens.

"Where are you parked?" The worried frown on Lynch's face makes me think he may have asked the question more than once.

"Oh, um, I got a ride." I can't help looking sheepish, remembering the way my hands shook standing in the parking lot with Winter.

He looks at me, his eyes searching for something.

"If you don't mind driving me back to campus—"

"I'm taking you home."

I stare at him, confused. "Home? But I've got to go back, clean up the lab."

"Already taken care of."

"What? How?"

"I made some calls. It's all cleaned up." He shrugs off my bewildered expression. "You've had enough to deal with today."

"Oh. Okay." The old Hannah's miffed at his presumption, stepping into her domain and taking initiative when he hasn't been asked. The new Hannah—one pummeled by the events of the last week—wants to cry with relief. As much as I hate to admit it, Lynch's take-charge decisiveness

is a balm. It's more than that, if I'm being honest. His protectiveness makes me feel safe in a way I haven't in years—
maybe ever.

"I canceled your classes tomorrow as well."

Now he's gone a step too far. "No, that's not—I have a
midterm to—"

"Hannah, come on." He plants his hands on my shoulders and levels his gaze at me. "You've got to take a breather.
Today was enough to knock anyone on their ass."

"I know, but—" I break off, searching for the right words.

"But what?"

"It's how I cope. When things get intense, I bury myself
in work."

He nods, compassion bringing new warmth to his face.
"I understand. I do the same thing."

I adjust my bag on my shoulder. "Then you know why I
can't take time off. If you'll just give me a ride back to campus, I'll call the office and let them know I'll be in tomorrow."

"Too late for that. Trudy's already emailed your students.
They're good and drunk by now, celebrating the reprieve
from midterms."

"But it will throw my whole semester—"

"I'm staging an intervention." Lynch takes off his wool
coat and hands it to me.

I didn't realize until now, but I'm shivering. When I left
campus, I didn't even think to grab my coat. "No, you keep
yours, I—"

"Think of this as therapy."

"Therapy?" I echo, still holding his coat, comforted in
spite of myself by the clean, masculine, Lynch-ish scent wafting from it.

He looks me straight in the eye. "You're a strong, inde-
pendent woman. You're tough as shit. You saved that girl's
life today, Hannah."

"I just did what anyone would—"

"People who always take charge need to take the back seat now and then. Let somebody else drive." He grins. "It's therapeutic."

"I appreciate what you're trying to do, but it's really not—"

"Do you trust me?"

His question catches me off-guard. I meet his probing gaze. In spite of having listed him as a suspect less than a week ago, having accused him of the worst sort of sabotage, I have to admit I do trust him. Standing there before me, his blue eyes searching mine, I can't deny my deep conviction that Lynch is one hundred percent on my side.

"Yes." It comes out in barely more than a whisper.

"Then put that damn coat on and come with me." He seizes an umbrella from a stand near the entrance and pops it open.

"Is that yours?" I ask.

"Nobody likes a backseat driver," he chides. With that, he holds the umbrella over me, links his arm in mine, and pulls me out into the storm.

* * *

We sit in Lynch's study, a fire burning in the grate. My hands are wrapped around a glass mug full of something that's warming more than my hands.

"What is this?" I ask.

"Aunt Clare's patented hot toddy. Cures anything."

I take another sip, feeling the heat spreading through my chest and then my extremities. I'm sitting on the green velvet couch I first encountered the day of Isabella's housewarming party; a thick wool throw covers my legs. Now that I'm finally warm, I suspect I've been freezing most of the afternoon and didn't notice. It's been a surreal day. A surreal fortnight.

Lynch sits near me in the same worn leather chair I caught him reading in during the party. Though it was only a week and a half ago, it feels like a lifetime. He's got his own hot toddy in his hands. The firelight flickers over his face as he stares into the hearth, his expression pensive. Lynch's dog, Ruby, lies on the Persian rug before the fire, her big paws stretched out and her muzzle pressed flat against the floor. Her red fur looks burgundy in the firelight. She watches us, her eyebrows twitching a little as she gazes first at me, then at her master, then back at me again. The scene is cozy and domestic. Being here adds to the unreality of the day, but I've decided not to fight it. The simple truth is, there's no place I'd rather be.

We sit in silence for a long moment, the crackling of the fire mixing with the patter of rain. I'm surprised to realize it's a comfortable silence, not the awkward sort that begs to be filled. There's a charge in the air, but I don't feel the need to make small talk. Since banter is something I'm abysmal at, it's a great relief knowing I don't have to think up things to say.

When Lynch speaks, he keeps his gaze on the flames. "Hope you don't mind how we're in here rather than the living room. The rest of the house is so . . ."

"Floral?" I suggest.

He laughs. "Yes, floral."

Ruby sighs, resettles herself on the rug, and closes her eyes.

"Do you miss her?" I ask in a tentative voice. I'm not sure if Isabella is a subject that should be avoided or explored. She feels like such a presence in the house, a ghost wafting through the rooms.

Lynch frowns, sipping his drink as he considers. "Not as much as I should, if that makes sense."

"Why is that?"

"We met thirteen years ago. I was barely thirty, she was twenty-seven. We were living in LA, she was modeling, I was just finishing my PhD. We knew we were very different people, but that was part of the appeal, I guess."

"Opposites attract."

"Exactly. But that only takes you so far, if the differences are fundamental." He puts his drink down, leans back. "To be honest, we were already running out of things to say by our third date."

I can feel my brow furrowing in confusion. "Why did you get married then?"

"The oldest reason." He looks at me, eyebrows rising with an expression of helpless resignation. "She got pregnant."

"You have a child?" My bewilderment deepens.

He shakes his head. "She miscarried."

"I'm sorry," I say.

"She was heartbroken. We both were. By then, of course, we were already married, and suggesting we go our separate ways seemed churlish at best—cruel, even. I knew we had very little in common—living together was already taking its toll on both of us. But she wanted a family very badly. Her modeling career was winding down. I think she felt motherhood would give her life more purpose, more meaning. We kept trying. Isabella had two more miscarriages, then . . . nothing."

"That must have been so hard."

He picks up his mug again, blows steam from its surface and takes a healthy swig. "I don't have any illusions that a baby would have fixed things. To be honest, fatherhood was never high on my list of wishes. I figured I'd try it for her sake, but I didn't want a child the way she did."

I nod, thinking of my own aversion to parenthood.

"We just never really fit—that's the truth of it. Sometimes, I wondered if there was some fatal flaw in our chemistry, some fundamental lack of compatibility that prevented us from creating life."

I don't say what I'm thinking—how plenty of horribly mismatched couples have children. I have a feeling this falls into the category of taking a statement too literally.

His mouth curves up at the corner. "What are you thinking?"

"I—it's not helpful."

"You don't have to do that with me, Bryers."

I look at him, surprised. "Do what?"

"Censor yourself. Go on, just say it."

I breathe out a laugh. "I don't think it works that way. Lots of people with nothing in common—people who hate each other, in fact—have children."

"Fair point." His smile is sad. "What about you? Any desire for a mini-Bryers?"

I shudder. "God, no. One of me is all I can handle."

"Seriously?" He studies me. "No yearning for kids at all?"

"None." I hope this won't turn into one of those conversations where I end up feeling freakish for my lack of maternal drive.

"Why do you think that is?" His stare is curious, open, devoid of judgment.

I shift in my chair, searching for an honest answer. "I'm not a very nurturing person, I guess."

"That's not true. I've seen you with your students. You nurture them."

This time my laugh comes out as a bark. "Hardly! I work them half to death."

"You nurture their intellects," he amends. Then, softer: "You care about them, though. Anyone can see that."

"I do. That's true. I'm just not a very soft person. Some even consider me prickly."

"You ever been married?" He takes a sip of his toddy, wincing a little.

"Never. I got close once, but when it came down to it, I couldn't see myself spending my life with him. Even spending the weekend together felt like a stretch." I turn my mug in my hands, relishing its warmth. "Maybe some people just aren't meant to pair up."

"Maybe." He looks unconvinced.

It's my turn to give him a look. "If I'm not going to censor myself, you shouldn't either."

He looks caught out for a moment. Then he tilts his head, studying me. "Okay, fine. It sounds cheesy, though, so be warned."

"Cheese away," I say.

"Maybe you just haven't found the right person." He drinks the last of his toddy, sets it down, and looks at me with intent. "If we're going fully uncensored, there's nothing I want more right now than to drag you into my bedroom—floral bedspread be damned—and tear your clothes off."

I can feel the warmth of the whiskey spreading lower. "Then why haven't you?"

"I don't want you to think that's why I brought you here. You've had a hell of a day." He smirks. "And then there's your bad pancake theory."

I cover my face with my hands. "I don't know why I said that. It just came out."

"No, it's a fair point." He holds his hands out. "If I were you, I'd be leery. My wife did leave me less than a week ago. My marriage was always shaky, though. The only difference now is we're admitting it."

"What's the statistical probability of you two getting back together?" I have to ask. As much as I hate to admit it, I've got a lot on the line here. Lynch is more than just a comforting port in the shitstorm that is my life. There's something real between us, puzzle pieces fitting together in a way I've never experienced before. If I allow myself to want that, to want him, having it taken away would mean the loss of something vital.

He leans forward and waits until I risk a look at him. Holding my gaze, he says, "There's zero chance of that. I promise you."

I set my mug down on the coffee table and go to him. Feeling daring and also a little stupid, I plant my knees on either side of him, straddling his lap. He watches me, his eyes going a little glassy. With one hand planted on Lynch's sternum, I push him all the way back in his chair. Then I do what I've wanted to do since I met him: I spread my palms over his head, feeling the smoothness of his skin, tracing the curves of his cranium with my fingertips.

He closes his eyes and lets out a deep sigh.

"I'm kind of obsessed with your skull," I admit, leaning closer to look at it from various angles. It gleams in the firelight.

He opens one eye. "Is this a scientific curiosity, or . . .?" He trails off into a faint moan as I plant kisses along his zygomatic bone, then his parietal bone. I kiss the place where his coronal suture must be, feeling the slight dip at the center of his skull. On impulse, I seek out the temporalis muscle, that hypnotically active, achingly tender place that had me transfixed the night of his presentation. I take my time with this spot, kissing a semicircle behind the curve of his ear, smiling as he lets out another moan, louder this time.

"You have a very active temporalis muscle," I whisper.

"Dr. Bryers," he says, pretending to be shocked. "I don't think I can control myself if you talk dirty."

I kiss his mouth, tracing the muscles around it with my fingertips. "Your orbicularis oris is pretty active too."

"You've got no idea what this orbicularis can do."

"So show me."

He holds my gaze for a moment. His orbicularis oculi push his brows up at my dare. In one deft movement, he sweeps me into his arms and stands, cradling me like a bride being carried over the threshold. "I have to warn you. The bedroom's an orgy of floral."

"Flowers never sounded so good," I say. "Do your worst."

And he does.

CHAPTER

19

Hannah

I SPEND THREE DELIRIOUS days at Lynch's place. It's the most irresponsible thing I've ever done. With my classes canceled on Thursday and nothing scheduled Friday, it feels like the most delicious sort of snow day—an unexpected, joyful reprieve from the stressful demands of my life. Since most of my "vacations" are spent examining mass graves and identifying homicide victims spread across the globe, this is the first time in forever I've lazed about, doing nothing. Well, not nothing. Lynch and I have plenty to do.

We don't check out completely, though. Thursday afternoon we call the hospital and learn Kim's been moved out of ICU. She's in stable condition, the wound to her throat is healing, and she's reportedly feeling no pain. She's scheduled to go home the next day. This is such a relief, I almost cry. Then I picture Gil glowering at me, nostrils flared. He was filled with such unshakable conviction that I'd put his daughter in danger. A queasy feeling of dread threatens my delirium when I let myself dwell on this. Lynch assures me Gil was just channeling his stress and sadness at the most convenient target. I know this is true, but I also know I'm far from blameless. Somehow, Kim got her hands on an out-of-date compound. Either the expiration date slipped past my notice, or somebody tampered with it. Either possibility is distressing. On Saturday, I try to get dressed so I can go to the lab and examine the labels more closely, but Lynch manages to dissuade me from my mission. He can be extremely persuasive.

By Sunday morning, I feel so boneless and blissed out I can barely walk. My abductor and gracilis muscles ache with overuse. I haven't been this sore since the week I spent riding a camel through the Kyzylkum Desert. I stumble to Lynch's kitchen and pour myself some coffee. The first sip makes me smile. Lynch makes the best coffee.

He comes into the kitchen with today's paper in one hand. He wears boxer briefs and nothing else. His torso is shockingly toned for a man his age. His obliques, his transversus abdominis, even his latissimus dorsi are all so defined and sculptural he could pass for a professional athlete. I smile lazily, hopping up onto the counter and admiring the view.

"Good. You found the coffee. And you're sitting down."

As my gaze wanders at last to his face, something there alerts me to danger.

"Everything okay?" I ask.

He lays the paper down on the kitchen island. His movements are careful, precise, like it's not the *Salt Gulch Bulletin*, but an ancient scroll requiring deft handling. I catch sight of the headline, and my stomach drops with a sickening lurch: *"MRU Professor Endangers Lives, Tampers With Evidence."* There's my picture, a god-awful shot taken at a fundraiser from an unflattering angle. I look frumpy, unkempt, and a little drunk—my cheeks ruddy with wine, my dress askew, and my chin tucked in a way that gives me rolls of fat around my face.

"Jesus! What the—"

"Before you read it," Lynch warns, "take a deep breath. And remember, this is just shoddy, small-town journalism run amuck."

I jump off the counter, my lazy, relaxed mood souring inside me like curdled milk. With shaking fingers, I seize the paper and take it outside into the garden. I need air. Also, I need to be alone when I read this. Lynch and I may have crash-landed on Planet Intimacy this weekend, but if this article is as humiliating as I fear it's going to be, I need space to process the blow.

Outside, the air is cool with morning dew. Isabella's flowers glisten with last night's rain. The sky is a bright blue; the grass steams with dissipating fog. Hummingbirds swarm around the trumpet vine and morning glories. I'm wearing one of Lynch's big white shirts and nothing else, so the cool air nips at my bare legs, but I sit on one of the padded lawn chairs in the sun, ignoring the chill of the damp fabric against my naked legs.

With a deep, fortifying breath, I begin to read.

MRU Professor Endangers Lives, Tampers With Evidence
by Laila Tikka

Dr. Hannah Bryers is one of the most respected professors at Mad River University, but recent lapses in security have put students at risk. An explosion during one of Bryers's classes Wednesday afternoon nearly cost undergraduate Kim Matheson her life. Less than a week before the explosion, local sheriff Shane Brannigan was shocked to discover that a potential murder victim he had entrusted to Bryers for identification purposes had been mutilated, hampering the investigation and leaving loved ones with more questions than answers.

Bryers is a key figure in MRU's cutting-edge Forensic Anthropology Department. She is also a frequent consultant for local and international suspicious death investigations, a respected figure in the medicolegal community. In spite of these accolades, Dr. Bryers appears to have little to no lab security, making her classroom a veritable death trap.

"The negligence Hannah Bryers exhibited here is appalling," says MRU engineering professor Dr. Gilbert Matheson. On Wednesday, Matheson's daughter, Kim, was conducting a routine experiment under Bryers's supervision when her beaker exploded, causing a shard of glass to impale her throat. It narrowly missed her carotid artery, which would have resulted in certain death, instead puncturing her jugular, causing massive blood loss. According to student witnesses, Bryers exited the classroom just before the explosion, leaving her inexperienced undergraduates unsupervised.

Thanks to intervention by one of Bryers's colleagues, Dr. Mick Lynch, Matheson was rushed to the hospital, where physicians performed emergency surgery and managed to save her life. "Professor Lynch literally pulled his shirt off to stop the blood," recalls Brittani Landers, a student in the class. "Thank God he happened to be nearby, or I don't know what would have happened."

The classroom explosion isn't the only black mark on Bryers's recent safety record. According to Sheriff Brannigan, the remains of an unknown person—a possible homicide victim found in the Salt Gulch Community Forest—were mutilated beyond recognition while in Dr. Bryers's care. "She was apparently surprised when she showed me the victim's remains and discovered the body had been liquified by corrosive acid. In the course of my career, I can't recall anything of this nature having occurred. It's unheard of. We're back to square one in our efforts to discover the identity of the deceased."

> *Dean of Academic Affairs Eli Balderstone offered*
> *little commentary on these life-threatening incidents,*
> *saying only that a full investigation is already underway*
> *and that the safety of MRU students is the administra-*
> *tion's top priority.*

By the time I've finished reading, I'm gripping the paper so hard it's damp and creased. When I put it down, my fingers come away black with newsprint, as if I've been contaminated. The sickness stealing over me is overwhelming. I feel hot and cold at once. There's a raw ache in my center, like someone's kicked me in the gut. My scalp prickles with fear. I let my gaze wander around the garden, trying to absorb the information rushing at me like scenery flying past on the Autobahn.

In the last few days, I've gone from traumatized to blissful with whiplash-inducing speed. Now I can feel the chasm opening up before me, offering new levels of despair. I'm not generally inclined to place blame on mystical forces, but I can't escape the sense that the gods are toying with me. For years—most of my life, really—work has been my main source of fulfillment and stability, while my love life has remained a fallow garden, untended and choked with weeds. Now the capricious fates have turned that equation upside down, making my love life a haven and my work life hell.

Though it's hardly the worst part of the article, the paragraph hailing Lynch as the hero of the lab accident is especially galling. The reporter makes it sound like he swooped in and saved the day, tearing off his shirt to staunch the blood. Technically, the part about his shirt is accurate, of course, but the quote from Brittani Landers skews the story in a way that makes the feminist in me seethe. It implies the woman in charge was MIA and ineffectual, off in the staff lounge drinking tea while her helpless charges nearly bled to death.

"How you doing?" Lynch's voice makes me jump. I didn't hear him come out onto the verandah.

"Not good" is all I can manage around the lump in my throat.

Lynch sits on the lawn chair beside mine, elbows propped on his knees. "It's bullshit, Hannah. That much is clear. I wouldn't be surprised if MRU sues the Bulletin. They can't print blatant lies and expect to get away with—"

"It's not bullshit." My voice sounds small, tight. "It's slanted, yes, but nothing in this article is technically inaccurate."

He stares at me. I can feel his gaze burning into the side of my face, but I can't bring myself to look at him.

"I know you mentioned the incident with the sheriff, but was the body really—"

"Yes. And Brannigan's right. It's unprecedented. The corpse was more or less liquefied. His investigation is ruined." I cover my face with my hands. Shame sweeps over me like a dark, suffocating tide.

I feel him get up and sit on my lawn chair, nudging my legs aside to make room. A part of me wants to be alone right now, to wallow in this pain without a witness. Another, newer part of me is so glad he's here I want to cling to him like a child waking from a nightmare.

"Hey." With gentle care, he pulls my hands away from my face and makes me look at him. "Whatever's happening here, it's not your fault."

"They're calling me negligent, Lynch. And they're right."

"No. I don't accept that."

"Kim almost died, and where was I? Out in the hall, flirting with you."

"I was *there*." His voice is firm. "That's not how it happened. You heard the doctor—you saved that girl. This stupid article paints me as a shirtless superhero. We both know that's a lie."

"I shouldn't have left," I protest. He's saying all the right things, wrapping me in the reassurance I'm desperate for. He can't stop the rising tide of guilt, though. I feel small and frightened, exposed in a way I've never experienced before.

"The fact that you stepped out for two minutes was just bad timing," he insists. "It could have happened to anyone. If anything, that was *my* fault for distracting you."

"But I allowed myself to be distracted."

"Hannah." He cups my thigh with one hand. The warmth of his fingers feels like the only real thing, something solid and tangible anchoring me to the earth. "Don't let these bastards get you down. You need to stay strong. Believe in yourself. Otherwise, whoever's trying to ruin you wins."

I allow myself to bathe in the steady light of his gaze. It's rare for me to cry, but I feel tears stinging at my eyes. To my great annoyance, one slips down my cheek.

Lynch lets out a grunt of frustration, leaning forward to swipe the tear away with this thumb. "God damn these small-town hacks. I hate that their bullshit can make you cry."

"Me too." I try for a brave smile, but it feels wrong.

"What do you say we break our self-imposed exile and go have a decadent brunch? I'm afraid we've eaten everything in the house."

I frown, my stomach writhing uncomfortably at the thought of facing the outside world. It's a small town. Everyone will have read the article.

"I know what you're thinking." He tucks a finger under my chin, tilting my face up to his. "But hiding doesn't help. You need to get out there right away and show them this shit doesn't faze you."

"Except it *does* faze me."

"You're the Amazing Dr. Hannah Bryers. Indiana Jane, Globetrotter, Intrepid Explorer of Decaying Human Flesh."

I can't help but smile. How is it possible for Lynch to save even a train wreck of a morning like this? His belief in me, his unwavering confidence in my ability to weather this, is infectious.

"Fine," I say. "But you're buying. And I want a Bloody Mary."

"Done and done." He grins, warming me with the heat of his steady blue eyes.

* * *

Winter

"Morning, gorgeous." Cam climbs back under the covers. He's probably been up for hours.

I rub the sleep from my eyes. "Morning."

He's got his phone in one hand. He turns his attention back to the screen. "There's a crazy story about Bryers in the paper today."

"Really?" I sit up, fluffing the pillows behind me. "What's it say?"

He shakes his head, frowning, his eyes still glued to the screen. "It claims she's to blame for Kim's accident. They're even saying she tampered with evidence in an investigation."

"Wow." I can't suppress a tiny grin of delight.

Luckily, Cam's too engrossed in his screen to notice. "Total bullshit. Hey, isn't Laila the name of that girl you were talking to the other night at Tom's?"

"Tom!" I clap my hands. "That's his name. I was thinking either Tim or Todd."

"It was Laila, right?" He looks at me.

"Maybe. Or Lilly? Not sure."

"Is she a journalist?"

I wrinkle my nose, feigning uncertainty. "I don't know. She said something about writing, but I thought she was talking about fiction."

He leans closer, nuzzling my ear with his nose. "What do you say we go to breakfast?"

"I thought you were going to make your famous waffles."
I'm dying to see the story, but I can't afford to look eager in
front of Cam. I'll read it later, alone, so I can pore over it in
depth at my leisure.

"Out of milk." He runs his nose along the length of my
jaw. "You know you want to. Magnolia Café. Best French
toast in town."

"I could be persuaded."

Twenty minutes later, we're following our hostess to a
table. Magnolia Café is at the north end of town. The inside
is cozy and quaint, but the garden patio is the real draw. As
we step outside, my senses fill with the colorful flowers and
the comforting clink of silverware. Patches of fog still cling
to the blue dome of sky, but only in thin, picturesque swaths.
The place is packed. The intoxicating scent of bacon and hash
browns fills the air. Cam and I sit near a cascade of nastur-
tiums by the back fence. Our vantage point is slightly elevated,
the perfect place to survey the garden patio, watching as the
guests file in and order their Instagram-worthy breakfasts.

We study the menus, though I already know what I'm
getting. I always order their French toast, which comes piled
high with berries. They make it with the best bread in the
world. God knows where they get it. Maybe they bake it
themselves.

I'm trying hard not to think about the article, though it
takes great willpower. My fingers keep twitching toward my
phone. I can't read the thing with Cam sitting right here,
though. He grew up in a no-phones-at-the-table sort of family, and unlike most people our age, he gets weird if I ignore
him in favor of a screen. Besides, I'm not sure I can keep the
joy from my expression if I read it now. Knowing it's out
there in the world is enough to put me in a good mood.

We've just ordered and we're sipping our coffee, enjoying
the spring sunshine, when Bryers walks in. I almost spit out
my coffee when I see who she's with.

THE PROTÉGÉ   219

"Oh my God," I murmur under my breath.

Cam follows my gaze, then turns his attention back to me, his expression dour. "Poor Dr. Bryers. We should go say hi."

"Did you see who she's with?"

He looks unfazed. "Dr. Lynch. Why? What's the big deal?"

Sometimes I think Cam's a cyborg. How can he be this immune to gossip? The boy doesn't have a catty bone in his body. "Lynch is married, you know."

"They're having breakfast. It doesn't mean anything."

I roll my eyes. "Please. Look at them. They totally spent the night together."

He shakes his head. "Nah. She's not like that."

"Not like what?" I can hear the frosty edge in my voice, but I can't help myself.

"Slutty?"

I blow out a breath, annoyed. With effort, I change the subject, but it's impossible to stay away from Bryers entirely. She's out of earshot, but she's in my line of sight. "Tell me more about this article you mentioned."

He rubs his face. "It's a terrible piece. It makes her sound negligent and sloppy, which is just—well, you know. She's meticulous. If anything, people criticize her for going over-board on the safety stuff—lecturing even grad students about expiration dates and PECs every single time we work with chemicals."

"I know. It's annoying."

He blinks at me. "It's not annoying. It's necessary. People get lazy, and that's when bad shit happens."

"Well, apparently she did get sloppy this once." I notice several people at nearby tables shooting Bryers covert glances and whispering behind cupped hands. Bryers and Lynch keep their eyes locked on each other, though. She even lets out a laugh I've never heard from her before—husky and full, like she's having fun for once in her miserable life.

How dare she laugh when Kim Matheson almost died?

"That's the thing," Cam's saying. With effort, I turn my attention back to him. "I don't buy it. Bryers didn't do anything wrong. First that stupid prank at her presentation, now this? I think somebody's trying to mess with her."

I look at him coolly. I have to play this just right. It won't do to show the rage rising inside me like a bloodred tide. "She's not perfect, Cam. She screws up."

"Not like this." He shakes his head, stirring more cream into his coffee. "Somebody's out to get her. I don't know who. Probably some unstable asshole with a grudge."

"You're not objective," I snap.

His gaze darts to my face, his interest piqued. "What do you mean?"

"You're half in love with her." I lean closer, lowering my voice to a whisper. "You refuse to see her as a human being."

"That's not true." He squints at me like he's trying to make out who I am. "Why would you even say that?"

"It's not important." I snap my napkin into my lap. "Forget I said anything."

"No. I want to know what you mean." Cam's face is flushed. He looks angry.

I realize I've made a huge misstep and backpedal with all my might. "I didn't mean anything. She's your professor. You respect her, as you should."

Cam doesn't look convinced. "Are you saying you believe this story?"

"I haven't even read it." I sip my coffee. "I can hardly take a stance on something I haven't read."

"But you're inclined to believe the accident was her fault?" He's gone very still.

"Not necessarily."

He leans back in his chair, never taking his eyes off me. "I don't understand your attitude."

I focus on the salt and pepper shakers, willing myself not to lash out.

"Maybe you're defensive because you don't believe in her like I do." Cam's tone is accusatory.

"That's ridiculous."

"Do you or don't you believe she may have been at fault?"

I stare at him, pinning him with my eyes. "I haven't ruled out the possibility. I'm her TA, not a member of her cult."

The waitress brings our plates. My appetite has abandoned me. I hate Cam right now. He's so pompous. Where does he get off, acting like I'm the disloyal pretender to our queen? It's sick. How can he judge me when I'm the only one who sees Bryers for who she is—the only one who fully understands the damage she inflicts?

He surveys his breakfast and tries to lighten the mood by changing the subject. "This looks amazing."

I watch as he digs into his breakfast burrito. I pour syrup over my French toast, staring at it as the butter melts, raspberries and blueberries swimming in the golden tide. My stomach feels like an oil slick.

"You okay?" Cam takes a huge bite of burrito, a tiny thread of hot sauce on his lips.

"Fine."

"You sure?" He pauses. "You look a little sick."

"I'm super," I hiss.

Across the patio, Bryers lets out another throaty, secretive laugh. I seethe.

She'll pay. One way or another, I'll make sure of that.

CHAPTER

20

Hannah

I'M SEATED IN Eli Balderstone's office, trying to look comfortable. It's not an easy feat. He's on the phone, nodding and scowling at his desk. He has an air of beleaguered melancholy about him. He shoots me an apologetic look, holding up a finger to indicate he won't be long. He's saying very little: "Yes, understood, I'll do that." From his meek attitude and minimal responses, I deduce two things: first, that he's talking to someone higher up in the food chain, probably the president of MRU; second, they're talking about me.

Neither thought is comforting.

Eli summoned me to his office today with a rather formal email. That's not a good sign. Normally, if Eli wants to talk, he picks up the phone and rings my office or sends a text. I wouldn't say we're friends exactly, but we're friendly. He's not a formal person. A summons via email means he wants a paper trail. Paper trails are necessary when you're trying to get rid of someone. It gives you more to lean on if the fired party sues.

The sourness in my stomach churns.

When Eli hangs up at last, he steeples his fingers and looks at me. "Sorry about that. How are you, Hannah?"

"I'm fine," I lie.

"Good. Glad to hear it. I suppose you know why I asked you here today."

I sit up straighter, trying to suppress an instinctive wince. "I have some guesses."

"This thing in the paper . . . well, it's not good."

"I agree." Again, I force myself not to do what comes naturally—defend myself. The damage to MRU's reputation is already done. Nothing in the story is patently untrue, so jumping in with excuses will only make me look more guilty. I watch Eli, keeping my expression as impassive as I can.

"You know I like you." He spreads his hands before him. "I've always liked you. I have so much respect for what you do."

"Thank you." My words are clipped.

"I know you're up for tenure, and I'm very much in your corner."

I can hear the imminent "but" in his tone. I brace myself, trying to breathe. My lungs feel like they've contracted to half their normal size. I can't get enough air.

"Which is why I feel obligated to be straight with you here: This is going to hurt your chances." He takes off his glasses, polishing them on the hem of his shirt. "Not just the article in the paper, but the incidents themselves, especially the lab accident. We take student safety seriously here, as I'm sure you know."

"I take it seriously too." My voice doesn't sound like my own. It seems to be coming from far away.

He nods. "That's what I've been telling the president. I know you, Hannah. You do good work. You're thorough. You care about your students. Nobody was more surprised than me when I heard about the accident."

I swallow hard, nodding. Speaking seems impossible, so I don't try. My mind is racing, trying to decide if it's rhetorically advantageous to tell him about my suspicions. Will

an unknown saboteur help or hurt my case? If I had any
proof, I'd tell Eli everything. Without evidence, though, I'm
afraid I'll sound paranoid. Only weak people point fingers
at shadow villains when they're cornered. Until I can find
out who's behind this—or at least cobble together a plausible
theory—bringing it up is more likely to damage my reputation than repair it.

God, I hate this person, whoever they are. I hate that
they're endangering the thing I love most—my work. The
terrible certainty that it's someone who knows me well washes
over me once again. The betrayal of this carves into me like
a knife.

Eli leans toward me. He puts on his glasses again, his
brown eyes squinting under thick brows. "Is there anything
at all you can offer in your defense?"

I take a deep breath, letting it out before I speak. "I *am*
careful. I'm thorough. You're right about that. I have no idea
how these things happened. I can only tell you I'm trying
very hard to find out what's really going on here. When I do,
you'll be the first person I go to with the information."

He's motionless behind his desk, as if waiting for more.
When the silence stretches too long to be comfortable, he
stands, holding out his hand. "Very good. I'll keep you
posted, and I ask that you do the same."

My legs feel wobbly, my knees soft as Jell-O. With effort,
I manage to stand and shake his hand. His grip is firm and
dry. My hand's the clammy one, slick and cold as an eel.

* * *

Winter

The faculty appreciation dinner is a peculiar MRU tradition.
It's an annual spring event where grad students serve the faculty a sumptuous six-course dinner. It's all funded by the college, a ritual where the already indentured grad students get

to bow and scrape even more than we usually do. We're all dressed in white shirts and black pants, serving up roasted bell pepper soup and chicken skewers, arugula pomegranate salad, and macadamia-crusted salmon. The faculty ooh and aah over our offerings, displaying how appreciative they are of our humble efforts. It's a strange, forced ritual of tight smiles and shrill praise.

Watching Bryers enter makes it all worth it. She's wearing an emerald-green sheath dress with a black shawl. She makes her way first to one table, then to another. She pinballs from spot to spot, ricocheting off the dirty looks and averted gazes. Her expression reminds me of a frightened rabbit searching for a place of safety.

I go to her, drawn by the vulnerability in her pale, shell-shocked face.

"Winter." She touches my arm. "How are you?"

"I'm good." I give her an empathetic smile. "You?"

"I've been better." She casts a quick glance over her shoulder. "Everyone here hates me."

"No way."

"They do. I don't even know where to sit." She clutches her chest. "I might be having my first panic attack."

"Do you need to go outside?"

She looks at me, her eyes full of questions. She has the face of a drowning woman groping for something to keep her afloat. "I shouldn't have come."

"You have nothing to apologize for." I say it with a decisive edge, the way she likes me to.

"You're right. I need to get a grip."

I look around. "Where's Dr. Lynch?"

She shakes her head. "Away at a conference."

I spot Eli Balderstone's table. "Why not sit over there?"

She follows my gaze. "I don't think so."

I widen my eyes at her. "You have every right to be here. Remember that."

"Everyone's avoiding me like I'm carrying an airborne pathogen."

I widen my eyes even more. "Dr. Bryers, if you can't sit at that table, I don't know who can."

She casts another furtive glance over her shoulder.

"Show everyone you're not afraid." I infuse my tone with just the right note of worship.

Her chin tilts in defiance. "You're right. Okay. I'm doing this."

With a determined stride, Bryers marches over to Balderstone's table. There's one seat empty. Too late, Bryers sees who she'll have to sit next to: Gil Matheson. His back was to us when I suggested she take the plunge. I can't help grinning as she dithers, one hand on the back of the chair, absorbing Matheson's poisonous glare. *This is priceless.* Joy flares in my chest like a match.

Under the pretense of filling everyone's wineglasses, I float over to their table, a full bottle of pinot in one hand. I go to Balderstone first. He doesn't look up as I fill his glass. The silence that falls over the table as Bryers stands there is toxic.

"Is anyone sitting here?" Bryers puts both hands on the chair, as if steadying herself.

"Yes." Matheson fixes her with a cold look. He doesn't offer apology or explanation; he shuts her down with the icy precision of a man used to giving orders.

I know Bryers. She's already off balance in any social situation; this should be enough to push her over the edge. I fill each of the wineglasses before me, keeping my eyes on the dark red liquid. It flows into their glasses with a velvety smoothness that matches the voluptuous victory filling me.

Bryers takes a deep breath, lets it out. "I understand. I'm a social pariah."

"Hannah." Balderstone's voice holds a note of warning. "We're here to—"

"It's okay, Eli. I get it. I'm not wanted here, and I don't stay where I'm not wanted." Her expression hardens as she surveys her colleagues, each one of them carefully avoiding her eyes. "But before I go, I just want to say, this could happen to any of you. Keep that in mind. I'm going to clear my name, prove I did nothing wrong. I won't forget who stood by me and who threw me under the bus."

Her speech concluded, she turns on her heel and stalks out.

*   *   *

Hannah

I drive through the dark streets of Salt Gulch, trying to catch my breath. A foreign panic is rising inside me, inch by inch. Each block I pass seems to leave me with less lung capacity. I see myself jobless and ostracized, set adrift from the academic community I've thrived in all my life. I see my credibility in tatters, my options for leaving and rebuilding cut off as my shame spreads like a pandemic, word of my thwarted tenure marking me as damaged goods.

You've confronted mass graves and corrupt government officials, I remind myself. *You can handle a few dirty looks.*

The problem is, all of the other dangers I've faced in my forty years have involved me going head-to-head with someone or something who stands in my way. This time, it's my reputation under threat. It's my self-worth. This shakes me in a way no other challenge ever has.

My identity is rooted right here, in Salt Gulch, at Mad River. This is my home. Sure, I venture out into the world and slay dragons when needed. But I always have this place to return to, this haven where I'm respected and—dare I say?—loved. At least I thought I was before now.

I park at the curb and hurry up the walkway, feeling like the wind's been knocked out of me. Lynch is in London for the week, presenting at a big tech conference. He offered to cancel, but no way was I going to stand in the way of his professional responsibilities just because my life is imploding. I finally reach the porch of Amy's bungalow, relieved. I ring the bell, my fingers shaking as I listen to the chimes reverberate inside Amy's small cottage.

A ribbon of laughter snakes its way through the open window. *Shit, maybe she's got one of her Tinder dates here.* She doesn't usually bring them home. She favors anonymous hotels or their places, since she usually hooks up with people in other towns, but who knows? Aside from the odd text, we've been out of touch these days. I've been distracted by Lynch and the ongoing destruction of my life. A part of me has been dying to tell her everything about Lynch. Another part of me wants to keep it to myself, nurture it as my little secret.

Now that I pause to consider, it's not just me who's dropped the ball on our usual get-togethers. Amy's been checking in a lot less than she normally would. The last time we hung out was almost two weeks ago, when we had dinner at Eye of the Thai-ger. She sent me a brief text about the article in the paper, offering to put out a hit on the journalist, but aside from that I've barely heard from her. Maybe she's met someone. As I stand there, concentrating on my breathing, I find myself praying she's alone tonight, that she's laughing at a movie or a book and not a random date. I need to fall apart properly without an unwanted audience.

I hear the sound of footsteps as she crosses to the door. It swings open. She's in old sweats and a stretched-out T-shirt, no makeup on her face. I breathe a sigh of relief. *No date.* Amy always pulls out all the stops for her Tinder boys, unworthy as they are. I can feel the final vestiges of self-control slipping away. At last, I'm someplace safe.

Her eyes go wide with surprise. She pushes open the screen door. "Hannah. Hey. Is everything—"

The words aren't even out of her mouth before I burst into tears.

Amy pulls me into her arms, stroking my hair as I cry. It's so unlike me, letting raw emotion overtake me without warning. As the dam holding back my pain and humiliation gives way, I lean against her, sobbing into her T-shirt. It's hard to catch my breath as my chest heaves with wave after wave of tears.

"Poor baby," Amy murmurs, rubbing my back. "It's okay. You're okay now."

When at last I extract myself from her warm embrace, movement in the kitchen catches my eye. Joe stands there, a beer in one hand, lingering in the entryway to the kitchen like an actor unsure of his cue.

"Oh my God." I swipe at my face, too confused to process this. "I'm so sorry. Didn't know you had company."

He shuffles closer, his expression sheepish. "Hey, Hannah."

"Hi." I'm desperate to blow my nose. Once again, I can barely breathe—this time not from panic but from sobbing-induced congestion.

Amy grabs a box of Kleenex from a nearby table and hands me a fistful. I take them from her, grateful. My dignity already destroyed, I blow my nose with a noisy honk. When I'm done, a silence falls over us. Amy and Joe have spent time together, but always with me, never on their own. I'm not sure how to read this situation. We're all at a loss for words, standing there motionless in the living room, like mannequins.

"Okay, wow." Amy looks from Joe to me and back again. "This is awkward."

Joe clears his throat, putting his beer down on the coffee table. "I should leave, let you two—"

"What's going on?" It comes out sharper than I intend. After the day I've had, the growing suspicion that my two closest friends are keeping something from me is too much. I've got no capacity for polite avoidance.

Amy chews her lip. "We're, um . . . together."

I look from Joe to her and back again. "You mean—"

"As a couple. We're dating." She gives me an anxious smile.

"Since when?" I'm stalling, trying to get my bearings.

They look at one another.

Joe's blushing. "Less than a week."

I'm not great at surprises, and I'm so distracted by my own worries it's hard to make space for this new information. I try to smile. "I'm happy for you guys."

"See, I told you she wouldn't be weird," Amy says to Joe, then turns back to me, beaming. "You're not mad?"

"Why would I be?"

"Joe thought you—"

"No, I didn't—" he protests.

"You didn't want to tell her—"

"I'm just embarrassed." Joe shoots me a guilty look. "I thought you'd see me as—after—you know."

"Because he came onto you," Amy clarifies.

I shake my head. "I don't think any less of you. Seriously. I want you to be happy."

"And you're not mad at me for not telling you?" Amy's still anxious.

I shrug. "At least now I don't have to worry about one of these Tinder guys chopping you up and storing you in his freezer."

"Oh, thank God." She throws her head back and lets out a groan. "I've been stressing."

I've always thought Amy and Joe would be great together. They have similar senses of humor, and they like the same stupid sci-fi movies. They're both gregarious and adventure hungry; they love to laugh. Plus they complement one another's shortcomings. Amy's financially stable, and Joe's not. Joe's creative and introspective, something Amy could use more of. So why do I feel so awkward?

"What?" Amy sees my expression and looks alarmed.

"Just don't break up and make me pick sides," I blurt. "That would be awful."

Joe runs a hand over his face. "We just got together. Can we maybe not fast-forward to the acrimonious divorce already?"

I laugh. It comes out brittle and hollow. "Fine. I'll hold off on the doom and gloom."

Amy tugs me toward the couch. "Enough about us already. What happened? Why were you crying?"

"No, it's okay, I don't want to intrude." I back up, heading for the door.

"You're not intruding, Hannah." Amy sounds upset.

As much as I need my friends right now, I can't adjust to all this newness quickly enough. I make my excuses and hurry back to my car. On the drive home, I'm annoyed at the tears that keep blurring my vision. I'm happy for them—*I really am.* I just wish I didn't feel so incredibly alone.

CHAPTER

21

Hannah

Driving to campus the next day, I talk to myself, administering a pep talk intended to lift me from my dull haze of sleep-deprived angst. I'm wearing my favorite blazer and my best boots. I'm like one of the Lakota Sioux I worked with in South Dakota, going into battle with my special buckskin decorated with ermine tails, hair, and beadwork. My regalia is made of cashmere, wool, and Italian leather, but it's the same idea—magical talismans meant to curry favor with the Great Spirit. I've never been superstitious or mystical. I do understand how clothing can serve as armor, though. It can bridge the gap between insecurity and confidence. I need all the help I can get today.

I have to believe my luck will change, that the tsunami of bad blood against me will finally recede. A niggling voice inside me whispers, *Whoever's plotting against you won't stop now. Success will only make them bolder.* This sends a flurry of fresh panic spiraling through me.

Hannah, stop. You can do this. You're one of the top experts in your field. No way is some random hater with a grudge going

*to bring you down. A week or two of bad press can't undo twenty
years of hard work.*

As I reach the end of the long, winding drive leading up
to campus, I see a large crowd of people amassed in front of
Thorn Hall. They're carrying picket signs. I can hear someone leading a chant on a megaphone. My spirits sink.

Political protests aren't unheard of, I remind myself. MRU
students are mostly STEM majors, so we might not be as
politically active as our neighbors to the south—campuses
like Humboldt, Berkeley, and San Francisco State—but we
have our share of protests. From this distance, I can't make
out what their signs say or hear what the chanting proclaims.
I tell myself it could be anything.

The sinking feeling in my stomach begs to differ.

I force myself to park and get out of my car. The scared
little girl in me wants to drive away, call in sick, do anything
except face that loud, angry mob. Instead, I march from the
parking lot straight to Thorn Hall, taking courage from the
staccato tap of my boots on the damp pavement.

As I get closer, I see around fifty people amassed on the
steps of Thorn Hall. Most of them are carrying signs, but at
least a dozen of them must be journalists, since they're taking pictures and shoving microphones at the spokespeople. A
crew is setting up a video camera emblazoned with the logo
of the local news stations while a perky reporter in a bright
pink blazer applies lipstick.

The signs are visible by now. The sick feeling in my
stomach deepens as I read them.

"Keep Our Students Safe"

"Sloppy Science = Deadly Science"

"Bryers Is a Menace"

And then, the most pointed of all: "Fire Bryers Now!"

That's when I figure out what they're chanting. It's the
classic call and response. A burly man in a flannel shirt holds
the megaphone to his mouth.

"What do we want?" he calls.

"Bryers gone!"

"When do we want it?"

"Now!"

I freeze, surveying the scene, feeling the blood drain from my face. Gil is there, holding a sign that reads: "My Daughter Almost Died. Stop Bryers, Save Lives!"

For a second, I contemplate rerouting to a side door, skulking to my office unnoticed. Then the fear morphs into something else. *Who do these people think they are? This is my campus, dammit.* I've been here since the beginning. I've given everything to this place. Just because they read an article that made me sound incompetent, that's it? They've decided I'm out?

Screw them and their signs. This is my world. If they want me out, fine, but I'm not leaving without a fight.

Anger boils up inside me, molten lava burning through the fear, leaving a hot, metallic taste in my mouth.

I take the steps two at a time, head high, shoulders back. When the news crew spots me, they perk up like dogs catching a scent. The reporter in pink hurries toward me, microphone outstretched. Flashes pop, blinding me. I cut through the mob with a walk I learned from my father, a lieutenant general who could intimidate heads of state with a single scalding glare.

"Dr. Bryers, is it true your student almost died in a lab accident?" The reporter shoves her mic at me while her cameraman inches closer, trying to frame me in a close-up.

"Kim was severely injured, yes."

"And do you agree with these protesters that the accident could and should have been avoided?"

"I do."

The reporter looks a little taken aback by this. Her pink mouth forms a tiny "O" before pouncing on the next question. "So you agree the accident was your fault?"

"There are many factors that contribute to lab safety. We are currently investigating the cause of the accident." More flashbulbs go off in my face, their stark brightness leaving squiggles at the edges of my vision. The protesters shout more loudly, their calls like tribal war cries.

The reporter brushes hair from her eyes and raises her voice to be heard over the din. "What about the sheriff's investigation? Did you tamper with vital evidence?"

"No. Absolutely not."

"What do you say to all these protesters who insist you should be fired?"

I pause, trying to gather my thoughts amid the chaos. In my line of sight, a little girl who couldn't be more than five holds up a sign. It has a big black circle with my name printed inside it, marred by a thick red slash.

My throat tightens, threatening to close up. I swallow hard. "I love this university. I consider it my home. These people have valid concerns about lab safety, but I don't believe firing me is the answer."

"Dr. Bryers, what about—"

I turn away. "No further comment."

"But people want to know about—"

I set my gaze on the massive double doors, carving through the crowd with my father's determined stride. Just as I pull the door open, I hear the protesters take up a new chant.

"Lock her up! Lock her up! Lock her up!"

* * *

Winter

The protesters are a gift. The sight of them gathered on the steps as I walk to Thorn Hall brings the sting of happy tears to my eyes. Finally, others see Bryers the way I see her: dangerous, reckless, a threat to innocent people everywhere.

I remember Ella, her dark eyes shining, her smile blinding in its beauty. We were identical, but somehow her smile had the extra brilliance of pure joy in it. I used to study pictures of us side by side. Even when we were little, she stood out. We dressed in the exact same clothes, right down to our underwear, but her smile outshone mine every time. It radiated pure delight. I'll never know how Ella kept that instinct for joy amid the swamp of our grandmother's hatefulness. Looking at us together, my face had the secretive glow of the moon, while hers flashed with the blinding light of the sun.

Walking up the steps of Thorn Hall, I long to join in the protesters' angry chants. Instead, I keep my head down and my mouth shut. I move through them slowly, savoring the jostling of their elbows, the fire in their eyes. There's a palpable sense of righteous rage rising off them; it matches what's inside me—or resembles it, anyway. None of these people can imagine my fury, the way it feeds me and sometimes drains me, driving me forward and guiding my hand. It's a comfort, though, knowing they see at least a glimmer of what I see in Bryers. Their hatred is a distant echo of my own, but I appreciate the moment of camaraderie as I pass among them.

My gaze falls on a girl in overalls, cherubic face pink with excitement. Her hair spirals up from her head in blond ringlets, unruly and wild. She holds a sign with Bryers's name inside a black circle, a diagonal line crossing it out. Our eyes meet. She grins, showing off her tiny Chiclets teeth. I can't help grinning back, feeling a rush of affection for the little imp. She'll make a great photo op. Hopefully, this gaggle of reporters and photographers aren't too clueless to recognize the golden opportunity she represents.

I feel a hand on my elbow and spin around. It's Laila, dressed in tight jeans and an oversized sweater, a camera hanging around her neck. She beams, looking pleased with herself. "What's up?"

"Oh. Hi." I nod at her, acutely aware I need to get away. I can't be seen talking to her, especially in this setting, with cameras everywhere. Nobody can ever know I'm the one who leaked the story to her.

"Quite the turnout."

"Yeah." I turn and hurry up the steps.

To my annoyance, she follows. "Whoa. Everything okay?"

"I'm late for class."

Laila makes an affronted noise in her throat. "I thought you'd be happy about all this."

As I reach the doors, I turn back to her, irritated but try-ing not to show it. In a low, warning tone, I say, "I can't talk to you. Not here."

"Really?" She raises an eyebrow. "Scared we'll run into your pretty boyfriend?"

There's something threatening in her tone I don't like. She pronounces the word 'boyfriend' with a taunting lilt that gets under my skin. She's acting like I owe her something, which never sits well with me.

She gives me a disappointed look, shaking her head. "You don't even know, do you?"

"Don't know what?"

"I could turn your world upside down." She pops one hip out to the side, a cocky smile on her plush lips. "Keep that in mind the next time you blow me off."

I lean closer to be heard over the shouts of the protesters. "Look, I'm not blowing you off. I like you. You know that. We just need to be discreet."

In answer, she raises her camera and points it at my face. The shutter clicks, and the flash goes off. She lowers it again with an insolent grin, letting it dangle off her neck at a jaunty angle.

I spin on my heel and push through the doors, furious. As I do, I hear her calling after me, "Have a nice day, *Bekkah*."

I stop dead in my tracks. *What did she say?*

I contemplate just walking away, leaving this behind me. Confronting her now is too public; it's only asking for trouble. Waiting until I cool down would be the smart thing. I'm not feeling smart, though. The rage spreading inside me is too violent to make room for reason.

I stalk back through the doors and get right up in her face. "What did you just say to me?"

"You know what I said." Her taunting lilt is gone. She's all business now. "And you know what it means."

"I don't think you understand who you're dealing with."

"I do understand." Laila smirks, stepping even closer to be heard over the frenzied protesters. "That's the problem, right? Or *your* problem, anyway. I know all about your childhood and why you want to bring Bryers down."

I shoot a quick look around, my throat going dry with fear. Everybody is too caught up in their chanting, though. Nobody's paying any attention to us, thank God.

"We need to talk."

"Oh, *now* you want to talk." Laila leans back, amused. "I see how it is."

"I said I wanted to talk, just not here."

She shrugs. "Whatever. Revisionist history."

"Can you meet me tonight? Eight o'clock at Misty Cove?"

"Ten. I've got shit to do."

"Fine. Ten." I turn away, rage pounding in my temples, adrenaline singing in my veins. This bitch has gone too far. She doesn't know what I do to people who threaten me, who threaten my mission. Jake Applebaum knows, but he's not talking.

Jake's not talking because he's dead.

* * *

Hannah

All day at work, I keep my armor on. In my 203 class, a large lecture hall, I can see the looks people are giving each other, the looks they give me. It's a little like those nightmares where I'm lecturing and I look down to see I'm not wearing pants; I feel overwhelmed by the collective smirk staring back at me from the rows and rows of raked seating. Instead of ending class early, though, giving in to the sinking dread in my belly, I use my discomfort to push harder, forcing my way through the intense unease. I burrow deeper into the material, challenging the class to answer questions and concentrate on the subject—in this case, the life cycles of blowflies and what they can tell us about a victim's estimated time of death.

Afterward, I retreat to my office, feeling wrung-out by my efforts. All my life I've taken refuge in my work, used it to distract myself from tricky emotions. Today, I've tried to use it in the same way, but it's harder now. I suppose that's because the problems I'm facing are rooted right here on campus. Whoever's trying to bring me down knows me well enough to poison the very well from which I drink.

I pick up my phone and notice a series of missed texts. Two are from Amy, one's from Joe; they're both checking in to see how I'm doing after the protests this morning. I'm considering my reply when I hear a soft knock on my door. "Come in," I call.

Eli pokes his head in, his expression carefully neutral. "Hey. Do you have a minute?"

"Sure." I silence my phone and stash it in my bag. "Have a seat."

He crosses the room, hands stuffed into the pockets of his chinos. When he takes a seat across from me, something in his face makes my blood run cold.

"What's up?" I try to sound light and casual, but my voice wobbles. The hornet's nest in my chest buzzes with trepidation.

"I don't know how to say this, Hannah." He sighs. "To tell you the truth, I shouldn't be here. Before I say anything, you have to promise you won't reveal this conversation took place."

"Okay. I promise." I force the syllables out through gritted teeth.

"I respect you. I value you as a colleague. So I feel like I should warn you. It's what I would want if our situations were reversed."

I don't speak. I can't make my mouth move. My body remains rigid, my spine ramrod straight. I wish he'd spit it out already. All this buildup is making me twitchy, like watching a dentist arrange his tools as you brace yourself for a root canal.

Eli takes off his horn-rimmed glasses and rubs his forehead. I've never seen him look this sleep deprived and disheveled. Normally he's impeccably turned out, sporting the finest Italian wool suits, complete with expensive-looking cuff links. Now he wears a rumpled jacket over his chinos. His shirt looks slept in, with a small amoeba-shaped coffee stain on the lapel. I feel oddly moved by that coffee stain. Is he bedraggled because of what's going on with me? I can't decide if this idea is touching or alarming.

"I can see I'm making this worse by dragging it out," he says, mercifully reading my awkward silence. "So I'm just going to come right out and say it. The committee met today. We've decided not to grant you tenure."

The room spins. I grip the edge of my desk, feeling woozy. After a long moment, I find my voice. "Are you saying you're not giving me tenure *yet*, or . . .?"

"Your request has been denied. As you know, when faculty are denied tenure, they're not asked back. It looks like this will be your last semester at Mad River."

My vision telescopes, making Eli look very small and far away. I slump in my chair like he's just kicked me in the gut.

"Our recommendation won't be official until it's approved by the board of trustees, but that's a formality." He clears his throat, tugging at his collar. This is hard for him, I can tell. His forehead crenelates with anguish. "I fought for you, Hannah, but the president is very close with the Mathesons, and this community protest, the bad press for the college—it's too many strikes against you at the worst possible time."

"I've given the best years of my life to this place." My voice is husky with emotion, ripe with accusation. I realize this approach will get me nowhere, so I try to change tack. "I know you've always been my advocate, Eli. Tell me honestly: Is there anything I can do to turn this around?"

He shakes his head, his eyes sad and tired. "I don't think so. I wish I could offer you hope, but I respect you too much to mislead you. Once President Foley makes up his mind, it's impossible to change it. I want you to know that several of your colleagues on the committee fought hard to give you another chance. It's a perfect storm of bad press and liability—two of Foley's least favorite things."

My eyes ache with unshed tears. I can feel the pressure pushing against my orbital plate, a storm brewing, begging for release. I have to get him out of here before I lose my last shreds of dignity.

With effort, I stand. "Thank you for telling me."

Eli's eyes are full of empathy. "I knew you'd want some notice, so you can start looking for—"

"Yes," I cut him off. "I appreciate that."

"Will you be—I mean, are you okay?"

"I'm—yes—I just—" I break off, terrified the sound clawing its way up my throat will escape before I can get him out of here. "I need a minute."

"Of course." He bows his head, eyes fixed on the floor as he makes his way to the door. When he gets there, he pauses.

I want to scream.

Eli looks back at me as he opens the door. "I'm sorry, Hannah. I really am." Then he's gone.

When I'm alone at last, I burst into ragged sobs.

22

Winter

MISTY COVE LIVES up to its name tonight. The whole beach is socked in with a thick, opaque fog. I sit in my car, bundled up but shivering. Sinister shapes roil in the dingy yellow light cast by the street lamps. I watch them twist and writhe through my windshield, all the while listening for the sound of Laila's Beemer.

It's after ten. I pull out my phone, checking for texts. My fingers hover over the keys, tempted to see what's taking her so long. I decide against texting her now. The fewer traceable links I have to Laila, the better.

I turn at the sound of Laila's Beemer jerking into the parking lot. She sprays gravel under her wheels, yanking the nose around, jabbing her car into the spot next to mine. She's a dark silhouette behind the wheel; the little hairs on my arms stand at attention. *This is it. I've got to get her on my side.* If I can't, steps will be taken. I can feel a backup plan taking shape in the dark corners of my mind.

She rolls down her window. I do the same.

"Your car or mine?" Her tone is perky, upbeat. It's fingernails on a chalkboard in my current state. How can she be so brisk and cheerful? My life is in her hands. She doesn't even do me the courtesy of treating me like an enemy. She has to know she's declared war. She can't think this is a flirty hookup.

In answer, I climb out and stuff my hands into my pockets. I'm wearing the smooth leather driving gloves Cameron gave me. It's such a rich-boy gift. Like I need driving gloves when I can't even afford a decent phone. Now, though, I'm glad I have them.

Once I'm settled into the front seat beside Laila, she gives me an appraising look. "You're mad."

"I'm worried."

One of her slender eyebrows arches. She pokes the side of her mouth with her tongue—the bulge appearing then receding—before she speaks. "What are you worried about?"

"Don't play games with me." My voice is sharp as barbed wire. I try to soften it. "I have plans. You need to trust me when I say it's all for a good cause."

"Revenge?" She eyes me, her gaze roving over my body.

I shrug one shoulder. She doesn't look away, doesn't blink. I'm the first to break our stare.

"You're trying to ruin her." There's a taunting lilt to her voice; she's goading me.

"It's got nothing to do with you," I say.

"It would make an intriguing human interest piece. The famous Dr. Bryers's protégé is the same girl whose twin sister killed herself after Bryers provided evidence that sealed her fate." She says this last part in a melodramatic voice, like a newscaster reading a teaser before a commercial break.

I glower at her, true hatred bubbling through my veins. "You can't do this."

"You have no say in what I do." She leans toward me, the deep "V" of her tight sweater revealing the curve of a lace bra.

"I thought we were friends." My voice has a sullen edge.

She snorts. "That pouty shit might work with your boy-friend, but it won't work with me."

"I'm serious." I try for just the right hint of indignation. "I thought we had a connection."

It's cheesy as shit. I'm grasping at straws here. I need an angle, and with Laila it's impossible to find one. She's too smart; she sees you coming from a mile away. We haven't known each other long. I can hardly pretend this is a true betrayal. We never pledged allegiance to one another, so she hasn't broken any pacts. We were sparring rivals from the start, enough alike to recognize the treachery in one another. Even the sex felt more like fighting than loving. There's plea-sure in pushing up against someone who meets you with equal force. Most people just give in, but not Laila. She's scrappy, fierce.

She's right too. If it was Cameron, I could pull all sorts of strings, get him so wrapped up in what he owes me and what our relationship means, he would do anything. All I'd need to do is get a little sullen, and he'd step right up, assure me he's the man who can solve all my problems. I've often wondered if he'd kill for me, but it's not a question I can afford to ask. He's such a noble, righteous human being. That's the main reason I picked him. When you have a boyfriend like Cameron—upstanding, rich, hardworking—people look at you differ-ently. If I asked him to kill for me, he'd see me differently.

No, I have to do the dirty work myself.

"You think we have a 'connection'?" Laila's smile is taunting.

Her question startles me. I flinch. Nothing comes to me—no snappy retort.

Her pupils dilate as she watches me, lowering her voice to a whisper. "You think because we had sex, I'll do what you say?"

"No—I—that's not what I meant." I hate that I'm stammering.

"Whatever." She produces a joint from the pocket of her flannel shirt and digs a lighter from the ashtray. With slow, measured movements, she puts the joint between her pink lips, flicks the lighter, and touches the flame to the tip. She sucks in as it catches. The fragrant smoke winds toward her cracked open window like a ghost making its escape.

We sit in silence for a long moment. The fog continues to wind its way around the parking lot. It's still empty except for us. In the distance, seals bark.

"The question is, how are we going to handle the situation?" She plucks a stray flake of weed from her lips and flicks it out the window. Her mouth is a glossy bubblegum pink. I wonder what color her lips will turn when she's dead. I've seen my share of corpses. Though everyone turns gray for a while, their coloring does vary, especially at first. Will Laila's lips turn a bruised lavender, or a chalky blue?

I swallow. "You're going to keep this to yourself."

"And . . .?"

"And what?" I see what she's getting at, but I take my time, playing stupid.

Her lips curve into a smug, tight grin, like she's in on a joke I haven't managed to catch. "What do I get out of it?"

I try a flirty smile, but it feels all wrong, like my face won't make the right shape. "My undying loyalty."

She scoffs. "Right. You've never been loyal to anyone in your life."

I think of Ella, her eyes pleading with me across the dank basement. Both of us tied to chairs, our mouths covered in duct tape. The nerve of this uppity, tattooed skank. She doesn't know a thing about loyalty. She's never shared a womb.

"You don't know me," I say through gritted teeth.

"Oh, but I do." There's that grin again, taunting, confident. I want to rip it off her face. "I know you better than anyone, don't I? And I've just met you."

"You're delusional."

"I don't think so." She glances out the windshield. Her gaze finds mine again with a piercing intensity, a dare in the arch of her brows. "It takes one to know one. We're the same. You know it, and I know it. The thing is, I used that knowledge to trap you in a corner. You don't like it, so you're trying to buy your way out with promises."

"I'm not, I just—if you understood why I have to—" I'm flailing now, desperate. With effort, I force my voice into a low, calm register. "I swear I have very good reasons for everything I'm doing."

"Fair enough." Laila shrugs, like my reasons are nothing to her. "The question is, how much will you pay to keep all that to yourself?"

I glare at her. "Blackmail? Really?"

"Not original, I admit, but tried and true."

"I have nothing." I hold up my palms. "I'm a broke grad student on scholarship."

"Your boyfriend has money."

"That's not—I don't have access to—"

"Bullshit." She takes another hit off the joint, tries to hand it to me.

I wave it away. "I'm serious. Cameron's money has nothing to do with me."

"Even his name sounds rich. Cam-er-on." She rolls the syllables around in her mouth like she's tasting a fine wine. Her head presses against the seat; she pulls a lever and lies back at an angle.

"It's not possible. I don't know how I can convince you." I stare out the windshield. The fog rolls over the hood of her car in gusty billows. The wind off the sea is picking up. It butts against the car with fresh determination.

I look at Laila's pale face in profile and know I can't let her leave this parking lot alive.

"Well, I guess it's human interest time, then. The protests made national news. Slow cycle, I guess. My piece ran in the *Press Democrat*. This adds a fresh angle." She tilts her head to the side, exposing the whiteness of her neck. "Supposedly loyal protégé harbors deep grudge, orchestrates mentor's downfall. The plot thickens. It's a story as old as time, but it never loses its appeal. Plus you both photograph well."

"You can't do this."

"I can." She's still reclined, looking relaxed and self-satisfied. She toys with her necklace, a stoned smile on her lips. Then she arches her back and turns to face me, stretching like a cat. "I've already written it, in fact."

"Has anyone seen it?" This is important. I have to stay calm through this part, find out everything. Getting rid of Laila might be step one in a longer to-do list. I hate how she's crushing my winning streak; it's so unfair. Now that I'm close to my ultimate goal, I should be celebrating, savoring how far I've come. Victory is finally a ripe enough fruit to taste, yet here I am, freaking out—all because this bitch thinks she's smarter than me.

She's so wrong.

"It's on my computer." She narrows her eyes at me. "Why?"

"Just—maybe it's not too late."

"That's what I'm saying." She reaches out, runs a finger up the side of my arm. Her touch is so light, it could be a breath of wind. "We need to think about what you have to offer."

I reach forward and kiss her lips. First softly, then with more force. She breathes into me, a soft moan vibrating against my mouth. I run my hands up her body, stopping when I reach her pronounced collarbones. My fingers linger there, caressing the fine, straight ridges. With slow caution, I slide my hands toward her neck, breathing in her smell— weed and cherry-flavored lip gloss. She breaks from the kiss and pulls back a little to look at me. My fingers close around her throat, my heart pounding.

Awareness dawns in her eyes a moment before I dig my thumbs into her windpipe. I watch the fear as it bleeds into her expression like the colors of a sunrise. She struggles, trying to squirm away, but there's nowhere to go. I've got her pinned to the driver's seat. I pivot so I can bear down with all of my weight. She thrashes, trying to wedge her fingers under mine, but her hands are small and ineffectual. I've got a good grip on her thin, pale neck, and I'm not letting go. There's no going back.

Laila's a fighter.

Just before the light leaves her eyes, she goes limp and seems to embrace her death. She's into altered states. It's the ultimate altered state, after all.

When she's still at last, I sigh, shoulders slumping. My heart's still racing, galloping like a wild horse. I release my fingers slowly, never breaking eye contact. Only now there's no contact because there's nobody there. She's an empty shell, a pretty husk; there's something perfect about her now. Her face is frozen in an expression that could be terror or it could be ecstasy. I'd like to think it's the latter.

I kiss her once on the lips.

Then I grab her laptop from the back seat, get in my car, and drive away.

* * *

Hannah

I'm working late Tuesday night, grading papers in my office. I try hard not to listen to the voice in my head screaming about how Mad River has given up on me, so it's pathetic to cling to my responsibilities here. It's not the students' fault my superiors have deemed me unworthy, though, so my duty is to them, not my bosses.

The truth is, though, I'm not here late out of loyalty to my students. The thought of returning home sounds too desolate. With Joe at Amy's and Lynch still in London, I've got my big house in the woods all to myself. I'm afraid I'll drink too much and indulge in a long, counterproductive session of self-pity. When I glance at the clock on my computer, I see it's after ten. I lean back in my chair, rubbing my stiff neck.

Since I'm in no hurry to return home, I decide this is the perfect time to take a more careful look at the lab. Ever since the accident last week, I've wanted to examine it in depth, but with midterms upon us, it's been in use almost constantly since I returned to campus, and I want to conduct my examination without students present. I lock up my office and hurry down the corridor, a little spooked by the silence of Thorn Hall. The automatic fluorescent lights flood the lab as soon as I enter. Not wanting to attract the attention of security, I shut them off. Yes, I have every right to visit my own lab, but now that I'm persona non grata around here, it feels like asking for trouble. If I were to get caught at the scene of my supposed crime after hours, it could be disastrous.

The small flashlight on my key chain is all I need. I know what I'm looking for. The lab is so familiar to me, I could navigate it in pitch-black. I move past the body storage cabinets to the shelves of peroxidizable compounds. I study the rows of chemicals, looking for the most unstable compounds. Moving the beam of light along the shelves, I home in on the bottles I'm searching for. They're arranged in alphabetical order. The first one I focus on is butadiene. I get up close, training the flashlight on the expiration date. At first glance, it looks normal, the dates written in tidy, upright numbers similar to all the others. I trace my finger over it. Sure enough, there's a slight roughness to the texture, almost imperceptible. Wite-Out. I scrape at it with my fingernails. Tiny flakes flutter to the floor.

"Son of a bitch," I whisper.

We label all peroxidizable compounds with the date received and the date opened. Those don't change. There's no reason to alter them.

I move on to the next suspects: chloroprene, chloride, divinylacetylene, isopropyl ether. Each one has a feathery stroke of Wite-Out applied so carefully it's invisible. Only the slightly rougher texture on the label, the telltale flaking, tells the real story.

The sting of betrayal hits me with fresh force. I've suspected for a while that one of my own students might have done this, but this new evidence hits me like a slap to the face. Not only is this person after me, but they're also willing to engineer a lab accident to make me look sloppy. They had no way of knowing how or when disaster would strike. They turned all of my students into sacrificial lambs. Anyone doing an experiment or running routine tests with unstable compounds could have been the victim.

It's one thing to want me humiliated, discredited, even fired. Putting my students at risk is a whole other level of evil.

I remember my dinner with Amy, back when the crimes against me were bad, but not quite this disastrous. I recall the list of suspects we drew up, focusing on people with motive and potential access to both the lab and my house. Nobody was a perfect fit, but by stretching our definition of "motive" and "access," we came up with four names: Joe, Lynch, Cameron, and Winter. I recall the ominous splash of sauce that fell on Cameron's name, a dark red dribble that made the letters look like they were bleeding. My stomach tingles at the memory.

A sound at the window makes me jump. I jerk around, my heart in my throat.

I peer out the window, but there's nobody there. The wind's getting gustier. Maybe a tree branch hit the glass, or an acorn. I hadn't even noticed the weather shifting. That's the thing about me—I get so focused on the task at hand, I block out everything else in my environment. This quality comes in handy when I'm performing painstaking analysis in chaotic, war-torn countries. Now, though, it's working against me. Keeping a myopic focus on my work has allowed someone in my inner circle to sabotage me without me even suspecting them.

I pull the bottles that have been mislabeled from the shelves and place them in a locked cabinet only I have access to. They'll need to be disposed of properly, but in the meantime, I need to keep them as evidence of what really happened here. I go to lock up the lab. As I fit the key in the lock, I notice with annoyance that my fingers are trembling.

A headache pounds in my temples as I head out into the windy night.

*   *   *

Winter

The silence in Bryers's house is broken only by the pulse of crickets. I stand in the doorway to her home office, smelling the clean, woodsy scent of pine. I wonder if she has a cleaning lady. Somehow, I doubt it. I suspect Bryers is the kind of freak who finds taking apart the stove and soaking it in lye relaxing. There is nothing extraneous, disorganized, or out of place in Bryers's world. Her home is the purest microcosm of the hyper-tidy universe she lives in. It's what makes her such a good scientist. She can compartmentalize. She can see where things go, how to pare back to the essentials.

She's a robot. No wonder Lynch is so into her.

Anyway, I've got a job to do. I go to her computer and take a seat. The plush leather conforms to my ass like a glove. It's the most comfortable piece of furniture I've ever sat in. I spin around for a moment, enjoying the cool luxury of

Bryers's life, the decadence. She's not a shopaholic, obviously, but you can tell when she does buy something, it's quality. I can't help but admire this about her. She's got taste.

I jiggle her keyboard, and the screen pops to life. The clock in the upper right reads ten forty-five PM. No password for Bryers. I guess she feels pretty safe, living all the way out here. The wind pushes against the windows in aggressive gusts.

I'm still edgy after Laila. It pisses me off that she made me do it. The whole thing was avoidable. If only she hadn't threatened me with exposure, the one thing I can't afford. It's not fair. The whole thing has my nerves strung tight. Every sound outside in the windy night makes me jump, and my body feels like there's electricity in my veins. I take a deep breath and will myself to calm down.

One last thing, then I'm done for the night.

I check the spy app on my phone and confirm that Bryers is still on campus. Just to be sure, I check the tracking device on her car. Still in the parking lot. It's risky coming out here so late, but there's something I need to do here, and though I have no way of tracking Shepley, I figure if he hasn't come home yet, maybe he'll stay out all night. After what happened with Laila, I need to stay in motion, need to keep my plan moving forward step by step. No way could I go home and sleep right now. There's so much adrenaline coursing through my system, I feel like I've been downing Adderall with Red Bull chasers. I need this challenge right now. It's a cold, bracing wind after escaping from a claustrophobic basement.

Is it weird that the only way for me to come down from taking a huge risk is to take a bigger one?

Checking my phone again, the tracking device shows Bryers is on the move. It will take her at least twenty minutes to get here, but I'll have to take backroads so she doesn't see my car passing her on my way back to town. Okay, Winter, stay calm. Just focus, and then you'll be done.

With a deep breath, I open Bryers's email. It only takes a few minutes to compose the letter. I read it over twice, then I hit "Send."

The wind shakes the trees outside like an angry giant.

CHAPTER

23

Hannah

MY PHONE YANKS me from the delicious refuge of sleep. It's in my hand and I'm talking before I've even seen the name on the screen.

"For the love of God, what?" I demand of my caller.

"It's me," Amy says. I can tell by her tone she's got bad news.

I sit up straighter. The acidic cesspool in my stomach has me rooted to the spot, my spine rigid as a totem pole.

"What is it?" I whisper.

She sighs. "I got called in at four AM. Body found down at Misty Cove."

"Who?"

"Laila Tikka. Mad River student."

I suck in my breath. "How?"

"Strangled. No sign of forced entry." She hesitates, and I know she's about to tell me the worst part.

"What?" I groan when she still doesn't speak.

"Does that name sound familiar to you?"

I search my brain, sifting through the layers of student names. Then I see it: not a face but the byline attached to the story in the paper, hovering right above that wretched photo of me.

"Oh, hell no." A tension headache's coiling at the base of my skull.

"You see where I'm going with this?"

"They have no idea who did it?"

"None." Her tone is grim.

"And you think they'll try to pin it on me?" I feel the walls of my bedroom closing in.

"No." She says it too quickly, though. I know that tone. It's the one Amy uses when she's lying. "Um, Hannah?"

"Yeah?" I pull the comforter up to my chin, trying to get warm.

"There's something else." The trepidation in her voice makes me shiver.

"Christ, what now?"

She's silent for a long moment.

"Just say it," I order through gritted teeth. "I can't take the suspense."

She sighs. "You didn't by any chance write a letter to the *Salt Gulch Bulletin*, did you?"

"A letter?" I echo, confused.

"To the editor?"

"Jesus, no. Why?"

"Google it," she says. "Shit, I've got to go."

"Wait—what are you talking—" I begin, but she's already hung up.

I flop back against the pillows. It's not even six yet. The dawn is an arctic blue. Rain lashes against the glass in thick torrents. I type my name and "Salt Gulch Bulletin" into my phone. It pops up right away.

Dear Editor,

Recent events have prompted me to take a stance in defense of my own character. Last weekend, you ran an article about my alleged safety violations and mishandling of an investigation. These claims were unfounded, but they have prompted an outcry from the community, nonetheless.

I just want to warn my colleagues and my neighbors. This could happen to any of you. Keep that in mind. When the press is allowed to run stories without proof, anyone can fall prey to character assassination. I'm going to clear my name, prove I did nothing wrong. I won't forget who stood by me and who turned their backs on me.

As for the reporter who started this chain of events, Laila Tikka, I have three words: You will pay.

Sincerely,

Dr. Hannah Bryers

My skin feels too tight. I can't get enough breath. My scalp tingles like the top of my head is dissolving.

My phone rings again.

It's Sheriff Brannigan.

I take a deep breath and hit "Accept."

* * *

I'm sitting in a small, airless interrogation room. It smells of stale air, new carpet, and air freshener. It's a sickly-sweet mélange with top notes of vomit. *God, did someone throw up in here?* I look around and identify a stain near my feet. Though the cheap Berber carpeting has been chosen in a color scheme obviously intended to camouflage stains—puce flecked with gray—an amoeba of darkness lurks just under my boots. I move to a different chair and order myself not to speculate about what sort of interrogation would inspire spontaneous vomiting.

Sheriff Brannigan comes in, cradling a travel mug. His eyes meet mine for a moment, and I see how tired he is.

Though he's youngish—probably still in his late thirties—
the violet half-moons under his eyes tell me he's operating on a serious sleep deficit. His usual friendly, gregarious
demeanor is gone.

"Morning, Dr. Bryers." It seems to take effort for him to
produce this nicety.

I notice a small abrasion on the skin covering his orbicularis oris. Shaving accident, no doubt. This all-important
investigation has been entrusted to someone without the skill
or focus to shave himself. The snide thought streaks like an
intruder through my brain. I make every effort to eliminate
this sort of thinking. Disdain is never endearing. I should
know. In the past, I've been accused of disdain and any number of its brethren: condescension, scorn, derision, supercil-
iousness. Nothing alienates a man faster than the suspicion
that you're smarter and more capable than him.

"Good morning." My words come out thin and brittle.

After turning on a video camera in the corner and
informing me our conversation will be recorded, he takes a
seat, setting his coffee mug on the table between us. "How
are you?"

The question throws me. "Not great."

"Why's that?"

I consider the list of reasons—framed for a variety of
crimes, fired from my dream job, humiliated in the most
public way possible. He knows all of that, though. This isn't
a therapy session. I opt to keep my answer minimal.

"It's been a difficult few weeks."

His brown eyes take me in with something like amusement. "Want to tell me about that?"

I can't help sighing with impatience. "Look, I know
you're trying to build rapport here, but I have class in"—I
glance at my watch—"less than an hour, so maybe we can
just skip the friendly chitchat and get to the point."

His smile is the opposite of friendly. "Works for me. Where were you last night between ten PM and two AM?"

"I was working in my office until late."

"Your home office?"

"No. At the college."

"Can anyone confirm that?"

I lick my lips. My tongue feels thick and uncooperative. "A janitor emptied my wastebaskets around nine."

"What time did you leave?"

"My office or campus?" I know I still sound prickly, but I can't help myself.

The sheriff's eyebrows pull together. "Did you go someplace else on campus?"

"I went to the lab briefly. That was around ten thirty maybe?"

He leans back in his chair, eyeing me with unmasked suspicion. "Why? What were you doing there?"

"I wanted to examine the compounds."

"The compounds?" His tone is that of a parent enduring a ridiculous excuse from a toddler.

"That's correct." I know I'm becoming less likable by the minute, but warmth is impossible right now.

"Why this pressing need to take inventory in the middle of the night?"

I can't see any reason to keep this from him, so I elaborate. "I suspected someone tampered with the dates of the more volatile compounds, resulting in the accident that injured Kim Matheson."

His eyebrows arch. "And . . .?"

"My suspicions were confirmed."

"Okay." He blinks a few times. "Any reason you went there so late?"

"No."

"No?" He's annoyed now.

I take a deep breath, forcing myself to stay calm. "I'd been meaning to examine the lab when it wasn't in use, so once I finished grading, that's what I did."

He leans back in his chair, folding his hands behind his head in a pantomime of relaxation. *Typical alpha male behavior—taking up as much space as possible, to signal dominance.* "After you examined the lab where did you go?"

"I went home."

He sips from his mug, watching me. "What time was that?"

I close my eyes, thinking. "I'm not sure, but I probably got home around eleven thirty, maybe a little after."

"Can anyone confirm that?"

"My tenant, Joe, wasn't home, so no." I look at my watch. "Sheriff, I'm not trying to be difficult, but I really do have class."

"We know you wrote the letter threatening our murder victim and sent it at 10:50 PM."

"What letter? The one in the paper?"

He nods, his eyes never leaving mine.

"I never wrote that. Somebody else did, posing as me."

"Then why did it come from your computer?"

I swallow hard, ignoring the clutch of fear in my chest. "It didn't. It couldn't have."

He tilts his head and studies me, his eyes scanning my face with the faintest hint of contempt. "We traced it. We know that email came from your desktop."

"My desktop at work? But that's not possible, I—"

"From home." He watches for my reaction, avid interest lighting his tired face.

CHAPTER

24

Winter

C AM WANTS ME to stay over. He gives me great big puppy-dog eyes when I climb off him and start putting on my clothes. I debated not even coming over tonight, but it's more important than ever that things look normal. Besides, after all the stress of last night, I needed a little release.

"Where are you going?" He manages to sound both hurt and accusatory.

"Got some work to do."

"Come on, stay." His voice loses its whine and shifts to playful. He knows I don't respond well to guilt trips. "I'll make you your favorite—grilled cheese with crispy bacon. You know you want it."

I pull my wool sweater over my head and button my jeans. "Tempting."

"It's settled then." He reaches for his sweats. "Take off those clothes, climb back under the covers, and let me spoil you."

"I can't—sorry. Too much to catch up on."

I go to the window and look out. Dusk has settled over the neighborhood; a chill's crept into the air. The sky's a bruised purple outside Cam's massive windows. The moon hangs like a sliver of ice above the black silhouettes of trees. A gentle wind pushes its way through the streets, eddying napkins and coffee cups along the sidewalk.

"We've barely seen each other lately." He stands there in his sweats, still shirtless, watching as I go back to gathering my things. I can tell he's trying to sound reasonable rather than bitchy, but it's easy to make out the petulant undercurrent.

It's irritating he's picked tonight of all nights to go needy on me. Still, I can't afford to alienate Cam—not now, when my plan has almost paid off in full. I've spent years following this path, focusing all my attention on this one goal, my North Star. Losing my camo boyfriend now—when I need him most—is not an option.

I go to him. My hand traces the indent between his pecs. My fingers are cold against his hot skin. Cam always runs hot. That's why he keeps his place at a cool sixty-five degrees, only turning up the heat when he sees me shivering.

"I'll make it up to you this weekend." I plant a kiss on his lips, lingering just long enough to give the promise a little mystery.

His brow scrunches up in consternation. "I worry about you."

"What are you talking about?" I heave my bag onto one shoulder.

He puffs out an exasperated breath. "Laila Tikka was murdered last night. The cops have no idea who did it. We could have another Ted Bundy out there, preying on hot college girls."

I turn away from him. Laila's name on Cam's lips has a strange effect on me. With Jake, I didn't have to deal with all this shit. Jake was such a loner, nobody even noticed he'd disappeared. The whole town's been talking about Laila all day—not just "Laila," but "Laila Tikka," over and over, like she's a damn celebrity. Every time I hear it, my nerves stretch tighter, like a wire being cranked until it sings with tension.

"Don't be such a worrier." I avoid his gaze. My eyes skim over his loft, searching for anything of mine I might have missed.

"Can't you work here?" he asks.

"No."

"Just for now? Until they catch this—"

"I said no." It comes out sharp—too sharp. I try to soften it with a hug. I mumble into his shoulder. "It's sweet of you—getting all protective—but I'll be fine."

He cups a hand behind my head, holding me close. "I know you're being stoic about this, Winter, but I can tell Laila's death has freaked you out. Do you want to talk about it?"

I pull away to study his face, my heart pounding. "What do you mean?"

"It's got to be a shock." He holds my gaze. "You knew her."

"Barely."

He tucks a strand of hair behind my ear. "You're not as tough as you pretend to be. It's okay, babe. You can be scared sometimes. I won't think less of you."

I try to arrange my face into a suitably meek, vulnerable expression. All the while, I'm boiling with rage. This rich, entitled little shit who's never had to do anything more odious than taking out the trash for his mommy thinks he can lecture me about danger? He's got some nerve.

"It is a little scary." I let my gaze go soft, as if imagining myself in the clutches of this serial killer Cameron's conjured. Really, I'm picturing myself ripping Cameron's arrogant, patronizing face off, but when I look up at him again, I'm confident my expression is pure kittenish adoration. "I do appreciate you looking out for me. Really."

He strokes my cheek with the back of his hand, and I know I've pulled it off.

I decide to push it a little further. It's a risk, but I'm counting on him being just gullible and pussy-whipped enough to eat this shit from the palm of my hand.

"Nobody's ever loved me like you do." I look down, then up again, pinching the inside of my arm until tears spring to my eyes. "It's a new thing for me. You'll have to be patient."

Cam wraps me in another protective hug, just like I knew he would. He kisses the top of my head just before I step from his arms and slip out the door.

*   *   *

Hannah

Wednesday night, Lynch is still away at his conference. Though I'm tempted to work late again, I force myself to go home at a normal hour. I haven't come this far in life just to cower in the face of danger. After the interview with Brannigan this morning, I've been holding my breath all day, wondering how long it will take him to decide he's got enough to arrest me. It doesn't bear thinking about. I've got to focus on the one thing I can control: figuring out why my life is falling apart.

I plan to sit down with a notebook in the silence of my clean, orderly home and think this through. I've been a consultant on countless homicide cases. According to my bio, I'm "internationally renowned" when it comes to catching devious criminals and finding just the right evidence to put them away. The trick is to approach this case like any other, with objectivity and logic. It may or may not be a homicide case; I have no way of knowing if the death of Laila Tikka is connected to the bizarre series of events robbing me of my sanity. Either way, the stakes couldn't be higher. I need to know who this is. Deep down, I know I've got all the clues I need to unearth the truth. The sick sludge in my gut tells me

I'm not going to like the answer, but I've got to find it just the same.

After a quick meal of soup and rice, I make a fire and plant myself in the leather club chair closest to the hearth. Fire always makes me think of my father. The fireside was his domain, the place where he would sip whiskey and get reflective. He's first-generation Irish, with a working knowledge of Gaelic. Throughout my childhood, he liked to utter Gaelic sayings from the depths of his tobacco-colored armchair. One of his favorites was *"Dá fhada an lá tagann an tráthnóna"* [No matter how long the day, the evening comes].

Well, it's been a hell of a long day, but evening is here. It's time to buckle down and figure out who's trying to destroy my life. I grab a pad of paper and begin to scribble names, struggling to find the clear-eyed objectivity I'll need to discover real answers.

I'm startled when my phone vibrates beside me. Picking it up, I see it's Cameron. Only a handful of the grad students have my cell number, since I don't like being too reachable. It's essential to keep a barrier up between work and home. Otherwise, I'd be at their beck and call twenty-four hours a day.

After a moment, my curiosity wins out over my irritation, and I hit the green button. "Hey, Cameron. Everything okay?"

"I'm sorry to call your cell," he says, sounding a little breathless.

"What's going on?" Normally, if a student calls me, it's because they're panicking about a paper they haven't finished or an exam they slept through. With everything that's happened in the last couple days, though, my pulse rate spikes automatically, bracing myself for bad news, the kind that has nothing to do with tests or deadlines.

"I don't know how to say this, but I'm worried about Winter."

There's a pause. Static crackles on the line.

"Worried, how?" I ask.

"She's been weird lately. Distant. You know Laila, the girl who—"

"Yes," I say. "Laila Tikka. What about her?"

"Winter says she barely knew her, but I saw them together." He hesitates, then adds, "At Misty Cove."

"Isn't that where—" I begin, but he cuts me off.

"Yeah, that's where they found Laila. But this was earlier—like a week ago, maybe." He sighs, and I can almost see him shoving a hand through his hair, his eyebrows scrunched together in worry. "I know Winter's keeping secrets, and maybe it has nothing to do with everything that's happened to you—all this stuff with the protesters and that stupid article—but I'm starting to think it might be connected."

I don't say anything. I can't. My body's gone cold, and my tongue is glued to the roof of my mouth.

"Doctor Bryers?" Cameron's voice is distant in my ear, like a faint cry from the end of a long tunnel.

"I'm here." The two words come out half croak, half whisper.

"It might be nothing, but I had to tell you."

"Anything else?" Again, I sound throaty and hoarse. I swallow hard and manage to get my voice back to something like normal. "Think hard, Cameron. Is there anything else about Winter's behavior I should know?"

After a long moment, he says, "She left here just now. I didn't want her to go, but she insisted. I have a bad feeling. I can't explain it."

"Thank you for calling me." I lean closer to the fire, trying to get warm. "I appreciate it."

Long after I've put the phone down, I stare into the flames, searching the past for answers.

25

Winter

It's almost eight o'clock when I knock on her door. I can see her through the window. She's sitting by the fire. A curl of smoke spirals from her chimney, drifting toward the canopy of stars. She's bent over a notebook, legs folded in her red leather chair, focused intently on her work. I have to knock a second time before she looks up, startled.

When Bryers opens the door, I can see the worry in her face, etched into the sharp grooves between her brows. "Winter. Hi. What are you—"

"Hey. I know it's kind of late, but I heard about the sheriff asking you questions, and I thought"—I hold up the bottle of wine in my hand—"maybe you could use this?"

She sighs, rubbing her forehead. Her surprise turns to something else—wariness? Indecision?

"I hope I'm not being invasive. I can go, if you want." I look down at my feet, then back up at her, going for the right blend of compassion and vulnerability. "We're just really worried about you—Cam and me. We wanted to make sure you're okay."

She frowns, glancing over my shoulder at my car in the drive. "Is he here?"

"No. I thought it might be easier to talk, Just you and me. Woman to woman." The phrase feels stiff and awkward on my lips. I backpedal again, knowing she responds better to tentative overtures. "You know what? I can see I shouldn't have come. I'll just hand this over and—"

"Don't be silly." She opens the door wider, ushering me in.

I take off my coat and hang it by the door. My eyes scan the room with an appreciative sweep as I remember to pretend I'm seeing it for the first time. "What a beautiful place."

"Oh, thank you. It's home."

This next part is crucial. I have to play it just right. "Such a cozy fire. Why don't you sit down, and I'll pour us some wine."

Bryers starts to protest, but I head toward the kitchen. With the open floor plan, it's right there. I'm already pulling the corkscrew from my purse. "Brought my own. Didn't know if you're a wine drinker." I open cabinets until I find one with glasses. "You sit down. I don't want you to feel like you have to entertain."

To my enormous relief, she settles back into her chair by the fire. Opening the wine, I turn my back to her so she can't see what I'm doing. I pluck the packet of ground sleeping pills from my shirt pocket and empty them into her glass. Should be enough to kill a man twice Bryers's size. I googled it—not from my computer; that would be too risky. I used hers. My hands are shaking just a little as I pour us both generous portions of pinot. I'm so intent on my work that a sound behind me makes me jump. I spin around, almost knocking over one of the glasses.

"Didn't mean to startle you." Bryers gives me a quizzical look. "Thought I'd grab us some snacks."

As she crosses to the fridge and yanks it open, I'm furious with myself for being jumpy. *It's okay,* I remind myself.

You're at your professor's house for the first time. You idolize her. She'll assume you're overwhelmed by this new and unfamiliar intimacy. I take a deep breath and will myself to calm down. All I need to do is get her to drink the damn wine. After that, nature will take over.

"You don't get skittish out here all alone?" I ask.

"Not really." She's got a melon and a hunk of cheese on a cutting board. She takes a large knife and starts slicing.

"I would. Isolation creeps me out."

"I like having my space," she says, arranging the melon and cheese slices on a plate. Then she rustles around in the cabinets until she finds some crackers.

I walk with our glasses to the fireside, taking a seat on the couch. For half a second, my heart freezes. Which glass did I put the drugs in? My knees go a little weak with relief when I remember. I push her glass along the smooth wood surface of the coffee table, close to her chair.

I'm way too edgy. I need to get a grip. I'm so close, I can feel my body throbbing in anticipation. I drink half my wine in the first gulp, then realize I'm swigging. The alcohol gushes through my food-deprived system, bringing with it warmth and ease. I press the back of my hand to my mouth, wiping my damp lips. My pulse charges forward, giddy. I don't know if it's fear or elation that has my heart thundering.

Bryers carries the plate of cheese, crackers, and sliced melon into the living room. She sets it down on the table, then sits in her chair, raises her glass to her lips. I watch, mesmerized. When she pauses, I force my gaze from her mouth to her eyes. She's watching me, a thoughtful expression on her face.

"You should try the cantaloupe," she says, her voice light.

I take a slice of melon obediently and nibble. I'm too nervous to eat much, but I nod in approval. "Mmm. That's really good."

"It's not in season, but I thought this one smelled just right."

"Delicious," I murmur, taking another bite before putting the rind down on the edge of the plate.

"What do you make of all this, Winter?"

I sip again, buying time. *Drink the goddamn wine, Bryers.* "All of what?"

She gestures with the wineglass, realizes she's about to spill it, and sets it down. I curse her.

"This accusation that I've put students in danger." She picks up her glass again and leans back in her chair. It's almost to her lips when she hesitates, adding, "And the one that I botched the investigation."

"It's all so stupid." I shake my head, rueful. "I can't believe you'd even ask me that."

She cradles the glass to her like it's something delicate she has to protect. I force my gaze to stay on her face, though the glass of wine at the edge of my vision taunts me. *Stay strong,* I tell myself. *You're winning. This is it. Your moment of justice.*

"The sheriff even thinks I killed this girl. What's her name?"

I blink at her. "Laila?"

"Laila." She searches my face. "What do you think of that?"

"It's ridiculous," I scoff. "You wouldn't kill anyone. Are they saying you had a motive?"

"Sure." She gives me a skeptical look, like she doesn't quite buy I could be this clueless. "Her article cost me my job."

I gasp. "Wait, *what*?"

She nods. "I'll finish the semester, but after that my career at MRU is over."

"Oh my God." I arrange my face into the appropriate expression of heartbreak. "That's terrible. They can't do that."

She puts her wine down on the coffee table and rubs her hands over her face, massaging her temples. For a second, I think she's going to cry. Normally, I hate it when people cry, but in these circumstances it's the sweetest sound I could hear. After a moment, though, she lets her hands drop again, and she heaves a sigh.

"They can, and they have." Her eyes are sad. "I don't have tenure."

"But we can protest—your students—we can—"

"That's kind of you, Winter, but I'm afraid it's already done." She waves a hand, dismissive. "Anyway, the point is, the cops think I killed Laila because her article ruined my life. And then there's the letter I allegedly wrote, threatening her."

"If you were going to kill someone, would you really write a letter publicly threatening them?"

"Exactly." She shakes her head in disgust. "It's insulting. If you're going to accuse me of committing a crime, at least give me credit for doing it with some degree of finesse."

The glass rises. At last she presses her lips to the rim, tips the ruby red liquid back. *Oh, thank God.* The rush of relief leaves me light-headed again.

A high-pitched beep starts up in the kitchen.

"Oh, that's the oven," she says.

"Do you want me to—" Bryers has barely taken a sip. I don't want her to lose focus.

She gets up, taking her wine with her, swiping my half-eaten melon slice as she goes. "No, it's fine. I'll be right back."

I hear her bustling around in the kitchen, opening cupboards and drawers. When she comes back, she settles into her chair and takes a healthy swig. It's half gone now. *There we go. That's more like it.* It takes all my self-control not to punch the air in victory.

She looks at her glass. For a terrifying second I'm afraid she's noticed the taste of the sleeping pills. She swirls the wine, raising it to examine it in the light. I hold my breath, wondering if the powder left a visible sediment. She pulls it close again and dips her nose into the glass, sniffing. My heart races.

Her smile catches me off guard. "This is really good." She takes another drink.

"Oh. Yeah." I pray the intense relief doesn't show on my face. "The guy at the co-op suggested it. I don't know much about wine."

"Very plummy. I like it."

"It's organic."

"So sweet of you to come here, Winter." Her eyes shine with gratitude. "I'm really touched."

I shrug, feigning nonchalance as I watch Bryers drain her glass.

It's done. Mission accomplished. Inside me, a symphony starts up, a great swell of triumphant music. I can hear the string section, the wind instruments, the timpani mallets pounding so hard they're vibrating in my chest.

Abruptly, the music goes silent. I see Ella standing there before me. I see the look she gave me right before she confessed. The sad, bittersweet half smile, her pleading eyes, as if I was the one who needed to grant forgiveness.

"Do you want some more?" I nod at her empty glass.

She shakes her head, puts the glass down. With one hand, she pulls her phone from the pocket of her sweatshirt, checks something, then tucks it away. She leans back in her chair, relaxed. "No, thanks. I'm so tired, another sip will probably knock me out."

Inappropriate giggles rise up in me like bubbles in champagne. I disguise them with a cough.

"Anyway, that's enough about my tale of woe." Bryers stands, grabs a poker from beside the hearth, stabs at the fire. Sparks rise like fairies chasing one another up the flu. With one hand, she picks up a small log and places it atop the glowing embers, watching as the flames lick and catch.

The distant whir of wind raking through the trees sounds ghostly. I watch the fire, mesmerized by the blue of the flames, the flickering orange fingers reaching out. I can feel Ella in the room with us; she's here, as palpable and real as the wine in my glass.

When she's satisfied with the fire, Bryers sits back down and hugs her knees, getting comfortable. "This has probably been the worst day of my life."

"What did the sheriff—"

She cuts me off with an outstretched palm. "I need a break. Distract me."

And so I do. Prompted by her questions, I babble about little things: life in the dorms, places I'd like to travel, research I'm interested in conducting. I try to keep it light and amusing, a buffet of bite-sized morsels chosen just for her. I'm careful to stay away from my childhood; a fictional past is too easy to screw up. One contradiction and the whole thing unravels. Bryers is sharp. She's compromised, of course, and if all goes well she won't be able to pass on my secrets even if I spill them, but still. I've got to play it safe, at least until I'm sure the drugs are doing their work. With calculated casualness, I perform the role of a self-obsessed twenty-three-year-old, the girl she thinks I am. My bright, meaningless chatter reinforces her assumptions, painting a picture of the ambitious grad student caught somewhere between girly daydreams and serious plans.

As we talk, I watch her body growing more and more relaxed. She sprawls in her chair, head lolling back, eyes blinking more and more slowly. I can almost see Bryers melting into the red leather like a blob of taffy left out in the sun.

After about half an hour, she rubs her eyes, shakes her head. "Sorry. I don't know what's wrong with me. I'm so tired all of a sudden. What time is it?"

I look at my phone. It's a little after nine.

"It's getting late," I say, keeping it vague. I don't want to alert her to anything odd about her exhaustion. "Do you want me to go?"

"No, no, I'm fine. Stay." She musters a smile with effort. "I like hearing you talk. It's soothing."

I breathe out a little self-deprecating laugh. "My stories could put anyone to sleep."

"Not at all." She lets her eyes close, hands limp on the armrests.

"You've been through a lot."

She sighs. "That's for sure."

Her breathing becomes more and more steady. She's asleep. It's done.

I start to stand, shifting my weight with painful slowness, watching Bryers the whole time. All I need to do now is tiptoe into her office so I can—

"What about you?"

I've just taken my first steps away from the couch. Spinning around, I see her eyes have opened to slits, and they're aimed in my direction.

I know, whatever I do, she's probably too far gone to reach for the phone, but there's no point in getting sloppy now—not when I've come this far. Something in her tone intrigues me. The air feels charged suddenly, the cozy living room dense with tension.

I take a breath, willing my voice not to shake. "What do you mean?"

"You've been through a lot too, haven't you?" She's slurring her words, struggling to open her eyes. The lids flutter, then close again.

I sit, moving with cautious slowness, watching her. "Sorry, I don't know what you—"

"I may not be a genius when it comes to people, Winter, but I know when someone's running from her past." Each word seems to take effort, every syllable a boulder she has to lift and stack with great care.

My brain spins like tires trying to find traction in thick mud. I've spent so many years hiding from everyone. My life has been cloaked in shadow since I was thirteen—before that, even. Nobody except Ella knew the whole story. When she died, my truth died with her.

The temptation to let my mask drop is strong. All the lies feel heavy and cumbersome—more than a decade of pretending hitting me all at once. It surprises me, this fierce hunger to tell someone the whole story—not just someone, but Bryers, the source of all my pain. *Should I use these final moments to let her know why she has to die?*

The answer hits me with a clarity as sharp as a slap across the face. I have to do this. I owe it to us both, a final reckoning; I owe it to Ella.

In movies and books, I always find it implausible when the killer confesses everything at the end. Now I realize the desire to confess is almost as visceral as the need to kill. I can't help but notice a hollowness to my victory, an emptiness in my chest that terrifies me. If killing Bryers doesn't repair what's broken inside me, then nothing will.

In her drugged stupor, Bryers has just offered me the solution: it's not enough to rid the world of Bryers. She needs to know what she's done, what it means. Only then will my mission be complete.

"Hold on," I say, heading for the kitchen. "We're going to need more wine for this."

*   *   *

I place the bottle between us on the coffee table and settle back into the couch. The wine tastes rich and velvety. After a few more sips I ask, "What did you want to know?"

"Hmm?" It takes work, but she opens her eyes. She looks disoriented, like she's not even sure who I am anymore. Then a slow, serene smile spreads across her sleepy face. The firelight dances on her skin, illuminating the high cheekbones, the sharp line of her nose.

I lean forward, speak a little louder. "You said I'm running from my past. What did you want to know?"

"Your childhood. Something happened." Her words run together, making her sound drunk. "Something bad happened to you, Bekkah."

I freeze. "What did you just call me?"

"Bekkah Jones." With a bleary-eyed grin, she takes in my shocked face.

"How did you—"

"Talon cusp. Rare dental an—anomaly." She pronounces it with the careful diction of somebody who's wasted. "Very unusual. Especially in females. I knew for sure when I saw the melon. Those bite marks proved it."

The talon cusp. I can't believe this. The bitch is trying to rob me even of this—my moment of revelation.

She can't rob you of anything, I remind myself. *She's as good as dead.*

"Maxillary lateral incisors." She wraps her mouth around each word.

"So you know then?" My voice is hard.

"I know you're Bekkah." She closes her eyes again, head tipped back, arms limp at her sides. "What I don't know is why you want me dead."

I get to my feet, staring at her, breathing hard. Her throat is exposed, white and smooth. It takes all my self-control not to close the small space between us and strangle her. The memory of Laila rears up hard and fast in my mind, taking me by surprise. I can smell Laila's breath—weed and cherry lip gloss. I can see my fingers closing around her throat, understanding sparking in her eyes half a second before my thumbs crushed her windpipe.

But no, that's not going to happen. Not this time. My work is already done. I can take off anytime, but I can't leave any marks. Nobody commits suicide by strangling herself.

"If you remember the talon cusp, then you must remember Ella." I start to pace, too agitated to stand still. "That's how you proved one of us killed her."

Her voice is weak, but she manages to mumble, "Your grandmother. Bite marks."

"Nana. Yes. And you were right. Ella did bite her. But it was me who hit her in the head with a crowbar. It was me who dragged her body out into the swamp to let the alligators finish her off."

"But Ella confessed." Her face screws up in confusion. "Why?"

"Because that's who Ella was." Fury rushes through me like a storm. I can feel tears threatening to close my throat, which only makes me angrier. "And I'm the coward who let her take the blame."

Bryers rouses herself again, blinking hard, as if to ward off bright sunlight. "Ella killed herself."

"Yes. Because of you. You found Nana's arm, you found the bite marks, you matched the marks to our 'extremely rare talon cusps.' If you hadn't been so damn good at your job, Ella would still be alive." I lean in closer, trying to twist the knife. "Except you weren't that good. You thought it was Ella. Well, it wasn't. You were wrong."

My face is only inches from hers when Bryers opens her eyes.

She fixes me with an almost lucid stare. "I'm sorry your sister is dead."

"Yeah, well, apologies don't cut it."

"Why did . . .?" She trails off, overcome again by sleepiness.

I cross the room again, too worked up to stand still. "Why did I what? Kill Nana? Because she was a sadistic monster. She tied us up in that basement. Did you even know that? We were thirteen years old and she invited men over so they could—I can't. I can't talk about—" My voice breaks. To my horror, tears have started streaming down my cheeks. This is supposed to be the happiest moment of my life. Bryers is ruining even this. She destroys everything.

"You were both minors in an abusive home." She keeps her eyes closed, mumbling. "The courts would have—"

"The courts," I sneer. "You think that matters now? She's *dead*. My twin sister is dead. She's the only person I ever loved, and she's gone forever. That's on you." I'm breathing hard now, almost panting.

Bryers sighs, still not opening her eyes. "So you came here for revenge."

I walk to the window and look out. The wind has picked up. Swirls of fog dance in the dim porch light. The trees around Bryers's house sway like a congregation. I watch them, remembering the double life of my childhood.

Nana, Ella, and I went to church on Sunday mornings. We'd recite the prayers and listen to the sermons, surrounded by our friends and neighbors, the good people of Apalachicola, worshipping a mighty God. All the while, Ella and I knew by nightfall we'd be tied up in a dank basement, getting raped by the hearty family men who were smiling and singing all around us.

With terrible clarity, I see Ella's body in the clawfoot tub. Her face pale as porcelain. Her dark, wet hair hangs about her face, clinging to her cheeks. There's blood—so much blood, the smell thick in my nostrils, tangy and coppery. I can still feel the way my heart caved inside my chest, a wet avalanche.

"I wanted to die, when I found her." My voice is quiet. I speak to the window, my breath fogging the glass. "A few years later, I almost did. I was going to end everything—the pain, the guilt, the fear. And then I thought of you. Your smug, self-satisfied look when you retrieved your precious evidence from that swamp. I realized then what I had to do: take everything from you, make you feel the despair Ella felt. Drive you so low that you no longer wanted to live."

"This isn't you." Her voice startles me.

I spin around. She's still limp in the chair, eyes closed, limbs heavy.

"This is your pain talking," she breathes, struggling to get the words out. "You're bigger than this."

Rage—pure and electrifying—surges through me. "You don't know me. All I've shown you is the girl you wanted me to be—worshipful, groveling. I've killed before, you know. Not just Nana—there are others."

"Who?" The syllable falls from her lips and hangs there.

This is my one chance to tell someone everything. The lure of confession is powerful. It's like a drug, speeding through my blood, loosening my tongue. I pick up my wine again and take a deep drink.

"Jake Applebaum. Your John Doe from the forest." I lick my lips, tasting wine on them, take another swig. "I killed him."

"Why?" She can only manage weak single syllables now. It won't be long. She's hanging by a thread.

"He knew who I was. I couldn't risk it." I drink more wine, comforted by the heat it sends coursing through my chest. "And Laila. She found out about my past, threatened to expose me. I killed them, but their blood is on your hands. I did it so I could get to you."

"You . . ." She trails off, head tipping forward, then lolling back again.

I lean over and put my face close to hers. "What was that?"

"You need help."

I laugh. "No, Bryers. I'm fine. You're the one who's almost dead."

"I . . ."

"Yes?" I take in her slack facial muscles, her limp, helpless body. I wait for joy to fill me, but there's nothing. The ecstasy I was so sure I'd feel at this moment eludes me. "Go on. Tell me. These might be your last words, so make them good."

"I want . . . you to"—she works hard, forcing the words from rubbery lips—". . . get help."

I cup her face with my hands. "And I want you to die. At least one of us will get what she wants tonight."

Her eyes pop open. With the speed and agility of a snake, she grabs my wrists. Her fingers clamp hard, almost crushing the bones. A searing pain shoots from my fingers to my shoulder as she twists as she stands, spinning me around.

"One of us will get what she wants." She's got both my hands behind my back now locked in her impossibly steely grip. "But it won't be you."

CHAPTER

26

Hannah

USING THE ROPE I grabbed in the kitchen when I dumped my wine, I struggle to tie Winter's hands behind her back. She's so shocked, I almost get her on the first try. She's young, though. Quick reflexes. Her body jerks away from me, twisting toward the door.

I crouch down and tackle her. We fall to the floor in a heap. My muscles trembling with effort, I wrestle with her. She yanks my hair, and I scream in pain. A howling fury for everything she's taken from me rises inside me. It fills my whole body.

After a minute or two of grappling, I get her face down on the floor. I manage to wrap the rope around her hands, trying to ignore how much my fingers shake. A bowline and two half hitches does the trick. She'd have to be Houdini to get out of that. I drag her over to the couch, push her down onto the cushions, and stand over her, panting.

Adrenaline's coursing through my system, the kind that makes everything clear and sharp. The heat from the fire pressing against my back, the wind in the trees howling like demons, her face staring up at me—it's all so vivid. The anger I felt when I realized who she was and what she'd done smolders in my chest. My sense of betrayal isn't white hot anymore; it's been tempered by the pain I heard in her voice when she talked about her sister.

Winter glares up at me, mute. Her body wriggles, trying to free herself. I watch her struggle. Though I'm relieved to finally have this over, I feel no pleasure seeing her helpless and tied up before me. My pity is so much stronger than my righteousness.

This girl has experienced horrors I could never even imagine. It doesn't justify what she's done, but it does help explain things.

I pull my phone from my pocket and turn off the recording app. "I've got your confession. It's all here."

"You—what?" She's too incredulous to form sentences.

"That letter you wrote to the paper—the one that was supposed to be from me?" I wipe sweat from my brow with my forearm, trying to catch my breath. "It was clever. You used practically the same words I did at the faculty appreciation dinner."

"Lots of people heard you that night."

"True. That's part of what made it so effective. Anyone who heard my little speech would read it in the paper and think it sounded just like me."

"So? That doesn't prove any—"

"Except you were the only one who heard me that night who also had access to the lab—the only person who could have stolen my keys. Means before motive. The secret to any investigation."

She glares at me. Her face is different, altered in some way I can't quite put a finger on. There's something raw and unguarded there now. Winter was always so good at wearing the mask of the devoted protégé. I never saw her hatred before. Now it's all I see. A vein at her temple throbs, the superficial temporal artery. The masseter muscles of her jaw work like a wild animal getting ready to tear flesh from bone.

"I didn't want to believe it was you, Winter." I can feel the sadness, the exhaustion, creeping over me, threatening to pull me down. It's only adrenaline that keeps me from melting into a puddle. "In fact, you were the only person I couldn't bear to consider."

She wrenches so hard against the ropes I'm worried she'll dislocate a shoulder.

"But once I looked long and hard at the letter to the editor this evening, it was like a door opened to a terrible, hidden room, and I couldn't deny it anymore. I started digging, finding connections."

Her efforts to free herself have only tightened the ropes. She slumps against the couch in defeat, her eyes boring into mine with feverish intensity.

"Jones is a common surname, but Winter is more unusual," I say. "I always knew there was something familiar about your face. You've changed since you were thirteen, of course. Tonight, I reviewed my notes from the Apalachicola case, and that's when I saw your middle name. I knew if I could just confirm you've got the talon cusp, that would be the final piece of proof I needed to be sure of your identity."

She glowers at me, saying nothing. Only the crackle of the fire and the wind in the trees fills the room.

"Then you showed up here out of the blue, and my suspicions were confirmed." I don't mention Cameron's phone call, the most helpful clue of all. She doesn't need to know he had any part in this. If I have my way, she won't be able to hurt anyone ever again, but it's better to play it safe, just in case.

When she opens her mouth to speak, it comes out low and dangerous, almost a growl. "How did you know about the wine?"

I shrug. "You've taken everything from me. The next logical step would be to take my life. I know your sister committed suicide. There's a kind of symmetry to it, right? Stage my suicide after driving me so low nobody would doubt I wanted to die."

She says nothing. Anger and frustration rise from her like heat waves off asphalt.

I dial 911, never taking my eyes off her. When the dispatcher answers, I speak in a calm, measured voice. "Hello. I've got a suspect tied up on my couch who just confessed to three murders."

After I've answered the dispatcher's questions and she's assured me help is on the way, I put the phone down and sit in the chair closest to the fire. As we wait for the cops to show, an eerie calm comes over Winter. She's preternaturally still, gazing with glassy eyes at the fire. There are matching pink dots of color high on each cheek, remnants of her anger, but aside from these she could be a statue.

I study her, thinking of the many months we worked together. Though it's probably futile, I can't help mentally sorting through the wreckage of lies, searching for scraps of truth. I sift through our shared moments like flipping through old photos. I see the first time I met her, during our first forensic anthro seminar—the way she watched me with dark, inquisitive eyes, always ready with pertinent questions. I see the day she started work as my TA, the brisk efficiency in her hands as she prepped the lab, the determined frown she wore as she assured me everything was ready. I see her warm, compassionate face as she sat right here in this room, assuring me she believed in my innocence.

I know it will take a while to sink in. The full extent of Winter's betrayal hasn't quite hit me. All the same, it feels like a gaping wound in my chest, one the morphine of shock has anesthetized me to for the moment. I know, when it hits, it will be bad. In all my years of teaching, Winter's my most promising student. It's the pain of losing this promise that's most devastating.

Her gaze is so distant now, I wonder if she'll acknowledge me if I speak. I decide it can't hurt to try. This will
probably be my last chance to talk to her face-to-face before
lawyers and law enforcement usher us both into a maze of
barriers and obstacles.

"Can I ask you one thing?" I speak softly.

She doesn't move. Her eyes remain locked on the flames
in the fireplace, her expression stony.

I decide to interpret this as a yes. "Were you even interested in forensic anthropology, or was your entire education
an elaborate ruse to get to me?"

She remains silent for so long I'm sure she won't answer.
I wonder if she's dissociating, floating away to some distant
shore, where none of this can touch her.

When the sirens are a faint whine far off down the road,
she blinks a couple of times and looks at me. Her expression
is so full of cold fury I flinch.

"Timing is everything. Know your enemy, know yourself."
Her voice is quiet, composed. Narrowing her eyes, she whispers, *"All warfare is based on deception."*

CHAPTER

27

Hannah

"THAT'S NOT FAIR," I say, exasperated. "I'm not an extraterrestrial. I just happen to enjoy decomposing flesh."

Joe sets down his beer with a thunk. "How can you *enjoy* it? We're designed as human beings to be repulsed by it. It's like a built-in safety mechanism."

We're at the pub, out on the back porch. The warm spring air swirls around us, carrying cherry blossom petals. It's the Sunday after graduation, always a glorious day. After the semester I've had, "Pomp and Circumstance" never sounded so sweet.

"I have to agree." Amy wrinkles her nose. "I put up with decaying corpses, but I don't *enjoy* them."

I slap her arm. "You're supposed to be on my side."

A flurry of laughter carries from across the porch. I spot Cameron with a bunch of other grad students, pints in their hands. He notices me watching him, and his smile turns sad for a moment. Then it passes, and he gives me a little salute. I return the gesture.

Lynch arrives with two fresh pitchers of Scrimshaw and a basket of fries. While he refills our glasses, we fall on the food. We've been hiking all afternoon, and we're starving.

"Look at you." Lynch laughs as we shovel the fries into our mouths. "Like a pack of wild dogs. There's more where that came from, kids. Take it easy."

I gesture at Amy and Joe. "They're saying I'm an extraterrestrial."

Lynch considers this with a frown. "That would explain a lot, actually."

Amy and Joe burst into laughter.

"Just because I enjoy decaying corpses, that doesn't make me weird."

Amy points a fry at me. "I'm pretty sure that's the definition of weird."

"Decomposition is beautiful," I pout, taking a sip of beer.

They all groan in unison.

I hold my hands out. "I'm willing to admit it's an acquired taste."

"You've acquired a taste for rotting flesh." Joe winces. "I take it back. You're not an alien. You're a zombie."

I throw a fry at him. Annoyingly, he catches it in his mouth. *Showoff.*

I take a moment to close my eyes and savor the sunshine on my face. It's been two months since that terrible night with Winter at my house. The betrayal still stings. I process emotion a little differently from most people, from what I've been told. At Amy's insistence, I'm in therapy. I'm not sure I believe in it—talking about my emotions ad nauseam bores me—but I do find it easier to put what I'm feeling into words now. I'm pretty sure my therapist thinks I'm an alien too, but I'm used to that.

Sheriff Brannigan comes out onto the porch, holding a pint. When our eyes meet, he gives me a sheepish wave, then slopes off to a table of other cops. A few days after my final confrontation with Winter, he heard from his missing deputy. Apparently, Dan Fowler has a pretty serious problem with alcohol he managed to keep from his coworkers. A weekend trip to Vegas turned into a monthlong bender, and after that he was too ashamed to even try returning to work. He's in rehab now, attempting to dry out. Brannigan had the decency to come by and offer a face-to-face apology. By then I felt generous enough to accept it. He told me I wasn't the only one to be fooled by Winter. I didn't dig for details, but I sensed there's more to that story. Since then, our working relationship has been better than ever.

Winter's in jail, awaiting her trial. She gave investigators the silent treatment for weeks, but from what I hear she's confessed to almost everything by now. When it's all over, I'm hoping to go see her. I don't know if she'll talk to me, but I'd like to try.

Lynch asked the other night if I hate Winter for what she's done. I don't think I do. My predominant feeling when I think of her is pity. She believed, if she could make me suffer, her own suffering would dissipate. She harbored so much hatred for so many years. The fury she felt when her sister died guided and shaped her life until it consumed her. When I looked into Winter's eyes that night at my house, her face had a haunting hollowness. Once she dropped the mask of devoted protégé, there was nothing left but the cold emptiness of rage. I can't imagine what that must be like—to loathe someone with such intensity you're willing to do anything to destroy them. Now that she's been robbed of her mission, I worry about what will keep her going. Amy says I'm crazy to feel concern for someone who tried to kill me. Maybe it is crazy, but I can't help it. I want Winter to be okay.

Of course, I'm not sorry she's behind bars. As a result, my reputation has been salvaged—mostly. I was granted tenure and even won the prestigious faculty of excellence award. The local paper's been running lots of sycophantic pieces about my work in the last couple of months. Lynch says they're trying to buy me off with extravagant praise so I won't sue. They don't need to worry. I've had enough time in the limelight. For weeks after the news of Winter's arrest, the national media hounded me for quotes. All I want now is to go on teaching and assisting with investigations, quietly examining my beloved decaying flesh.

At this point, the only black mark on my reputation is this persistent rumor that I'm an alien.

Lynch puts an arm around me. "Zombie, alien, shape-shifter—whatever you are, it's working for me."

"You better watch yourself, buddy." Joe swigs more beer and flashes Lynch a conspiratorial grin. "If she acquires a taste for *your* flesh, it's game over."

I lean over and nip at Lynch's neck. His beautifully shaped cranium gleams in the sunlight. I run my hand over his smooth scalp, tracing the shape of the parietal bone, landing on the zygomatic arch, massaging the tender muscle behind his ear that's always preternaturally active. He slants me a sideways look that tells me all I need to know.

"Man, look at you two." Amy shakes her head in mock disgust.

"What?" I hide my smile in my beer.

She arches an eyebrow at me. "Never thought I'd see you so happy, that's all."

"Aliens can fall in love too," I say.

"Okay, that's it." Lynch swigs the rest of his beer and stands.

We all look at him, mystified.

Joe holds up the empty basket of fries. "I thought you said there was more food on the way."

"There is." Lynch pulls me up by the hand and wraps an arm around my waist. "You two knock yourselves out."

"Where are you going?" Amy asks, smirking.

Lynch's hand wanders to my hip. He tugs me closer. "I'm abducting this alien so I can teach her how we do things here on Earth."

Amy's eyes widen in delight. "Shameless!"

We're already halfway to the steps. I manage a quick wave before Lynch pulls me around the side of the pub and kisses me. His mouth is so full of longing I can taste it. It's the taste of salt and stardust and a thousand nameless things I never knew existed before this strange man stumbled into my life.

"I'm sorry. That was rude. I just couldn't wait another second to get you alone." He buries his face in my hair. His breath is warm on my scalp.

I cup his face with my hands. "You can abduct me anytime, Dr. Lynch."

"Let's get out of here," he says with a wolfish grin.

And we do.

ACKNOWLEDGMENTS

I'D LIKE TO offer my heartfelt appreciation to the brilliance, generosity, and hard work of all the people who helped shape this book.

First and foremost, a big thank you to my agent, Jill Marr, for her guidance and support. A round of applause goes out to everyone at Crooked Lane Books for their tireless work on my behalf, especially Melissa Rechter, Rebecca Nelson, Dulce Botello, and Madeline Rathle.

Research for this one proved more challenging than past novels. I'm indebted to Rebekkah Steinbuck for medical details and Aum Bolton for Humboldt County crime scene insights.

To my family and friends, thank you so much for your ongoing love and support. I'd be lost without you.